COME SUNDAY MORNING

COME SUNDAY MORNING

TERRY E. HILL

www.urbanbooks.net

Urban Books, LLC
78 East Industry Court
Deer Park, NY 11729

ISBN 13: 978-1-60162-245-7
ISBN 10: 1-60162-245-7

First Trade Paperback Printing February 2011
Printed in the United States of America

10   9   8   7   6   5   4   3   2   1

Distributed by Kensington Publishing Corp.
Submit Wholesale Orders to:
Kensington Publishing Corp.
C/O Penguin Group (USA) Inc.
Attention: Order Processing
405 Murray Hill Parkway
East Rutherford, NJ 07073-2316
Phone: 1-800-526-0275
Fax: 1-800-227-9604

Acknowledgments

For Scot Harrison, who taught me to love unconditionally and to laugh without fear.

For Michael Pincus, who taught me it's okay to get mad as long as you remember that love and integrity trump all.

To Sha-Shana Crichton, for her commitment to writers, readers, and literature.

1

Sunday Morning

Cynthia Pryce scanned the pages of the Sunday paper. A silk robe sloped gracefully around the calves of her slender legs. Hair, the color of burnt caramel, curved leisurely over cheekbones that most women would gladly pay thousands to replicate. Cynthia looked perfect even with no one there to impress. She had no choice.

It was six o'clock on Sunday morning. The city lay at her feet as she looked from the twenty-third floor of the rooftop condominium. Morning light drifted into the penthouse while floating clouds peeked through the windows for a glimpse of the beautiful woman.

Crystal vases and glass tables throughout the condominium sparkled from the light flowing through the floor-to-ceiling windows. Soft beige carpet served as a lush backdrop for Cynthia's expensive and eclectic taste in furniture. Scandinavian leather sofas and chairs stood in the center of the living room, and a Louis XV armoire held a state-of-the-art sound system and music collection that ranged from classical to gospel and included every genre in between.

Original paintings by Bearden, Barnes, and Motley hung in places of honor above the fireplace, behind the sofa, and at the head of the dining-room table. Freshly cut flowers, magenta, mauve, and pink, arranged by the skillful and nimble fingers of Cynthia's favorite florist, were poised to greet visitors in the large foyer, as well as the dining and living rooms.

Hands and fingernails that never went a day without special attention lifted a second cup of coffee to her lips as she searched for mention of her pastor, Hezekiah T. Cleaveland, in the paper. Cynthia slammed the paper to the coffee table when the last page was turned, rattling her coffee cup and plate, which held the remains of a half-eaten poppy seed muffin. The story she had waited for was not there, as had been promised. She looked again to the front page. The headline read, FATHER KILLS FAMILY AND SELF, DESPONDENT OVER FINANCIAL LOSSES.

Cynthia pushed the paper to the floor.

Who gives a fuck? she thought while reaching for the cell phone on the dining-room glass table.

She entered the number that had been called frequently in the last month.

"Hello," a raspy voice answered. "What do you want? It's six o'clock in the morning."

"Lance, it's Cynthia. Where's the story? You told me it would be in this morning's edition."

"My editor won't run it until I give Hezekiah a chance to respond. I tried to convince him the evidence stands on its own, but he wouldn't budge."

Lance Savage sat up in bed and rubbed his squinting eyes. "I've got a meeting with Hezekiah tomorrow. He thinks I'm doing a story on the new cathedral. I can't wait to see his face when I drop this bomb on him."

"He'll deny everything," she said. "When you meet with him, make sure Naomi isn't there."

"Naomi isn't available for the interview. I think Catherine will probably sit in, though."

Cynthia laughed. "That's fine. You'll certainly get a reaction from Catherine if you can't get one from Hezekiah."

"That's what I'm hoping. Does she know anything about this?"

"I doubt it. As far as Catherine is concerned, Hezekiah walks on water. If she does, let me know and I'll deal with her later."

The joy in the Sunday morning church service at New Testament Cathedral was palpable. Brass instruments, drums, violins, guitars, and pianos caused the auditorium to pulsate with rhythmic music. Images on the twenty-foot-high JumboTron screen alternated rapidly between sweeping images of the 15,000-member congregation standing, clapping, and singing, to the 200-member choir and orchestra performing songs of inspiration.

Shots of Hezekiah and Samantha Cleaveland standing at the front row, smiling and waving their hands in the air, filled the screen throughout the morning. The captions below their images read, "Visit our Web site at www.New TestamentCathedral.com to make your love offering today!"

On cue, the pace of the music gradually shifted to a more melodic and reverent tone. A soprano sang a hypnotic tune and the audience obediently chimed in. A billowing hum from the crowd rolled from the front of the church to the top rear row and filled the room as congregants softly sang in unison and looked upward to heaven.

The camera followed Hezekiah as he walked up the steps to the center of the stage. Behind the pulpit to his left and right were waterfalls made of a series of stacked boulders, greenery, and gently flowing ribbons of water. The stage backdrop was an electric wall of light that periodically changed from blue to green, lavender and a hazy yellow to accompany the desired mood of each moment during the service.

"Good morning, New Testament Cathedral," Hezekiah said when the music began to subside and the audience settled into their seats.

The room replied in unison, "Good morning, Pastor Cleaveland."

Hezekiah was well over six feet tall. He wore a crisp white shirt and a sleek tailored black suit that was stitched to perfection around his muscular frame. A cranberry-colored necktie complemented perfectly his flawless skin, which seemed to glow under the bright lights.

Hezekiah flashed his radiant signature smile approvingly in acknowledgment and continued, "This is the day the Lord hath made. I will rejoice and be glad in it."

For the next fifteen minutes the jumbo screen was filled with the image of Hezekiah Cleaveland delivering the Sunday sermon, interspersed with shots of members of the audience reading a verse in their Bible that he had referenced, nodding their head in agreement to a word of wisdom just shared, and his wife, Samantha, looking lovingly up at her husband and pastor. The sermon ended on a euphoric note that had all the attendees up on their feet, clapping, and Hezekiah looking pleased and exuberant at the podium.

After a final uplifting song from the choir and orchestra, Samantha joined Hezekiah on the stage. The last shot that appeared on the screen was that of the beautiful couple waving to the camera with a caption that read, "Always Remember, God Loves You And So Do We! To make a love offering, call us toll free at 1(800) 555-4455 or visit our Web site at www.NewTestamentCathedral.com."

The service had ended and members of New Testament Cathedral gathered in the Fellowship Hall. The cavernous room was filled to capacity. It served as the meeting place for thousands of congregants after the morning service. Sunday hats, which seemed to defy gravity, dotted the room: swirling turbans, perfectly erect feathers, fluttering satins, and wilting silks crowned freshly coiffed heads and made-up faces. Colorful dresses and well-constructed suits filled every inch of the room.

The space vibrated from the roar of laughter and gossip. Words of encouragement were exchanged, assignations planned, schemes plotted, and reputations ruined. The multiple conversations fused into an indecipherable buzz above their heads.

"Pastor Cleaveland outdid himself this morning," came a comment from a cluster of women in the center of the room.

"Jason got laid off last week. I don't know what we're going to do now," was heard from two women huddled near the entrance.

"I can't believe she wore that to church. Looks like she should be at a cocktail party," a woman said while rolling her eyes and shielding her mouth.

"She should have left him years ago. He's slept with half the women here," was observed simultaneously by three different sets of women referring to three different men in the hall.

"Look at him over there in the gray suit. Girl, that man

is fine. All he would have to do is smile at me and I'd give him whatever he wanted and a little more just to make sure he came back for seconds," said a woman as she peeked from behind her leather-bound Bible.

Children balancing cookies on paper plates and spilling fruit punch from plastic cups wove through a forest of high heels and freshly shined leather shoes. The elder women of the church had taken seats against the rear wall of the hall, beneath a stained-glass window. Parishioners took breaks between animated conversations to kiss the church mothers weathered cheeks and tell them, "You're looking good this morning, dear," and that they were praying for them.

Rev. Willie Mitchell stood in his usual spot in the center of the room. His bulging stomach made it impossible for him to button the coat of his favorite cream-colored suit. A red necktie formed a puddle on the top of his belly and then sloped down like a neon arrow advertising his oversized gold belt buckle. The thick hand in his pocket unconsciously caressed and massaged keys to a new appliance-white Mercedes-Benz. He threw his head back and laughed as Reverend Pryce's wife, Cynthia, commented on the abrupt ending of the morning sermon.

"I guess Samantha was afraid she'd be late for her afternoon manicure," she said, checking to ensure no one other than Reverend Mitchell had heard her. The silk flowers on her hat shook as she spoke.

"I'm glad he cut it short. I could hardly stay awake," Reverend Mitchell responded.

Unlike Cynthia, the reverend didn't look over his shoulder. He wanted everyone to hear his harsh critique of the morning service.

Hattie Williams graciously accepted kisses from the

younger members. She sat embraced in the glow from the window and soothed by the warmth on her shoulders. Hattie was the senior mother of New Testament Cathedral. She had been a member since the first service held in the little storefront building ten years earlier.

Hattie was eighty-two years old. She was a stately and imposing woman but her warm smile could melt away the fears of any troubled soul fortunate enough to be in her presence. Her silver upswept hair was held in place by a row of well-positioned black bobby pins. A shiny patent leather purse filled with tissues and peppermints matched her sensible Sunday shoes perfectly. Hattie wore a simple lavender floral-print dress with a white ruffled collar which she had made herself. In one hand she held a handkerchief used to occasionally dab perspiration from upper lip and in the other, the smooth curved handle of a wooden cane for maneuvering the steps in the church.

A barrage of emotions suddenly pulsed through Hattie as she clutched the handle of the cane leaning against her swollen knee. She knew the feelings were not her own but instead belonged to others in the room. Sifting through the hidden passions and pain of others each Sunday morning had almost become a game for her. She inherited the empathic gift from her grandmother. Once she thought it a curse but now she considered it a blessing. Silent prayers were said for the more desperate cases and stern rebukes issued to those with nefarious intentions.

She immediately recognized the pool of jealousy surrounding Willie Mitchell. *That man's going to have a heart attack worrying about how much money Pastor Cleaveland has*, she thought.

Hattie looked to her left and saw Scarlet Shackelford handing a cup of red punch to a little boy in a black suit with his crumpled white shirttail hanging from the rear. Scarlet's chiseled face resembled a tormented angel imagined only in the mind of an artist. Her pastel silk dress twirled gracefully around the calves of her slender legs.

Hattie preferred to keep a safe distance from the young woman. The pain she experienced in her presence was sometimes even too much for her to bear. *That girl needs to forgive herself for having the pastor's baby*, she observed as she fought to block the still raw emotions pouring from Scarlet. *It's been over five years and still nobody knows anything about it.*

Hattie suddenly felt Samantha Cleaveland enter the hall. Only Samantha carried with her such extreme feelings of anger and hate and only Samantha could so skillfully conceal it from others. The hate however, was transported in a body that rivaled the beauty of a marble statue intricately carved by the hand of a master.

Shoulder-length glimmering black hair surrounded her flawless pampered skin. The mint linen suit she wore had been designed to accentuate her sensuous curves. The heels of her elegant shoes were the exact height to contort her calves into the perfect feminine silhouettes. Proud, commanding, and in control, her body moved through the room as though carried on a horse-drawn chariot.

She's going to hurt somebody one day. Lord, you better keep an eye on that one, Hattie thought as Samantha passed. Hattie acknowledged her only with a slight nod of her head.

The few remaining worshippers said their final goodbyes in the parking lot.

Reverend Mitchell honked the horn of his lumbering Mercedes and waved to the security guard at the gate as he turned onto Hezekiah T. Cleaveland Avenue. The street had been named in Hezekiah's honor the year he broke ground for the senior citizen housing complex behind the church. If there were any other exit from the parking lot Reverend Mitchell would have taken it. He often wondered why his backroom lobbying against the street name change had failed. *Maybe I should have made a bigger contribution to the mayor for his reelection campaign,* he thought while plunging the car into oncoming traffic.

Samantha Cleaveland waited patiently in the rear of the black Lincoln Town Car and watched as Hezekiah handed a twenty-dollar bill to a young man wearing a wrinkled shirt and pants too short for his long legs.

"Who was that?" she asked as Hezekiah folded his body in next to her.

"That was Melanie Jackson's son, Virgil. He used to play drums for the youth choir. I had to fire him after the police caught him trying to break into the church. He was released from jail a couple of months ago. He said he's been off drugs for over a year. You remember him."

"Yes I do remember him. He doesn't appear to be off drugs. Don't get involved with him, Hezekiah. He looks like he could be trouble," Samantha said with contempt as the limousine turned onto Cleaveland Avenue.

She prayed the driver would go faster and turn quickly off the street that bore her husband's name. The sooner she was off that road the better she would feel. She regretted all the campaign contributions she had made and the luncheons she'd hosted to get the street named in his honor. *Now I've got to look at those damned signs every time I come to church,* she thought as the car idled at a missed red light. *Maybe I should pay that thug Virgil to knock them all down. It would take the city years to replace them in this neighborhood.*

"What did you think of my sermon?" Hezekiah asked. "I think I should have spent more time on the Twenty-third Psalm. People hear it their whole lives but never really understand its true meaning."

"It was fine, Hezekiah," she said. The tiresome chore of reassuring him of his oratory prowess had been part of their Sunday-sermon debriefing for the last ten years. "I'm sure everyone enjoyed it very much."

"Next time I think I'll do a sermon on the entire chapter." Hezekiah looked pensively out the window and continued. "Willie Mitchell slept through my entire sermon. At least he pretended to be asleep. Why doesn't he go to another church if he dislikes me so much?"

"I've told you before, we need him here. He's already donated a million dollars toward construction of the cathedral and he's hinted that he might double that. Just smile, shake his hand on Sunday mornings, and let me handle him."

"I know you like him, Samantha, but sometimes I'm not sure if the money is worth the trouble."

"That's where you're wrong. I don't like him either but we need him."

"One day he's going to push me too far and . . ."

"And what, Hezekiah? You'll kill him?"

Hezekiah laughed. "No, something worse. I'll sic you on him."

Samantha quickly changed the subject. "You should use the cordless microphone more often. You look stiff standing behind the podium for the entire sermon. I wish you'd move around more. The audience and the cameras would love it."

"I'll try to remember next Sunday," he said as he laid his head on the headrest. Without looking in her direction,

Hezekiah continued to speak. "Do you want to preach next Sunday? I think I could use a break."

Samantha's heart fluttered when she heard the words. She was rarely offered the opportunity to preach at the coveted Sunday-morning service. She had earned her doctorate in theology six years earlier and was a gifted and inspiring ordained minister, but her more frequent role was that of the expensively dressed mannequin smiling at Hezekiah's side on their weekly television program.

The 15,000-seat sanctuary had always been filled to capacity on the rare occasions she had been given the opportunity to preach. Television ratings would skyrocket, primarily due to channel surfers forced to pause by the striking and charismatic woman who flashed on their screens.

Men loved Samantha for one reason. She was beautiful. At thirty-five she commanded the adoring attention of deacons, cameramen, lighting technicians, and every heterosexual male within range of her seductive voice. She never flaunted her looks. Everyone in her presence took notice of them without any effort on her part. Instead, she focused her energy on perfecting the image of a sacrificing wife and mother who stood by her man, come what may.

Women had the predictable love-hate reaction to Samantha Cleaveland. They loved her devotion to the man they admired but envied the command she had over every inch of her body. No part of her was unattended, unnoticed, or unappreciated.

She only wore clothes designed especially for her voluptuous figure or those from her favorite boutiques in Beverly Hills, New York, and Paris. Even if other women could afford the clothes and accessories she took for granted, they could never assemble them as masterfully as she. It took years to perfect the look and most people didn't have her patience, skills, or her means.

"Why didn't you ask me earlier?" she hissed. "I won't have time to prepare a sermon by next Sunday. I've got a busy week." Anger took over after the initial shock from the unfortunate timing of his request. Titles of the dozens of sermons she'd written but never had the opportunity to deliver flashed through her mind.

"You don't have to do anything new. How about preaching the one on wives supporting their husbands?"

Samantha marveled at the arrogance of her husband. His one-dimensional view of her caused her blood to run cold. She had spent their entire marriage in the shadow of Hezekiah's greatness. Her beauty and talents only served to propel him higher.

She responded sharply, "I've got more important things to say than to remind women of how great their husbands are."

"I know you do, honey. I just thought it was a good sermon."

"Drop it, Hezekiah. I won't be able to preach next Sunday."

"All right, baby, maybe the following Sunday," he said while rubbing her knee. "I think I've got at least one more good sermon in me."

Hezekiah stared out the tinted limousine window. He braced himself and hoped that the next exchange would be quick and painless. "Reverend Duncan is in town," he said, closing his eyes.

"Who's Reverend Duncan?" Samantha asked with a hint of suspicion.

"He's from Shiloh Church of God in Detroit. I'm having dinner with him today."

"I wish you would have told me this morning. Etta has been home all day preparing dinner for us." She knew there was no Reverend Duncan.

"I didn't know about it then," Hezekiah snapped defensively. "He called before this morning's service. Where was Jasmine? I didn't see her at church."

"She wasn't feeling well." Samantha had no intention of allowing him to use their daughter as a diversion for his lies. "I can go to dinner with you."

"He wants to talk to me alone. I think he's having marriage problems."

Samantha was almost embarrassed by the perverse pleasure she took in his obvious discomfort. "Then he might benefit from a woman's perspective," she said looking directly at him.

"Damn it, Samantha, he said he wanted to talk to me alone." Hezekiah knew he had overreacted as his words reverberated through the car.

"Hezekiah, I know you're seeing someone. You haven't been yourself for months now. The least you can do is come up with more original lies."

"Can I have dinner with a fellow pastor without you thinking I'm sleeping with another woman?" he snapped. "Your paranoia is getting out of control."

"It's not just dinner, Hezekiah. You've been sulking around the house for weeks now. You could never hide your feelings from me."

"Maybe if you had a life of your own I wouldn't have to hide my feelings."

Samantha sat erect in the plush leather seat. "A life of my own? You wouldn't have a life if it weren't for me. You'd still be in that storefront preaching to neighborhood kids and old ladies. Everyone knows I made you and without me you'd be nothing."

"I don't want to argue with you, Samantha."

"I'm not arguing. I simply want you to tell me the truth for once. I can't keep pretending not to know something is wrong. I deserve better than this."

"I'm not seeing anyone, Samantha. I've just had a lot on my mind. You can believe it or not. I don't care anymore."

The intersections rushed by in a blur. Samantha's mind raced as she thought. *When this is done, I should send his body to whoever the bitch is and let her bury him.*

The car turned onto Sunset Boulevard, toward the whitewashed towers at the West Gate of Bel Air, and began the familiar ascent up the hill. Rolling estates quickly replaced the grime and congestion of the city streets below. Lush trees on each side of the winding road tilted inward and formed a green lace canopy over the street. The center median was filled with vibrant flowers and cement fountains poured water from the mouths of lions at each intersection. Pristine terra-cotta-tiled roofs peeked over the tops of densely clustered shrubs and waving palm trees. Couples wearing matching jogging suits strolled leisurely along the paved sidewalks with their sprightly Lhasa Apsos and prancing Irish setters in tow.

Samantha's thoughts shifted to her daughter, Jasmine. She remembered the therapist's recommendation to admit their only child into a drug rehabilitation program. Her stomach tensed at the thought of the public scandal it would cause. The daughter of a prominent pastor spending the tithes given by grandmothers on pensions to support her addiction to Ecstasy and alcohol.

No further words were exchanged until the car turned into the driveway of the Cleaveland estate. Hezekiah never liked the enormous house that overlooked Los Angeles but Samantha felt it appropriate for a family of their prominence. An eight-foot white stucco fence surrounded the grounds. Lower points in the rolling fence allowed passersby brief glimpses of the magnificent home. A wrought-iron gate emblazoned with the initials "HC" quietly parted at the sight of the car and gently closed behind it. Palm trees that lined the winding driveway quivered gently as the car drove past. Meticulously manicured grounds surrounded the home and seemed to spill down the hill into the skyline. To the left was a freshly painted green tennis court with sharp white lines. A whitewashed gazebo stood to the right, overlooking the Pacific Ocean, and a two-story guesthouse could be seen tucked behind a grove of trees. At the final curve of the driveway, the trees unfurled like a stage curtain and the house could finally be seen. It was an off-white Mediterranean villa, nestled behind pine and oak trees, sitting on a sloped crest with spectacular views of the city and Pacific Ocean. Double stone stairways ascended to the grand main entrance under a covered porch, which was held by four twenty-foot-high white carved pillars. Each window on the front of the home was topped by cream-colored arches and flanked by stone columns. Branches dripping with lavender and white wisteria spilled from a deck on the second floor.

The car stopped at the foot of the stairway.

"Are you coming in?" she asked coldly.

"No," came the abrupt reply.

"What time will you be home?"

"I won't be gone long."

Samantha slammed the car door and walked up the steps to the house without turning to see her husband being driven back down the hill.

Etta Washington, the Cleavelands' housekeeper and cook, opened the massive double wooden doors as Samantha approached.

Etta had been with the Cleavelands for five years. She was forty-eight years old but appeared much older. She wore a white apron, knotted at the waist, over a simple black dress which fell just below her knees. Samantha insisted she wear the uniform at all times. Etta had never married and had no children. To Etta, the Cleavelands were her family, but to Samantha, Etta had never risen above the rank of hired help.

The opulent exterior of the house was mirrored in its interior. Sunlight poured through a skylight in the two-story foyer and coated the oval-shaped room in a warm glow. Double living-room and dining-room doors framed in oak were to the right and to the left. A round marble table holding a massive floral arrangement sat in the center of the room and on each side symmetrical stairways molded into the curve of the walls and climbed to a second-floor landing which overlooked the room. Black wrought-iron banisters provided a stark contrast in the bright room. Directly ahead hung the first of two original Picassos in the Cleaveland home. The painting was in the center of the foyer rear wall and the first thing seen when entering the home. The dreaming woman's hands rested suggestively in her lap. Her head was slightly tilted to the right and her closed eyes hinted of erotic sweet dreams. Parts of her deconstructed face provided a glimpse of the thoughts that seemed to give her such serene pleasure.

Antique furniture and European oil masterpieces were skillfully displayed throughout. A well-thought-out floor plan of wing-backed chairs, marble and glass-topped tea tables, and satin-swathed couches created the optimum setting to impress and entertain the rich, the pious, and the famous. Crystal chandeliers and Lalique vases glittered throughout, while plush pastel carpets softened the hard edges of each room. A sleek black baby grand rested in front of a wall of glass which overlooked the grounds and a shimmering cobalt blue infinity edge swimming pool. The second Picasso hung over the fireplace in the living room. The five women of *Les Demoiselles d'Avignon* looked approvingly over the elegant room. Their faces resembled primitive tribal masks and the jagged edges of their pink flesh formed sharp angles that pointed in every direction.

An oil painting of Hezekiah and Samantha was on the opposite wall. The two smiling faces countered the seductive and horrifying image of the five women across the room. Hezekiah's and Samantha's smiles in the painting absorbed all the light that streamed through the room's many windows. As lovely and masterfully executed as the dueling paintings were, their beauty was eclipsed when Samantha entered the room.

"Good afternoon, Mrs. Cleaveland." Etta took her coat and hung it neatly over her arm. "How was church today?"

"It was fine, Etta. I'm sorry you had to miss it."

"Will Pastor be home for dinner?" Etta asked.

"No," Samantha said. "He's having dinner with a pastor from out of state. How's Jasmine? Has she been out of her room today?"

"No, ma'am, she's been up there all day. I knocked on the door a few times but she told me to go away." Etta knew an addict when she saw one but had been sternly warned by Samantha not to get involved in Cleaveland family matters. "Will you be having dinner in the dining room, ma'am?"

"No. I think I'll have it in my study. I'm going to check on Jasmine first. I'll ask if she wants dinner."

"Yes, ma'am."

From birth Jasmine had two strikes against her: she was an only child and a pastor's kid. To others her life was a fantasy: two loving parents, a beautiful home, the finest private schools, a new convertible BMW on her sixteenth birthday, and lots of attention from the many people who loved her parents. But it was a nightmare for her. She often referred to herself as "a theater prop" used by her parents to illustrate their idyllic Christian life.

Years of being "the perfect little angel" had taken their toll on her. She ran away from home for the first time at thirteen. Her first abortion was at fourteen and the second at fifteen. She added the use of Ecstasy to her already nagging alcohol problem at the exclusive Catholic high school. Jasmine ran with the most privileged kids in the school, and soon she even ran them. The drug use turned from recreation to abuse. Now, at sixteen, she was rapidly heading for what appeared to be a tragic ending, but only her mother was able to see the signs.

Samantha put her black patent leather Gucci clutch under her arm as she climbed the staircase. At the top she looked over the banister into the vestibule below to ensure Etta had gone back to the kitchen.

"Jasmine, honey, open the door," she said, accompanied by a gentle tap. "Jasmine, it's Mommy."

"Go away," came the hostile reply from a hoarse voice behind the door.

"Young lady, open this door right now."

Jasmine crawled out of bed and abruptly swung open the door. "What do you want?" she moaned as she crawled back into bed.

Samantha, with determination, stepped into the room. It was dark and musty. The room still looked as it did when it was designed especially for Jasmine when she was ten years old. Pink was the dominant color. A dusty pink floral paper covered the walls and a pile of satin and silk pink pillows lay jumbled beneath a brass headboard.

Cherubic faces of the favorite boy bands from her innocent years still hung on the walls. A collection of over one
hundred dolls from exotic lands she and her parents had
traveled stared down on the groggy teen from shelves
around the room. Pink shades were drawn and designer
clothes were strewn on the bed and floor. Samantha
immediately pulled up the blinds and began picking up
clothes.

"Why are you still in bed?" she asked. "Get up this
minute, take a shower, and get dressed. Dinner is ready,
and I want you downstairs."

Jasmine shielded her eyes from the light and asked,
"Where's Daddy?"

"He's having dinner with a minister from Detroit."

"Then why do I have to come downstairs?"

"Because you don't need to be in this dark room all
Sunday."

"I'm not hungry. I still feel sick. Just leave me alone,
please."

Samantha threw her purse onto an overstuffed pink
chair under the window and sat down on the edge of the
bed, which was partially covered by a satin pink down
comforter. She pulled the comforter back to reveal Jasmine's tired face. She was a young and beautiful female
version of Hezekiah Cleaveland. Her skin was still taut
and clear but her eyes told of the troubles she had seen.

"Honey, you've got to let me help you with this problem."

Jasmine recited her well-rehearsed denial. "I've told
you, I don't have a problem. I was just out too late last
night. I'll be fine if you would leave me alone."

She knew well the fine line between her mother's love
and rage. Jasmine skillfully stopped short of pushing her
to the edge.

"Jasmine, I'm not stupid. You smell of alcohol. Your eyes are red and you've been in this room all day. I won't have this in my house. You're going to have to get some help, or else . . ."

"Or else what?" Jasmine blurted out. "You'll throw me out? How would that look? The daughter of the perfect Samantha Cleaveland living on the streets and begging for food. Maybe I could sit on the steps of the church with a sign that says, 'Pastor's daughter—will work for food.'"

Samantha's eyes tightened. "You know that's not what I was going to say. Why are you doing this to me? I love you and it's killing me to watch you destroy yourself like this."

Jasmine turned to avoid her mother's eyes. "I'm not destroying myself. I told you I'm just tired. Now please leave me alone."

"I won't put up with this much longer." Samantha stood and picked up her purse from the chair. "I'm not going to let you embarrass this family with your behavior."

She slammed the door of her daughter's room and stood for a moment to compose herself before walking back down the stairs.

Samantha took keys from her purse and unlocked the door to her private study. Hezekiah had never understood why she needed a private study but he didn't protest when the locksmith came and installed the dead bolt. The room provided a startling contrast to the décor of the other rooms in the house. A sleek Swedish couch and two modern leather chairs, too perfect and erect for comfort, floated on a bloodred island rug in the center of the room. Sparkling modern light fixtures served more as art than illuminators. Stark teak planks covering the floor guided every step taken in the room. Samantha's glass desk glowed at the rear of the room from light shining through floor-to-ceiling French doors that overlooked the lush grounds of the estate.

Samantha locked the door behind her. Sitting at her desk, she opened the purse and removed her BlackBerry. Next she removed a pack of cigarettes and then a small black revolver. She found the weight and cold steel of the pistol strangely erotic as she held it in her hand. A sudden knock on the door startled her and she quickly placed the gun back into the purse.

"Mrs. Cleaveland," Etta called through the locked door, "I have your dinner, ma'am."

2

Monday Morning

Muted light filled the large conference room at New Testament Cathedral. The ministry's staff looked as rested and eager as possible considering it was nine o'clock on a Monday morning.

The room bulged with a mix of young technology whiz kids, religious zealots, ministers, accountants, administrators, and wide-eyed interns who were clueless to the gravity of their role in running the renowned megachurch and television ministry. Hands clung to coffee cups. Expensive leather attaché cases and purses littered the floral-print carpet.

Five to six bodies sat at tables placed around the room in no particular order. Pastor Hezekiah Cleaveland stood at the front of the room and addressed the gathering of sixty-two employees.

"Good morning, everyone," he said with enthusiasm. "I'm sure you've all heard by now, Sunday's broadcast was seen by a record number of viewers. This is largely due to the great new marketing campaign launched by our PR department."

Everyone applauded to acknowledge the good news.

"We've got a busy week ahead of us," Hezekiah continued. "We officially entered the final phase of the capital campaign for the new cathedral and media center. To date, twenty-five million dollars have been raised and, as a result of the recent jump in viewership, contributions are still pouring in. We are going to need each of you to double your fund-raising efforts. We've got twenty million more to raise in the next six months."

The rear door opened and Samantha Cleaveland walked in as he spoke. She sat down at a table near the door. Her beige pantsuit was constructed with skilled precision to complement her body. A silk scarf, knotted to perfection, hung over her shoulder, revealing the subtle red tones in her unblemished skin.

Hezekiah paused midsentence and greeted Samantha. "Good morning, honey," he said. "I was just reminding everyone that we have to increase our fund-raising efforts over the next six months. . . ."

"Correction, Hezekiah," Samantha interrupted. "Everyone who expects to keep his or her job will have to double the amount of contributions, publicity, and the number of new members they bring to the church in the next month."

Hezekiah attempted to change the subject. "Thank you, Samantha. We received more good news last week. The Trinity Broadcasting Network has asked us to allow them to air the opening ceremony for the new cathedral."

Samantha ignored Hezekiah and stood abruptly. She walked to the front of the room and peered into the now mortified crowd.

"Some of you don't seem to realize this job is not just a paycheck. It's a calling. People all over the country depend on this ministry to fill the empty void in their lives.

Every Sunday morning New Testament Cathedral gives hope to millions of viewers who, without us, would have no reason to live.

"Let me remind you that you represent Hezekiah and Samantha Cleaveland, and if you don't do your jobs and raise more money the ministry suffers and if the ministry suffers, so will each of you."

Everyone sat frozen as all eyes in the room searched each other's faces for the humiliation they all now shared.

Samantha exited the room through the door she had entered without further comment. The staff meeting continued for the next half hour. Several brave staff members asked pointless questions in attempts to appear unfazed by the thrashing delivered by Samantha.

Bodies retrieved briefcases and coffee cups and filed solemnly through the double doors into the cavernous hall and retreated to their designated cubicles and offices.

Catherine Birdsong, New Testament Cathedral's chief operations officer, gathered her belongings and darted through the crowd behind Hezekiah. Public relations director Naomi Preston followed closely behind. Both women ignored comments and questions from staff members as they passed through the crowd. They focused on catching up with Hezekiah who had exited the room and now moved rapidly toward the elevators.

Naomi was a tall woman who, regardless of the season, always wore two-piece monotone suits. Her stiff hair bobbed like a straw hat as she maneuvered around people whose names she never felt the need to remember. A costume bracelet rattled with each step she took.

The two women caught up with Hezekiah and together they fell quickly into step as if they had been at his side the entire length of the hall. Lesser staff members moved to the side as Catherine and Naomi took their rightful places beside the pastor. Hezekiah stared directly ahead.

"What time am I scheduled to be interviewed by Lance Savage and what's the article he's writing about us?"

Naomi's throat dried as she strained to respond.

"Eleven o'clock, Pastor Cleaveland. I believe he wants to get an update on the cathedral construction."

The three stepped into an elevator heading up to the fifth floor. The doors closed and Hezekiah's firm body slumped against the back wall with a thud.

"Catherine, get me the most recent construction figures," he said, peering directly at the doors ahead as if a face were looking back at him. "How much we've spent and how much we've raised. I want to be ready for Lance."

Catherine scribbled the pastor's instructions and answered, "Yes, Pastor Cleaveland," as the elevator doors slid open.

Hezekiah, Catherine, and Naomi exited the elevator and walked directly toward the pastor's suite of offices. Floor-to-ceiling glass double doors stood before them. Naomi took a double step ahead of the pastor and opened the door. Hezekiah entered the suite without altering his stride as she stepped aside.

The outer office now held many of the same faces from the staff meeting. Attractive young women shuttled important-looking documents from one side of the room to the other. Handsome men wearing cheap suits and expensive neckties huddled in various corners of the office as they conferred on urgent church business.

Lush burgundy carpets muffled the sound of multiple conversations. Mahogany panels covered the walls from which architectural renderings of the new towering 25,000-seat glass cathedral hung.

Hezekiah scanned the room. His eyes rested on no one in particular. They were all just bodies. Empty faces serving at his whim. The people he and Samantha surrounded themselves with were there simply to do their bidding— not to think, analyze, or make decisions.

A lanky man with wavy black hair approached him. Associate Pastor, Rev. Kenneth Davis was the only staff member brave enough to break bad news to Hezekiah so early in the morning.

"Good morning, Pastor Cleaveland," Kenneth said as Hezekiah looked up from a stack of telephone messages.

"Sorry to start your week like this but there is another protest going on in front of the church." Kenneth pointed toward open French doors along the rear wall.

"What is it now?" Hezekiah asked sharply.

"It seems another group of homeless advocates are angry about the amount of money we're spending on the construction of the new cathedral. They think we should be spending the money on the homeless instead."

The sound of a man speaking through a megaphone met Hezekiah's ears as he looked from the third floor onto the grounds of New Testament Cathedral.

A group of over 200 people waved protest signs that read: LOS ANGELES NEEDS MORE AFFORDABLE HOUSING, NOT SHRINES TO GREEDY PASTORS AND HEZEKIAH CLEAVELAND DOESN'T CARE ABOUT POOR PEOPLE.

New Testament Cathedral was a two-block-long, five-story stucco structure with a row of stained-glass windows lining each side of the building. Park like settings wrapped around its perimeter. Cobblestone paths dotted with benches, curved brick walls, gurgling rock fountains, and lush greenery provided parishioners with aesthetic justification for the millions of dollars they gave to the Cleavelands each year.

Worshippers were greeted by a sweeping flight of steps that spanned the width of the building and led up to a two-story-high glass wall containing six sets of double doors. Through the windows a massive crystal chandelier could be seen dangling in the sun-drenched lobby. A twenty-foot sapphire blue cross was the centerpiece of the stained-glass window that dominated much of the front of the building. Massive birds were on each side of the cross. Their outstretched glass wings were made of blue, red, yellow, lavender, and white opaque panels, and they held olive branches in their powerful beaks. Visual proclamations proudly declaring the edifice to be the home of New Testament Cathedral and presided over by Dr. Hezekiah T. Cleaveland, pastor sat above the stained-glass center-piece.

"Hezekiah Cleaveland is spending forty-five million dollars to build a shrine to himself while homeless people, sick people, and mentally ill people are living and dying on the streets all around him," the megaphone-toting man below shouted to the crowd. "New Testament Cathedral and Hezekiah Cleaveland should be spending that money to build affordable housing, shelters, and clinics for the poor in this community!"

The crowd cheered and the grounds of New Testament Cathedral were alive with the sounds of boos, whistles, and clapping hands. Burly men hoisting television cameras on their shoulders captured the scenes for the evening news.

Hezekiah could see the construction site of the new cathedral directly across the street, on Imperial Highway. Bulldozers kicked up dust as they moved dirt to clear a space for the new parking structure. Men in yellow hard hats and wagging tool belts walked around the site carrying blueprints, lumber, and power tools. Cranes carefully positioned steel beams onto the rising structure. The new site was twice the size of the one the church now occupied. It included a 25,000-seat sanctuary to hold even more generous congregants each Sunday morning, three thirty-two-by-eighteen-foot JumboTron screens, the Hezekiah T. Cleaveland elementary, middle, and high schools, a theological seminary complete with dorms to house future missionaries, a sprawling park with two restaurants, a bookstore and gift shop, and a 5,000-seat amphitheater for outdoor summer concerts. The new campus also included a fitness center and an automotive repair complex.

Hezekiah spotted the *Los Angeles Chronicle* reporter Lance Savage talking to a man wrapped in a trench coat that looked like he had slept in it for months.

"Maybe you should go down there and address them," Naomi said, walking up behind Hezekiah and Kenneth. "Since there are so many reporters, maybe this would be a good opportunity to tell the public how we already help the homeless."

Hezekiah's smile quickly vanished. His shoulders tensed as he stared directly into her eyes.

"Are you crazy? Do you want me to be on the six o'clock news, being yelled at by a bunch of bums?"

"I didn't mean . . ."

"That's your problem. You don't seem to know what you mean most of the time."

Hezekiah spun on his heels and stormed through the door leading to his private office suite.

Everyone present pretended not to have heard the lashing Naomi had just received. Nervous hands throughout the office frantically groped for telephones on the first ring; papers were shuffled and feet darted toward the nearest exits when she turned from the window.

Kenneth looked at Naomi with a sympathetic eye and said, "He's in one of his moods today. What is going on?"

"He's been like this for weeks now and it seems to be getting worse," replied Naomi as the crimson hue slowly drained from her face.

Hezekiah retrieved more telephone messages from an assistant positioned outside his office.

The scheduling secretary greeted Hezekiah as he approached.

"Good morning, Pastor Cleaveland," she said. "Senator Swanson's office is on the line. The senator will be in town next week and wants to know if you're available for lunch."

Hezekiah looked unimpressed as he retrieved more telephone messages from her neatly appointed desk. "That's fine," he said. "Go ahead and set it up."

When he entered his office, the private telephone rang. After dropping the stack of telephone messages on the desk, he picked up the receiver.

"Hello. This is Hezekiah Cleaveland."

"Good morning, handsome," said the voice on the line.

The tension in Hezekiah's shoulders slowly dissolved. "Good morning, baby," he said in a whisper.

"I'm driving down Imperial Highway past your church. I'm on my way to give out condoms and socks to a group of homeless guys at an encampment under the freeway near your church and I just wanted to hear your voice."

"Condoms?" Hezekiah asked, laughing. "Why do homeless people need condoms? They shouldn't be having sex under the freeways."

The voice on the phone laughed with him.

Hezekiah lowered his body into his huge black leather

chair and said, "I loved being with you last night. I miss you already."

"I miss you too."

"Do me a favor?" Hezekiah said. "Drive in front of the church and tell those protesters to get off my property. I think they might be friends of yours."

"Friends? What are you talking about?"

Hezekiah could hear the blaring horn of a city bus through the receiver. "It's those homeless advocates who've got nothing better to do on a Monday morning than harass me."

The voice on the line began to laugh again. "Don't let them get to you, Hezekiah. Everyone knows you do a lot for the homeless."

"I've got a meeting in a few minutes," Hezekiah said as he spun around in his chair to watch the protest escalating outside his window. "When am I going to see you this week? I miss you."

"How about tonight?"

"I can't tonight. I think I'm free tomorrow evening. I've got to meet with my attorneys at six but I should be free by seven."

"Sounds good. I can hold out until then."

Hezekiah whispered seductively, "You know I love you. Be careful out there and tell those guys to stop having sex near my church."

The voice laughed again and said, "I'll give them the message. I love you too, Hezekiah. See you tomorrow night."

3

One Year Earlier

Hezekiah first saw the young man kneeling at a corner on skid row. His green canvas backpack lay on the sidewalk beside him, filled with the daily rations of vitamins, warm socks, and condoms for homeless people he encountered on his rounds of the city.

The sounds of horns honking and public-transit bus engines revving echoed off glass towers and graffiti-marred hotel facades. The block was cluttered with wobbly shopping carts filled with plastic trash bags, aluminum cans, plastic bottles, soiled clothes, and half-eaten cans of beans and sardines. Cyclone fences served as the only barriers between the human debris and parking lots filled with BMWs, Jaguars, and other nondescript silver foreign automobiles.

The pungent smell of urine and human feces was everywhere. Emaciated dogs foraged through piles of trash, looking for the morsel that, for them, stood between life and death. Drivers sped by, making extra efforts to avoid looking to the left or the right. The human misery was too painful to witness, and the filth too disgusting to stomach.

One man lay sleeping in the middle of the sidewalk. His limbs were twisted and his face was pressed into the cement. His blue denim jeans were stained from being worn for over two months. Alcohol fumes were almost visible as he breathed. He looked as though he had been dropped from the roof of a five-story building.

A woman sat on the curb with her legs spread to the street. She wore a dirty pink scarf wrapped around her matted hair, a dingy, tattered yellow sweater, and no shoes. Her feet were covered with scabs and open wounds. "I told you ta stop bring'n dose peopo in'ta my mothafuck'n house. I'm mo kill that mothafucka if he do dat ta me again," she cursed to the air as it breezed by.

Other men and women lay coiled and hidden under oily, lice-ridden blankets and behind cardboard fortresses.

When Hezekiah first saw Danny St. John, he was speaking to a homeless man named Old Joe, who was sitting on the curb, rattling a paper cup filled with coins. Everyone who lived in or walked through the shopping cart shantytown knew Old Joe. He was a tall man with matted black hair, wearing oil-stained clothes.

Brakes screeched, a car barely missing elderly pedestrians, as Danny and Old Joe talked below on the sidewalk. Lights flashed green, yellow, and red, and pigeons danced amid the remains of half-eaten burgers and discarded French fries. The two men spoke of warm places for Joe to sleep when the cold returned for the night.

Danny reached into his bag for a clean hypodermic needle sealed in cellophane. He searched in the bag around packages of alcohol wipes, a tin canister filled with condoms, bottles of Purell hand sanitizer, and bundles of clean socks until he found the syringes. He looked over his shoulder to ensure a private moment for the exchange and found himself staring into the eyes of Hezekiah Cleaveland.

The pastor was watching him intently from the driver's seat of a silver Mercedes-Benz. Before Danny could look away, Hezekiah called out, "Excuse me. Are you a city employee? May I speak to you for a moment? I have a question for you."

Danny recognized the handsome face immediately. He excused himself from Old Joe and walked to the car.

"No, I don't work for the city," Danny said bending to the window. "I work for a nonprofit homeless-outreach agency downtown."

Hezekiah's brain went uncharacteristically blank as the tall, attractive young man looked into the car. He hadn't expected to see such a beautiful face or hear so gentle a voice come from a man who worked so closely with the outcasts of the city.

At twenty-eight Danny looked as though he had never had a difficult day in his life. He was a handsome man, with smooth almond-brown skin, who attracted admiring glances from both men and women. Just over six feet tall, his slender body was modestly hidden under a baggy T-shirt and green army fatigues.

Hezekiah quickly regained his composure and introduced himself. "My name is Pastor Hezekiah Cleaveland. There's a homeless woman who sleeps near my church on Cleaveland Avenue at Imperial Highway," he said. "She's obviously mentally ill and has a dog in a shopping cart. You can't miss her. She's always there. Can you go over and talk to her?"

"I know her. Everyone in my agency knows her but she has a long history of refusing services from our agency."

As Danny spoke, Hezekiah became distracted again by a glimmer in the beautiful young man's eyes.

There was an awkward silence after Danny finished his sentence. Then Hezekiah replied, "I would appreciate it if you would speak with her again."

Danny looked surprised. He never thought Hezekiah Cleaveland had any interest in people who couldn't send him a donation.

"I'm glad to hear you're concerned Rev. Cleaveland. When I've seen you and your wife on television it seemed you were only interested in people who could make large contributions to your church."

"Don't believe everything you see on television," Hezekiah said, smiling. "I was poor once myself and I've never forgotten it."

As Danny walked back to Old Joe he heard Hezekiah call out again. "After you talk to her would you mind stopping by my office at the church? Just to let me know how it goes," the minister explained.

"I'll stop by and see her this afternoon."

"Thank you," Hezekiah replied with an odd sense of relief. "By the way, what's your name?"

"Danny. Danny St. John."

4

Monday

It was 10:50 A.M. Catherine Birdsong rushed to gather the information Hezekiah had requested.

Her office was small compared to others in the administrative wing. There were no pictures on the walls. Newspapers, magazines, and press releases occupied every available surface. A silver frame on the desk held a picture of her seven-year-old daughter, Sarah.

Catherine jumped when the telephone rang.

"Yes, Pastor Cleaveland. I'm on my way," she said before the voice on the line could speak.

She hurried through the winding halls to Hezekiah's office.

Without stopping at the receptionist's desk in front of Hezekiah's door, Catherine snapped over her shoulder, "He's expecting me."

Hezekiah was laughing on the telephone when she entered the room. He concluded the conversation with, "Don't worry, Barry. Just let me know if you need me to call him. He's good for at least another hundred thousand."

Hezekiah hung up the telephone.

"Where have you been? It's almost eleven o'clock."

Catherine did not respond while handing him the reports. She stood over his shoulder and attempted to explain the numbers as Hezekiah studied the pages.

"Pastor, no one seems to have an accurate number on how much the project has cost to date. The figures range from twenty to twenty-five million. That would mean we have between twenty and twenty-five million more to raise. I recommend going with the lower number because of all the controversy surrounding the building project." Catherine continued quickly before Hezekiah could ask a question. "The second page is a geographic breakdown of contributions to date. As you can see, the majority of our contributions are coming from the southern states. The Midwest is coming in at a strong second. It looks like we need to put more emphasis on the East Coast, though. For example, donations from Maryland, Rhode Island, and D.C. are falling short of what we projected for this final phase of fund-raising.

"The last page shows the donor demographics. Of course, women between twenty-five and sixty-five years of age are our most prolific donors. Followed by men thirty-five to sixty-five. The number of single white female donors has increased significantly in the last two months."

Catherine refrained from offering further explanations as Hezekiah continued to scan the reports.

The intercom on his desk cut through the silence.

"Pastor Cleaveland," said the receptionist, "Mr. Lance Savage is here for your eleven o'clock."

"I'll be out in a minute," Hezekiah said sharply.

Moments later Hezekiah and Catherine emerged from the office and Lance Savage jumped to his feet. Lance was a tall man of thirty-five years who never left home without a slightly wrinkled sport coat, thick corduroy pants, and a pair of well-worn suede shoes. His pale yellow shirt had gone several wearings without benefit of dry cleaning.

"Hello, Lance," Catherine said as she approached him. "I'm going to join you in this meeting if you don't mind."

"No, I don't mind. I've just got a few questions for Pastor Cleaveland."

Hezekiah approached Lance with a welcoming grin. "Lance," he said, extending his hand. "You here to rake me over the coals again?"

Lance laughed and shook Hezekiah's hand.

Hezekiah directed Lance and Catherine to attractive, yet uncomfortable, chairs in front of his desk. He sat behind the desk surrounded by plaques, awards, and framed magazine covers with pictures of the perfect Cleaveland couple which served to remind all who entered the room that he was one of the most famous ministers in the country.

Hezekiah spoke before Lance could settle into the chair. "Lance, I've pulled together some information on the new sanctuary and media center building project. The community is going to benefit greatly from the expansion of our ministry."

"I'm sure the project is very impressive, Pastor Cleaveland, but I'm not here to talk about the new cathedral." Lance retrieved a small notepad from his breast pocket and continued. "Pastor Cleaveland, are you familiar with a man named Danny St. John?"

With no discernible signs of surprise, Hezekiah responded, "The name doesn't sound familiar."

Lance continued his questioning. "Is that so? Would it jog your memory if I told you Mr. St. John is a homeless-outreach worker with whom, my sources tell me, you've spent a considerable amount of time over the last year?"

Hezekiah's face hardened as he felt the muscles contract in his shoulders. "I'm sorry, but I don't know of anyone by that name. My ministry, however, is very concerned about the growing number of homeless people in Los Angeles."

"Pastor Cleaveland, I have been given information by a reliable source that you and Mr. St. John have a relationship that . . . How can I put this? A relationship that goes beyond your mutual concern for the well-being of Los Angeles's indigent population."

"I'm a busy man, Lance," Hezekiah said impatiently. "What is this about?"

"All right, sir. Would you care to comment on the fact that we have information which suggests that for the past year you've been involved in a homosexual relationship with Danny St. John?"

The chair bumped the bulletproof window behind the desk as Hezekiah leaped to his feet.

"What are you talking about? This is ridiculous! Who told you that?"

"I'm sorry, sir, but I am not at liberty to say."

"How dare you come into my church and make a libelous claim like that? I'll sue you and the *Los Angeles Chronicle* if any word of this lie appears in it."

Lance stood to his feet. "Pastor Cleaveland, there's really no point in denying it. My source's proof is irrefutable. I'm here to give you the opportunity to respond, even if that response is simply 'No comment.'"

"I won't dignify this nonsense with a response. Now get out of my office."

"That is your choice, Pastor Cleaveland. However, please know that we will run this story within a week, with or without a quote from you."

Hezekiah rushed from behind the desk to Lance and pointed to the door. "Get out."

Catherine stood. "Lance, this is outrageous. Pastor Cleaveland said he never met this Danny St. John person!"

"Shut up, Catherine." Hezekiah turned his anger to her shrieking face. "Stay out of this."

As Lance walked to the door, he turned and said, "If you change your mind, you know how to reach me."

Catherine collapsed into the chair after Lance left the room. "Pastor, a story like this could ruin you. Would you like me to call our attorneys?"

Hezekiah's eyes glazed over. He stood in front of her and slammed an open palm on the desk.

"No," he snapped. "Don't say a word about this to anyone, and especially not Samantha."

5

Associate Pastor Kenneth Davis sat alone in his office on the second floor. His was one of the largest offices in the church, second only to the pastor's. The size of his space reflected the tremendous influence he wielded in the ministry. His power came from his shameless tendency to flaunt his close association with Hezekiah Cleaveland.

Kenneth paced the floor. *Stupid idiot*, he thought angrily, not of Lance Savage but of Hezekiah Cleaveland. *So close to completing a multimillion-dollar construction project and he pulls a stunt like this.*

The framed picture of his twelve-year-old son from a failed attempt at marriage stared helplessly at him each time he walked past the desk. His mind was awash with thoughts of private school tuition, braces for the crooked, bright smile, monthly child support, his car note, and mortgage payments for the Tudor mini-mansion he had purchased behind the gated walls of Hancock Park only a year earlier.

His clenched fists slammed together repeatedly as he

continued his silent assault on Hezekiah. "All the work that went into this fund-raising campaign, down the drain," he muttered. His steps grew more agitated as he silently tabulated his monthly bills.

"I've got to stop that story," he said loudly. "There's no way I'm going to let him screw up all I've worked for. I'm not going out like this."

Kenneth had first heard the name Danny St. John two weeks earlier at a gay bar in West Hollywood. He had always taken painstaking efforts at church to conceal his predilection toward men, but the idea of being spotted in a gay bar by some other "closeted queen" seemed a risk worth taking in exchange for the camaraderie he felt with others who had similar tastes in companions. He was having a drink with Larry Kennedy, a fellow closeted minister from another congregation.

The small neighborhood bar was filled with men who looked like they had just returned from long weekends in Palm Springs. Toned, tanned, and well-dressed bodies packed the room. Music blared from below, above, and everywhere in between. The two men had just ordered their second round of beers.

"So what's up with the latest gossip going around about Hezekiah?" Larry asked while reaching for his drink.

"Why? What have you heard? Who's he supposed to be sleeping with this time?"

"Everybody's been talking about it. I'm surprised you haven't heard. I hear it's some guy who works with the homeless downtown. Danny something. A buddy of mine who works for the same agency told me he is gorgeous."

Kenneth laughed loud enough to be heard over the pul-

sating music. "A guy?" he said dismissively. "You're joking. What else have you heard?"

"Well," Larry said, leaning forward, "supposedly it's been going on for about a year now, but I don't know how true that is."

"Larry, if you're dumb enough to believe a story like that, then you deserve to be an assistant pastor for the rest of your life."

Larry smiled. "Yeah, I know. It sounded ridiculous to me when I first heard about it, but what if it's true? Can you imagine the fallout? The gay community would be pissed because he's a closeted high-profile minister. The black community would feel betrayed and embarrassed, and God only knows what the evangelicals would do."

"Nobody is ever going to find out, Larry, because there's nothing to this. Hezekiah's not dumb enough to sneak around banging some guy in the middle of a forty-five-million-dollar capital campaign."

"For his sake and yours, I hope you're right. By the way, who's Lance Savage?"

"He's a reporter with the Los Angeles Chronicle. *Why?" Kenneth asked.*

"Because he's been asking questions around town lately. Apparently, he's working on a tell-all story."

Now sitting alone in his office, Kenneth recalled the conversation with Larry Kennedy. He began to wonder if the gossip could be true. He hoped the possibility of Hezekiah being gay or even bisexual was too far-fetched to be real.

If it is true, he thought, *he can kiss his church good-bye. This country isn't ready for a powerful gay black preacher and especially not one who cheats on a woman like Samantha.*

* * *

Collard green stalks peeked over the pink brick fence surrounding Hattie Williams's garden. Green tomatoes waited for the day Hattie would say, "You're just right for picking." Green beans on the vine protected their precious contents from the sun, and bright yellow squash provided a beautiful contrast in the emerald sea.

The neat stucco house was quiet except for the gospel hymns playing on the radio. Hattie sat at her kitchen table, which overlooked the garden.

Her Bible was open to John 3:16.

She read aloud, "For God so loved the world, that he gave his only begotten Son, that whosoever believeth in him should not perish, but have everlasting life."

As she pondered the words and gazed out the window, the image of Hezekiah Cleaveland flashed before her. His face expressionless and his eyes hollow. He wasn't looking at her but rather looking at himself.

All she could hear, see, and feel at that moment was the battle of emotions that raged in his soul. The pastor's conflicting feelings of torment and relief, anger and fear, drowned out the crackling of the radio. She sat motionless and silently watched the battle that played out in the reflection of her garden window.

"Lord, what has the pastor got himself into now?" she said aloud as the melee in her window raged on.

She had never seen so many warriors on the battlefield of one man's soul before. Fear violently thrashed his sword at the breastplate of peace. Contentment protected his head from the deadly blows of confusion. Love cowered under the pounding leveled by a white horse whose rider was death.

The image of the equestrian made Hattie shiver. She

had seen him before: at the bedside of her mother and in the hospital room of her late husband. On each occasion she pleaded that he ride away and allow her just one more day with her loved ones. Each time he did not hear her. She knew he would not hear her today.

Hattie had learned to separate her emotions from those of others. But today she sat helplessly and succumbed to the tears that welled in her eyes as the horseman delivered the lethal blow to the man lying on the ground.

"Oh Lord, not the pastor. Not Pastor Cleaveland!" She cried out as the scene faded from her window.

Catherine Birdsong instructed her secretary to hold all calls after the startling meeting with Lance Savage. Her body trembled as she reached for the small flask of bourbon tucked beneath an even smaller bottle of minty green mouthwash, tissue, and a silver makeup compact.

The office was quiet. Only the muffled white noise of traffic passing below her window could be heard. Cool pale light hovered around oil canvases and ceramic vases filled with yellow and white lilies. With shaking hands, she took the first sip of the brown tonic, then a second, and third.

Catherine had been with Hezekiah Cleaveland for over ten years, throughout his various business and religious incarnations. She was thirty-three years old and always impeccably dressed, accomplished by frequent and extended-lunch shopping excursions throughout Beverly Hills.

Her expensive tastes in clothes and jewelry far exceeded her salary as a chief operations officer. That of her husband, however, generously supplemented her own. He was a prominent real estate developer who sold New Testament Cathedral the property across the street for the new church. This deal had bordered precariously on a conflict of interest for Catherine. She naively believed that her position in the church never influenced her husband's sweetheart deal but silent observers knew otherwise.

A knock on the door shattered the private moment between her and the bottle. Catherine returned the now half empty bottle to the safety of her purse. It was Kenneth Davis.

"Kenneth, this isn't a good time for me. Is this something that can wait?"

"Catherine," he said, "I want to know what's going on. He's been snapping at everyone for weeks now. There are rumors going around that Pastor Cleaveland is gay and supposedly a Lance Savage is working on a story about it. Do you know anything about this?"

The alcohol had temporarily sharpened her defensive skills. Catherine bolted to her feet. "Kenneth, I said now is not a good time."

Kenneth's long legs made light work of the distance between the door and her desk.

"Catherine, you need to tell me what's going on. We need to do damage control. You can't hide in this office and pretend this will go away. The entire ministry might be at stake. If Hezekiah is destroyed, we'll all be destroyed with him."

Catherine's knees buckled under the weight of his statement causing her to wilt back into the soft leather chair. Her eyes filled with tears as she scrambled for the tissue in her purse. There was a tense silence shared between the two while she stared vacantly out the window. Reverend Davis held his gaze firmly on her quivering face.

Then, through mounting sobs, Catherine said, "Close the door, Kenneth. I don't want anyone to hear this."

Kenneth closed the office door and sat in front of her desk.

"So what is this all about?"

"Kenneth, you've got to promise me you won't repeat this to anyone. He'd kill me if he knew I spoke to you."

"Who am I going to talk to? Now tell me."

Catherine took a deep breath and proceeded to recount the amazing confrontation she had just witnessed between Hezekiah and Lance Savage.

"Savage claims to have proof that Pastor Cleaveland is having an affair with a man."

Catherine looked away to avoid Kenneth's bulging eyes. Her lips longed for another encounter with the flask in her purse.

"His name is Danny, Danny St. John. He's a homeless-outreach worker."

"Catherine, that's crazy," Kenneth said. "A gay rumor surfaces about Hezekiah every few years but no one has ever proved anything."

"I know, Kenneth. I've heard them too, but . . . but it was the way he reacted when Lance said it. I've never seen him that angry before. He snapped. I thought he was going to attack him. It was horrible."

"So what makes you think he can prove it? Did he identify his source?"

"No. Pastor Cleaveland didn't give him a chance to. He exploded and threw him out. Lance would have never confronted him the way he did unless he knew something. He was so cocky and bold."

Kenneth stood and walked abruptly to the door.

"I'm going to call Savage. We'll sue that paper for slander if they print the story, even if it is true."

Catherine sprang from her desk. She grabbed Kenneth by the arm as he reached for the door handle. "Kenneth," she said through tears, "you said you wouldn't repeat this to anyone. You promised."

Kenneth pushed her away. The force of his thrust, and the alcohol, caused her to lose her footing and stumble backward.

"You're crazy, Catherine, if you think I'm going to sit by and allow Lance Savage to destroy this ministry."

"You bastard," Catherine said as the reverend darted down the hallway. "You liar. You're going to make him even angrier. Stay out of this, Kenneth."

Her words echoed without reception, through the hall as Reverend Davis vanished from sight.

6

Monday Afternoon

Fortunately for Hezekiah, the protest on the grounds had ended before he left the church. A group of smiling tourists stopped him and requested photos with him as he walked through the first-floor lobby.

Always gracious to visitors, he shook their hands and posed for pictures. Hezekiah spoke kindly to the small group. "You should all move to Los Angeles," he said. "We could use more dedicated Christians like you in our city."

The group laughed and snapped more pictures as he walked through the doors.

It was a crisp clear day in the city. The grounds were now filled with office workers from the surrounding buildings leisurely reading newspapers and eating homemade lunches.

Dino Goodman stood next to the black Lincoln at the foot of the church steps. He was to drive Hezekiah to his standing Monday lunch with three of his oldest friends.

Dino was perfectly suited for the roles of muscular bodyguard, driver, and loyal keeper of all things secret. His brown trench coat wafted in the breeze, revealing a revolver nestled in a leather shoulder holster as Hezekiah approached.

Dino was the one person in the church who consistently saw the vulnerable Hezekiah Cleaveland from the unobstructed vantage of his rearview mirror. What would have shocked his flock the most were the countless hours Dino had spent late at night waiting in the limo outside the old converted Victorian in the Adams District.

Hezekiah was already ten minutes late when they arrived at the restaurant. It had taken him more energy than expected to recover from the confrontation with Lance Savage. His hand shook as he steadied himself to step from the rear of the car.

He heard a man yell out as he walked to the entrance, "Hey, it's Hezekiah Cleaveland!"

Hezekiah looked to his right and saw a wiry little black man with disheveled hair approaching. He wore ragged pants and walked with a limp.

Hezekiah waved, hoping the gesture would provide ample fodder for the little man to recount future stories of "the day I met Pastor Hezekiah Cleaveland."

The tattered man was not satisfied. Dino saw the rapid pace at which he advanced and stepped in front of the man.

"Hey, Pastor Cleaveland!" the man blurted out as he tried in vain to walk around Dino. "You ought to be helping poor people in this city instead of building that megachurch."

A lengthy barrage of insults from the scraggly man caused Hezekiah to halt in his tracks. He placed his hand firmly on Dino's shoulder and moved him to one side allowing the little man clear passage and said, "Maybe you should go back to wherever it is you came from?" With that, Hezekiah took a one-hundred-dollar bill from his wallet and threw it at the stunned man's feet. "That should be enough for a bus ticket out of town."

The little vagrant stood speechless as Hezekiah disappeared through the restaurant door.

Hezekiah's first inclination had been to cancel the lunch with his three buddies. After anguished deliberation, he decided to meet with them to learn just how far rumors of his affair had spread.

Franco, the maître d' at Petro's Steak House, greeted his most famous customer. "Pastor Cleaveland," he said, "good to see you, sir. Your party is waiting for you at your usual booth."

Faded black-and-white photographs of famous Los Angeles athletes covered the walls of the dimly lit room. Booths with seating covered in cracking red vinyl were occupied by lawyers, construction workers, and every occupation in between. Dishes clanked and waiters moved through the room in a frenzied blur balancing trays piled with steaming dishes.

Rev. Jonathon Copperfield, a ruddy-faced pastor from Anaheim, was the first to see Hezekiah walking to the table. Hector Ramirez, the mayor of Los Angeles, was sitting next to him, and Phillip Thornton, the owner of the *Los Angeles Chronicle*, sat across the table.

All three men were natives of the city. If there was a secret worth telling in Los Angeles, one, if not all, of these men knew it.

Hezekiah was immediately struck by the absence of boisterous chatter that normally greeted him.

"Hello, gentlemen," he said as he placed a linen napkin on his lap. "What's going on here? Who died?"

The three men exchanged momentary glances. Jonathon Copperfield was the first to speak.

"Nobody died, Hezekiah. We were just talking about some gossip Phillip heard last week."

"All right, boys. Who's going to fill me in, or are we just going to change the subject to one you feel won't offend my delicate sensibilities?"

A heavyset waiter wearing a black vest, which barely concealed his bulging belly, came to the table and handed Hezekiah a menu.

"Good afternoon, Pastor Cleaveland," he said jovially in a thick Italian accent. "Will you be having your usual or would you like to try something different today?"

Hezekiah placed his order and the waiter left the table.

"All right, Phillip," Hezekiah said. "Who's trying to screw me over now? Come on, spill it."

Phillip drank the last of his red wine.

"It's not about who's screwing you, Hezekiah," he said. "It's more about who it is you're screwing."

Hezekiah sat silent. There was a hush at the table when the waiter returned with a basket of steaming bread.

"I'll have another drink, Luigi," Phillip said as the waiter walked away.

"I don't know what you're talking about," Hezekiah said.

"Come on, Hezekiah," Hector said. "You know what this is about. Don't try to bullshit us. We've known each other too long for that. We all get our share of pussy in this town." He leaned in and lowered his voice. "But a man? That's just sick. This country will never tolerate a faggot as the pastor of one of its largest churches."

Hezekiah looked to the source of the information. "Phillip, this is all a lie. It's Lance Savage at your news-paper. He's been trying to dig something up on me ever since I broke ground on the new cathedral."

"You say it's a lie," said Phillip. "But, Lance says he has

proof and can back up the entire story. Hezekiah, he's going to bury you with this one and there's nothing I can do about it."

Hezekiah grew agitated. "What do you mean, nothing? It's your newspaper, Phillip. Stop the story. Fire him. Transfer him to Idaho. You could get him off my back if you wanted."

"You know I don't have any editorial control, and besides, he's not the only one at the paper who knows about it. Lance has already briefed the managing editor and I understand he's just about finished with the final copy."

There was a long pause and then Phillip continued. "How'd you let it get this far, Hezekiah? I thought your people were supposed to be out there making sure things like this never leaked out. You've dug your own grave this time and I can't pull you out."

"You can do something about it," Hezekiah said, throwing his napkin on the table. "You just won't. Your bottom line is selling that paper, and if it's at my expense, then so be it."

"Hezekiah, wait a minute. That's not fair," Jonathon Copperfield interjected. "This isn't Phillip's fault. You've only got yourself to blame for this one. If you just had to get your cock sucked by a man, you could have gone anywhere in the world. Instead, you chose to do it in your own backyard." Jonathon stood from the table. "I can't take this anymore. This is just sick. Sick and stupid. I'm out of here."

Jonathon wove through the neighboring tables and disappeared out the door. The remaining men sat in silence for what seemed like hours. Hezekiah, with his right hand over his mouth, stared blankly at the untouched basket of bread. Hector tapped his fingers on the bare wooden table and Phillip gulped down the remains of his second glass of wine.

The quiet was finally broken. "So what am I going to do?" Hezekiah said with his hand still cupped over his mouth. The torment in his voice was deafening. "If that story runs I'm through. I could kill that bastard. . . ."

Hector cut him off. "Take it easy, Hezekiah. Look, you haven't denied it so I assume it's true."

Hezekiah's silence served as confirmation.

"Oh shit. This is crazy," Hector said. "You throw away your whole ministry for a dick. How could you let this happen? You're too smart for this, Hezekiah." There was a pause. Then, "I don't think you have any choice other than to step down."

Hezekiah sat astonished, unable to speak. At that moment life slowly began to seep from his body.

7

Tuesday

Samantha Cleaveland lay awake in the massive oak bed as Hezekiah slept at her side. It was 7:10 on Tuesday morning. She'd been awake since 5:30 A.M., staring out the window, watching the sun rise over the city. The bed headboard loomed above their heads like the facade of an Italian cathedral with peaks that almost reached the ceiling. Ornately carved mahogany pillars stood at the foot of the massive structure.

The bed had belonged to her deceased mother, Florence Weaver. A few porcelain figurines and the bed were the only items belonging to Florence that Samantha felt worthy of occupying space in her home after her mother died.

Samantha often wondered how Mama Flo, as everyone called her, could have afforded the magnificent piece of furniture. She wished her mother could have seen the bed in its opulent new home. Samantha knew that Mama Flo would have been very impressed.

A vanity with a large oval etched mirror was perfectly

positioned to catch the light from the window. The surface held expensive perfumes, which provided more evidence for discerning noses that Samantha wore only the finest of everything. Fresh flowers sat on a table between two overstuffed chairs. The mantel over the fireplace held more gold-framed pictures of the Cleavelands.

Hezekiah jerked as he grudgingly emerged from a fitful sleep. Silk pajamas stroked his skin with each twist of his body. For a brief luxurious moment he could feel Danny nuzzling his ear and stroking his thick black hair. He slowly entered the reality of his true location as his eyes adjusted to the light and saw the oak posts standing guard at his feet.

"What time is it?" he asked, sitting up abruptly.

Samantha looked up and then rolled onto her side with her back to him "Seven-ten," she curtly replied.

"Why didn't you wake me? You know I have to meet with the contractor this morning."

"Where were you last night?"

"Don't start, Samantha. I don't have time for your paranoia this morning," he snapped, and stormed into the adjoining master bathroom.

"You're not going to put me through this again!" she shouted, jumping from the bed and throwing a pillow behind him. "I won't stand by and let you humiliate me again!" Her rage was legendary behind closed doors in the Cleaveland house, but this time it was different.

The image of the pistol in her purse flashed as she continued to scream and burst through the bathroom door. "You can't do this to me again!"

Hezekiah had already removed his pajamas and was stepping into the shower when she entered. His long, muscular body gave no hint of his divine calling. Without his clothes he didn't look like the elegant clergyman most knew but rather like a man who could satisfy the most carnal of desires.

On most mornings Hezekiah would meditate under the flow of hot water, but this morning his ritual was interrupted by the attack escalating beyond the glass shower door.

"Who is she?" Samantha demanded. "Is she from church? Is it Catherine? I should have never let you hire that bitch!"

"Leave Catherine out of this," he sternly shouted over the shower door. "She doesn't have anything to do with this."

"Then who is it? You've already fucked half the staff. Who's left?"

Exhausted and broken by a long year of lying, and now her tirade, Hezekiah placed his hands against the tile above his head and shouted, "It's nobody from church, all right?"

He began to sob into the stream of water flowing on his face as the words fell without consent from his wet lips.

"I knew it. You fucking bastard. How could you do this to me again? Who the fuck is she?"

Samantha violently swung open the shower door. She reached in through the stream of water and grabbed one hand from his face. "I want to know who she is."

Hezekiah tried to pull away but her grip was too firm. His face, dripping with water and tears, turned away from her gaze.

Samantha stepped into the shower and pushed Hezekiah against the marble-tiled wall. Water from the gushing nozzle drenched her nightgown and caused her hair to flop and dangle over her eyes.

Hezekiah backed away to the rear of the space but she

matched him step for step. "Hezekiah, you can't do this to me again," she said, pulling his head toward her. "I can't go through this again with you."

Hezekiah jerked his hand from her grasp and leaned against the wall. "You're making a fool of yourself, Samantha. Get out of here. We can talk about this later."

Samantha then pulled Hezekiah's body from the shower.

"We'll talk about it now," she said, blocking his reflection in the mirror. "What if someone finds out? Everything we've worked for will be destroyed."

"I don't want to talk about it right now. I'm already late for an appointment," he snapped.

Samantha jerked his head up and looked him in the eye. "Fuck your appointment. There is nothing more important than this right now. You have to talk about it. I'm not going to let you ruin me. I'm not going to let you destroy everything we've built. Now tell me who she is."

Hezekiah did not respond.

"You're leaving me no choice, Hezekiah. I won't be humiliated. If you don't tell me I'm going to expose you. I'm not going down with you."

Hezekiah looked her in the eyes and grabbed her shoulders and held her steady.

"Don't threaten me, Samantha."

Samantha winced from his tight grip and demanded, "Let go of me, Hezekiah."

"Don't ever threaten me. This is my life and my ministry."

"It's not your life. It's *our* life and I made this ministry what it is. I'm not going to let you destroy it and me as well."

Samantha broke free and ran to the bedroom. Hezekiah ran behind and grabbed her bobbing wet hair. With one forceful yank he pulled her backward, causing her knees to buckle. She groped for a chair to maintain balance but he pulled harder, sending her tumbling to the carpet. Hezekiah straddled her chest, pinning her body to the floor. He jerked her head up and said, "If you tell anyone about this, I'll . . ."

Samantha thrashed beneath the full weight of his body. Her flailing legs toppled a table, sending a vase filled with flowers, and two of her mother's porcelain figurines crashing to the floor. Hezekiah grabbed her wrists to restrain her. Her hips bucked upward and from side to side. She twisted and turned but Hezekiah's weight held her pinned on her back.

"You'll what?" she screamed, clawing at his face. "Kill me?"

Blood flowed from the scratches on Hezekiah's face and dripped onto Samantha's as she yelled obscenities and clawed viciously. "Get the fuck off me!"

Samantha finally was able to squirm from beneath him and scrambled to her feet. Her wet, tangled, and tossed hair flew in every direction. The straps of her nightgown flopped from her shoulders, exposing her breast. Years of suppressed rage exploded onto her bloodstained face.

"You're pathetic!" she raved as she backed away from him. She picked up a book which was sitting on a table near the window and threw it at Hezekiah. "I can't wait for the whole world to find out exactly who you are. I hope the bitch is worth it because she just cost you every fucking thing you ever worked for."

Hezekiah looked up in amazement. He had never seen the woman who stood howling before him. He didn't recognize the rage nor had he ever encountered such unbridled anger from another human being.

Samantha picked up a silver dish from a nearby table

and flung it at Hezekiah. He ducked, causing the dish to whiz over his head and crash into the wall with a loud metallic clank.

"Break it off with her now or I'll tell everyone the truth about the great Hezekiah T. Cleaveland. You'll end up like all those other redneck ministers crying like idiots on television, begging the world to forgive you because you can't keep your dick in your pants."

Hezekiah stared blankly for moments at the raging woman; then he began to sob again.

"I can't break it off with her," he finally said.

"Oh my God, is she pregnant?"

"No," he said through mounting tears.

"Then why not, you coward?"

"Because . . . it's not a woman."

Samantha froze in place. Her heaving chest was the only thing moving on her body. Each breath she took caused her still exposed breast to rise up and down. She looked at him with a puzzled expression and asked through deep, gasping breaths, "What do you mean it's not a woman?"

"Just what I said. It's not a woman. It's a man."

Hezekiah came downstairs and was greeted by Etta. His eyes, behind dark sunglasses, were red and his face was puffy.

"Good morning, Pastor," Etta said as she wiped her hands on her apron. "Are you all right? I hope you're not coming down with that flu that's going around. Let me feel your head."

Hezekiah moved away from her like a frightened child. "I'm all right, Etta. My allergies are acting up again." He turned his back to her and walked toward the door.

"Aren't you having breakfast this morning? I made your favorite—eggs Benedict, blueberry muffins, and a strong pot of coffee."

"Not today. I'm running late." With that, he picked up his keys from the table in the foyer and left the house.

Samantha sat, still moist from the shower, curled on the sofa in the living room. Her silk robe held tight around her waist and legs under her body. Etta looked at the figure of the woman and knew something was seriously wrong. Samantha hadn't given the pastor her usual litany of directives before he left the house. She quietly withdrew to the safety of her kitchen.

Under normal circumstances Samantha would also have provided him with a better cover story for his unusual behavior. However, this morning she just sat and continued looking out the window. She no longer had the desire or strength to use her well-honed skills of deception.

"Sammy. Open the door, honey. It's me, Sandra," Sandra Kelly said, ringing the bell and pounding on the front door.

Sandra Kelly was one of Samantha's closest confidantes. They had gone to college together and over the years had remained friends and mutually supportive. Samantha had comforted Sandra through her first and second divorces, a series of abusive boyfriends, and the meteoric rise of her law career. In turn, Sandra had nursed Samantha through Hezekiah's many affairs and coached her through the political and social labyrinth that was the lot of every powerful pastor's wife.

Sandra was one of the most sought-after attorneys in California and represented only high-profile clients who could guarantee her prime-time coverage on CNN, or an interview with Anderson Cooper. They were sisters, but the only common blood they shared was the pain endured at the hands of the men they loved.

Samantha looked through the beveled-glass window-pane of the double front door to ensure that Sandra was alone, and then hurriedly unlatched the locks.

Sandra was an attractive woman with a slight mascu-line air about her. She frequently wore navy blue pant-suits with the lapel of a white silk blouse framing her full and deep cleavage. Today was no exception. "Sammy, are you okay? I came as soon as I got your message. Is he still here? Did he hurt you, honey?"

Samantha collapsed sobbing into Sandra's arms. The silk robe draped off her bare shoulder. "Oh, Sandra," she cried. "I thought he was going to kill me. I've never seen him like that before."

"Where is Etta?" Sandra asked.

"I don't know. As usual she disappeared after Hezekiah left."

"Stop crying, honey, and tell me what happened."

Sandra led her to the living-room sofa. As Sandra sat, she saw drops of blood on Samantha's face.

"Oh my God, Samantha. You're bleeding. What did that son-of-a-bitch do to you?"

Samantha wiped the blood from her cheek with a shak-ing hand.

"This isn't my blood. It's Hezekiah's. I confronted him about having another affair. We got into an argument and he went berserk. He attacked me. He jumped on top of me, choking me, and I scratched his face." She began to sob again. "It was horrible, Sandra. I swear he was trying to kill me."

Sandra retrieved a hand towel from a powder room off the entry hall and handed it to Samantha.

"All right, honey, it's over now. Everything is going to be fine. That cheating bastard will get what's coming to him one day, I promise you. When are you going to wise up and leave that asshole?"

The question registered slowly. *I won't have to leave him*, Samantha thought. Soon Hezekiah Cleaveland would be out of her life for good. She would be free from the man whom she now loathed. A smile, ever so slight, crept across her blood-smeared face.

The telephone on a side table rang and Samantha jumped. "I don't want to answer that. It might be him. Would you get it, Sandra?"

"Hello," Sandra said calmly. "Cleaveland residence."

"Who is this?" Hezekiah growled from the rear of the limousine.

"Oh, hello, Hezekiah. This is Sandra. Samantha can't come to the phone right now. She's busy wiping your blood off her face."

Sandra sat on the sofa and crossed her legs. Her face contorted into that of an attorney preparing for a fierce courtroom battle.

As Dino maneuvered the winding hills away from the Cleaveland estate, Hezekiah pressed the button to raise the window that separated the rear cabin of the car from the driver's section. He put the phone on speaker and calmly replied, "Don't start with me this morning, Sandra. I'm not in the mood. Put her on the phone."

"Hezekiah, do you need a building to fall on you to realize how much you're hurting Samantha?"

"This is none of your business. This is between me and my wife."

"It becomes my business when you hurt someone I love. If you're not careful, she might accidentally talk to the media about how you physically assaulted your loving wife and have been cheating on her since the day you married. You'd be a laughingstock, the butt of every joke on late-night talk shows."

There was a brief pause; then, "Are you threatening me? It all makes sense to me now. You're a lesbian. I always thought you were after Samantha, but I never figured you'd stoop this low. You would encourage her to do something stupid so you could run to her rescue and . . ."

Sandra put her hand over the mouthpiece and whispered to Samantha, "He's saying he's going to kick my ass the next time he sees me."

Hezekiah continued on the other end. "Does she know, Sandra? Have you told Samantha you're in love with her yet?"

Sandra looked stunned for a brief moment, and then whispered again to Samantha, "He's saying you're lying and that he never touched you. He said you attacked him."

"Well, I've got news for you," Hezekiah continued. "Samantha likes dick—the bigger the better."

Sandra laughed into the telephone. "Speaking of dicks," she said sarcastically, "you should try keeping yours in your pants."

Hezekiah slammed the leather car seat with three rapid strikes, and then yelled, "You can't talk to me that way!"

"He said I can't talk to him like that," Sandra said, mimicking Hezekiah's baritone indignation. "He's Hezekiah Cleaveland."

Hezekiah could hear Samantha's familiar laugh in the background. It was the same laugh he had heard when he told a bad joke on the night of their first date. The same laugh that teased him when he fell off the bed the night they made love in their first apartment together.

Sandra quickly grew impatient. She held the receiver

away from her ear as Hezekiah spewed a flurry of accusations.

"Hezekiah," she interjected, "you're fucking with the wrong person. I'm not impressed or intimidated by your holier-than-thou bullshit. If you don't watch your step, I will take matters into my own hands and believe me, I have more than enough shit on you to make your life a living hell."

Hezekiah stopped mid-insult when he heard the words.

"Shit? What are you talking about? You don't know anything about me. I told you, Sandra, I didn't touch her. Now stay out of this. Samantha and I will work this out without your interference."

"I know more than you think, and you'll find out soon enough. Brace yourself. Things are about to get even worse for you."

Sandra hung up the telephone. Within seconds the telephone rang again. "Don't answer it, Sammy," she said. "He's livid and screaming like a madman."

Samantha looked at Sandra with a puzzled expression. "What dirt are you talking about?"

"Nothing for you to concern yourself about right now, Sammy."

Samantha stepped dripping from the shower when she heard a knock on her bathroom door.

"Are you all right in there?" Sandra called out.

"I'm fine," she responded, startled by the intrusion. "I'll be out in a minute. Wait for me downstairs."

When Samantha came downstairs, Sandra greeted her in the living room with a steaming cup of chamomile tea.

"I feel much better now," Samantha said, sitting on the sofa. "I don't know if I could have got through this without you. I'm so lucky to have a friend like you."

"I'm the lucky one, Samantha. You've helped me through so much bullshit in my life. This is the least I can do for you. Sammy, can I ask you a question? Why do you stay with him? He ignores you unless the cameras are rolling. He's never cared about your career, or even acknowledged that you have one apart from him."

Samantha was silent for a moment. She laid her head on the back of the sofa. "I've asked myself the same question a thousand times," she finally said. "He used to make me so happy. But the larger the church grew, and the more famous we became, he seemed to change. The only time I think he notices me is when he thinks someone was watching. I honestly don't believe that he loves me anymore."

Samantha took a sip of the tea. "Now it's your turn. Why do you hate Hezekiah? You've never said it to me, but I can tell by the way you look at him sometimes. He has always been so good to you. He got you your first job out of law school. Loaned you money to set up your law practice."

Without hesitation Sandra responded, "It's because of you."

"But—"

"Wait a minute, Samantha. Let me finish." Sandra set her cup on the table and turned to Samantha.

"It's because I see how miserable your life is in his shadow. My heart aches every time I see you smiling dutifully behind him while people heap praise on him. I see how he went chasing after his dreams and left you to struggle through seminary alone.

"I didn't tell you this earlier, but when I spoke to Hezekiah, he accused me of . . . Well, I won't say exactly what he accused me of . . . but in essence he said I was in love with you. At first I was shocked and embarrassed.

But the more I thought about it the more I knew he was right."

Samantha showed no reaction.

"I am in love with you," Sandra continued. "But, not in the way he meant it. I love you like a sister. He accused me of being a lesbian. That's where his bruised ego caused him to miss the point completely. He'll be disappointed to learn that I'm just your average run-of-the-mill heterosexual. But I'm a woman who's blessed enough to have another woman in my life whose friendship, happiness, and well-being are as important to me as my own. If that makes me a lesbian, then fine . . . call me a dyke and sign me up for the standard-issue blue flannel shirt and Birkenstocks. At least I won't have to shave my legs anymore.

"I won't apologize or be ashamed of caring for you and for doing anything in my power to ensure that you have every opportunity to realize your dreams. The same thing you've always done for me."

A tear fell from Samantha's eye. For moments the two sat in silence.

Samantha turned to her with a smile and said, "So, does that mean you don't want to sleep with me?"

They laughed out loud together, and Sandra replied, "Sorry, girlfriend, but I like dick way too much."

Hattie Williams sat down in her favorite floral-print wing-back chair in her living room. She placed a round wicker sewing kit, which had belonged to her mother, on the tea table next to her. Hattie had raised three children in the house. Her husband died four years earlier and she now lived alone. The newest piece of furniture in the entire house was a small ottoman her husband had purchased twenty years earlier so she could elevate her leg and take the pressure off her arthritic knee.

Every other piece of furniture in the house had decades of stories to tell. There was the coffee table, which her youngest son hit his head on when he was four, and to this day he still had the scar. She recalled entertaining her in-laws for the first time on the tufted peach Barker Bros. sofa, which she and her husband had purchased when they first married. They took the bus to the high-end furniture store downtown and paid ten dollars a week to get the mahogany dining-room set and hutch with curved legs and claw feet out of layaway.

A pot of greens simmered on the stove, filling the small house with the smell of smoked neck bones and onions. Hattie turned on a ceramic lamp, which was shaped like a bird standing on one leg and covered with a frilly Victorian lamp shade, to provide the extra light she would need to mend the tear in her favorite housecoat.

As she searched the sewing kit for just the right thread, the image of a man in flight flashed before her.

It is Pastor Cleaveland. Hattie leans back in the chair with a look of cautious curiosity and watches Hezekiah, wearing a meticulously tailored suit that flaps with each twist of his flailing limbs, as he plummets through the air in the sanctuary at New Testament Cathedral.

Hattie drops the sewing basket in her lap and it tumbles to the floor, spreading bobbins, pins, and needles over the thick green carpet. She gasps and covers her mouth in disbelief. Hezekiah is falling and she cannot save him. Hideous flying gargoyles accompany him as he spirals downward. They dance rhapsodically in the air around him, cheering him on to his final destination below. Their wings flap in delight as Hezekiah tries in vain to find some hint of sympathy in their grotesque faces.

"Oh Lord, please don't let him fall," Hattie cries out loud. "Please catch him." But the harder she prays, the faster he falls. Then their eyes meet for a brief moment. Although he does not speak, she knows what he is saying to her. "Help me, Hattie. I can't stop. Help me."

She hears a chorus of screams echoing through the sanctuary as he continues his glide like a hawk toward its prey on the canyon floor below.

"Oh my God," comes as a howl from the balcony. Other shrieks of horror reverberate through the chamber. "It's the pastor. He's falling!"

Women in fashionable heels drop helplessly to their knees, unable to fathom the event unfolding before them. Men leave skid marks on the balcony floors, from rubber on their soles, as they dash in disbelief toward the rail for a clearer view.

"Tell me who did this, Pastor," Hattie says out loud to the falling man. "Tell me what to do."

But it's too late. The falling man becomes dimmer and dimmer until the image fades away.

Hattie cupped her hand to her mouth and sobbed into the housecoat she had planned to mend and said one last time, "Tell me what you need, Pastor. Lord, please tell me what to do."

Hezekiah tried calling Samantha again but still there was no answer. He struggled helplessly in an overwhelming sense of embarrassment and guilt as Dino drove the limousine along the now flat city streets. He had dealt the ultimate blow to the woman he once loved so deeply. She wouldn't leave him, but what dismal part of her soul would survive such a devastating assault? He resisted the urge to go back and comfort her, like he had done so many times before. *How could I put my family through this?* he questioned silently.

As he rode in the rear of the limousine through the city, he painfully navigated the emotional debris that accompanied infidelity, being caught, and confession. However, at the end of his silent process, there was no trace of the remorse he thought would greet him. Instead, he felt a sense of relief that he could not explain, although at times he ached at the thought of what Samantha must have been feeling at the moment. His breath seemed to pass freely through every organ in his body and then flow out the pores of his skin. The images he saw on the street seemed more vivid than they ever had before. Streams of energy rose from his belly, up his spine, and lifted an oppressive smoky haze from his shoulders and then flowed out the top of his head. He could feel the fog leave his body and evaporate into the light.

The car turned into the construction site across the street from his church and parked next to a pickup truck. He had been sitting for a moment when a tap on the window commanded his attention.

"Good morning, Reverend," said a jolly red-cheeked man wearing a plaid shirt and baggy denim jeans. "I didn't think you were going to make it. I was just about to leave."

"Good morning, Benny. Sorry I'm late. I had a little problem at home. The building is looking great."

Benny Winters was the general contractor for the cathedral that would soon be the new home of New Testament Cathedral and Media Center. Hezekiah never trusted the round little man, but he had a reputation for building some of the most impressive edifices in the country. As a result of his concerns, Hezekiah insisted on approving every construction change order, regardless of how small, and visited the construction site as frequently as he could.

"Thank you. We're right on schedule too. Come with me. I've got a few things to show you," Benny replied.

The two men put on hard hats and began a tour of the grounds and skeletal tower. Trucks drove on unpaved roads and dust filled the air. Men in hard hats and construction boots waved good morning as they passed. To their left a cement truck churned as a wet gray substance poured from its bowels.

"There is where we decided to put the satellite dish. Now everyone in the world will be able to see your pretty face live every Sunday morning," Benny said with a hearty laugh and pointed to a leveled piece of ground in the distance.

Hezekiah followed Benny into the cathedral and along corridors with exposed metal beams and wires. Workers were busy drilling and moving items through the halls. Benny pointed to a series of metal brackets along the corridor and said, "Those are where we're installing the smoke detectors and alarms. The fire inspector came by yesterday and approved the distance between each unit. He went over the building with a fine-tooth comb and said everything looked to be in order."

Images of Danny flashed through Hezekiah's mind as he walked and made him smile. He remembered bringing him to the construction site on several occasions. He always wanted Danny, more than anyone else in his world, to be proud of him. He often wondered what Danny would think of a decision he had made or a project he was considering. He never hesitated to call and ask his opinion.

Hezekiah suppressed a smile and asked, "Have you got the final bids in for the carpet and tile work yet?"

"They're in, and I think you'll be very pleased. Most of them came in under what we budgeted. It's tough out there now and all these contractors are desperate to get a job as big as this."

"I never understood the point of hiring the cost estimator. It sounds like he overestimated the market. Maybe I should underestimate his fee," Hezekiah said without humor.

Ben smiled only to appease Hezekiah. "I don't think it was his fault. No one knew the economy would end up in the toilet like this."

Hezekiah barely heard the words spoken by Benny in front of the building. All he could think about was Danny and holding him again. The pounding of hammers and the smell of freshly cut wood seemed only to remind him more of how much he was in love.

Samantha paced the floor of her study after Sandra had left the house. Her silk robe trailed behind as she retraced her steps in front of the desk.

I could survive an affair with a woman, but a man? she thought. *If I didn't have a good reason to kill him before, I sure as hell have the perfect one now.*

Her course was clearer now than it ever was before. She could survive the affair with that bitch from the restaurant they frequented, or the scheduling secretary she had immediately fired. But a man? She would never stand by and have the power of her feminine allure called into question. He handed her the verdict and read his own sentence. Death by shooting on the stage he had built for himself.

Samantha removed a pack of cigarettes from her desk.

She nervously inhaled the smoke and retrieved her cell phone.

Rev. Willie Mitchell answered. "Yeah? This is Willie."

"Willie, it's Samantha. Are you alone? Can you talk?"

Reverend Mitchell, like so many other men, worshipped Samantha Cleaveland. He had schemed to be a part of her inner circle from the first day he saw her standing next to Hezekiah at a fund-raiser for a state senator. Over the years he watched her become more confident and saw her naive good looks evolve into seductive and intoxicating beauty.

He willingly gave everything Samantha had requested of him: one million for the new cathedral, substantial contributions to the politicians of her choice, or playing the "heavy" with any misguided bureaucrat or church trustee who dared to challenge her wishes.

Years earlier, he had bravely confessed his true feelings for her. She was repulsed by his proposition but kept her sentiments private. Instead, she used his adoration as a leash to keep him securely within her reach. The unspoken agreement was that if he acted upon her every wish, then maybe someday she would return his affection.

Willie quickly sat up on the edge of his couch and turned down the volume of the television with a remote control. Striped boxer shorts bunched between his legs and a tight white T-shirt stretched around his belly. "Yes, I can talk. What's up?"

"Have you found someone to do it yet?"

"What's the rush? The guy I've got in mind won't get out of jail for at least three more months."

"I don't have three months. It has to be done this Sunday."

"This Sunday? Are you fucking crazy? How the hell am I going to find anyone to do it in less than a week?"

"If you can't handle it, then I'll find someone else who can."

Willie rubbed his eyes and released a heavy sigh. "Wait a minute. I didn't say I couldn't do it. You just caught me off guard. Where do you want it done? Inside the house? A drive-by?"

"No. I want it done at church. Hezekiah always said he wanted to die in the pulpit. I want him killed this Sunday morning while he's giving the sermon. That's the least I can do for him."

"Where the fuck am I going to find someone stupid enough to kill him in front of the whole damn church and broadcast live all over the fucking country?"

"I know of someone who I think will be perfect for the job."

"Who?" Willie asked suspiciously.

"Virgil Jackson. He used to play drums for the youth choir. Now he's a crackhead living on the streets. He just got out of jail and I'm sure he's desperate. He bummed twenty dollars from Hezekiah this past Sunday."

"Yeah, I know him but that's kind of close to home, don't you think?" Willie asked. "I don't know, Samantha. This seems unnecessarily risky. What if he gets caught?"

"That's why he's perfect. Hezekiah fired him a year ago, when he was caught trying to break into the church. That's what he was in jail for. People will think he was just settling a score."

"What if—"

"No more 'what-ifs.' Just talk to him and make sure he says yes and offer him enough money to leave Los Angeles permanently. I'll make sure the church balcony is empty. He can sneak up there at about eleven thirty. If he stays low behind the seats, no one will see him, and he'll be out of the range of the cameras up there."

Unable to deny the woman he had loved for years, Willie responded, "I still say this is fucking crazy, but I'll talk to him."

"Get back to me as soon as you've spoken to him," Samantha concluded.

Samantha disconnected without saying good-bye. She took one final drag from a cigarette and dropped the almost extinguished butt into a tepid cup of tea.

Willie adjusted his body on the sofa to relieve the pinching from the tight boxers. He reached for his bottle of Mylanta sitting on a cluttered coffee table. Samantha's sudden need to speed up the murder of Hezekiah concerned him.

Why the rush now? he thought. *We've planned this for almost a year, but now she wants it done within a week.* He worried that her haste would cause mistakes. His stomach growled as he tensed his body to force the release of a trapped air bubble. She had never been that terse with him before. In the past she had convinced him to do her bidding by dangling the hope of sex in front of him. This time, however, was different.

His thoughts continued to whirl. *If she could do this to her own husband, what would she do if I disappoint her?* Would she ever allow him to touch her, or was it just another game? He feared she would shun him and his life would change dramatically if he disappointed her. The source of much of his power in the city came largely from his relationship with her. She made him worth talking to. Her association with him prompted others to look past his portly and crass exterior and tolerate his company.

His mind turned to Hezekiah. The man who embodied everything Willie ever wanted in life: looks, wealth, fame and, most important, Samantha. Only Willie truly knew the depth of his hatred for Hezekiah Cleaveland.

His stomach continued to rumble after he drank the last of the medicine. He pictured Samantha running to him for comfort and protection after Hezekiah was gone. He would be her hero and those who laughed behind his back would then clamor for his attention.

8

One Year Earlier

The first time Danny had ever been in the church, and also the first time the two men had ever been alone together, had been one year earlier. Hezekiah had asked him to come by after he talked with the homeless woman near the church. Danny was nervous about speaking for the second time in one day with the pastor of New Testament Cathedral.

Danny sat with his backpack at his feet in Hezekiah's outer office. A dark-haired young woman opened envelopes at a desk near Hezekiah's door. Danny thought her face was exceptionally attractive for a church employee. After reading the content of a letter, she looked in Danny's direction and smiled.

"I'm sure he'll only be a few more minutes," she said as her hands reached for the next envelope. "He's running behind schedule today."

As he thumbed through a religious periodical, the door opened and three expensively dressed people walked out, with Hezekiah close behind. The first was a woman wearing a blue suit. She smiled from ear to ear as Hezekiah shook her hand. The two men accompanying her waited their turn to shake the pastor's hand.

"Thank you for your generous contributions," Hezekiah said to the three. "I'm going to have my staff contact you to work out the details. It's good to know the corporate community is also concerned about spreading the gospel."

"It's our pleasure. I only wish we could do more," came the eager reply from the youngest man.

Hezekiah saw Danny as the three spouted their support. His mind became blank for the second time that day. Each lapse had been prompted by the sight of the attractive young man. The three executives assessed that their fifteen minutes of face time had expired and politely exited the room.

"It's Danny St. John, right?" Hezekiah asked without moving forward. "Thank you for stopping by. Please come in."

"Pastor Cleaveland," the receptionist reminded him, "your next appointment is on his way. You're running a little behind schedule."

"This will only take a few minutes," Hezekiah replied without removing his eyes from Danny.

Hezekiah sat with Danny in chairs in front of his desk. "So, did you have a chance to speak with that woman? What's her name? Is she mentally ill?" Hezekiah asked as Danny placed his backpack on the floor.

"I'm sorry, sir, but I can't say too much about her without breaching her confidentiality. As I said to you earlier, she refuses to accept any assistance. She said she makes enough money panhandling to survive without our help."

"For God's sake, she's homeless. That's no way to live. Can't you at least talk her into going into a shelter?"

"I've tried. She thinks they're too dangerous. Her belongings were stolen a few years ago at a shelter. Now she refuses to go back. Women are exceptionally vulnerable in shelters, especially women with mental disorders. They often feel safer out in public, where there are other people around, and they can keep all their belongings with them."

Hezekiah found himself lost once again in the melodic tone of Danny's voice. His full lips were forming words, but Hezekiah could hear only music.

Why does this kid have such an effect on me? Hezekiah thought. God, he's beautiful.

"Danny, what exactly is it that you do on the outreach team? It must be very difficult to see human misery on a daily basis."

The intercom sounded before Danny could answer. "Pastor Cleaveland your four o'clock is here. He said he has a plane to catch in forty-five minutes and will only take a few minutes of your time."

"Excuse me, Danny," Hezekiah said as he picked up the telephone. "Why did he schedule a four o'clock appointment with me if he had a four forty-five flight? Tell him I'll be right out."

Hezekiah returned his focus to Danny. "I'm sorry I have to cut this short, Danny." The two men stood up and walked toward the door. Hezekiah put his hand on the doorknob. He hesitated for a moment and then said, "I've got a proposal for you. If it wouldn't be too much trouble, I'd like to go with you one afternoon on your rounds." The words escaped effortlessly from his mouth. "I'd like to see firsthand how people live on the streets."

Danny raised his eyebrows at the suggestion. "I think you will be surprised if you've never seen it before. I'd be glad to take you around to a few shelters."

"I've been to shelters before," Hezekiah said. "No, I want to see where people live on the streets, under the freeways, in the parks. I'll put on some jeans, tennis shoes, and a baseball cap. No one will recognize me."

"Sir, I think people would recognize you even if you went in drag."

Hezekiah laughed out loud. "In drag? I won't go that far. I don't think my congregation would like that."

"Well, they'd love it in West Hollywood," Danny said, laughing along with Hezekiah.

"Maybe, but I think I'll stick with jeans. Do we have a date, then?" Hezekiah asked as his laughter subsided.

Danny picked up his backpack and shook Hezekiah's hand.

"Anytime you'd like, Pastor Cleaveland," he said as the two walked to the door.

"Good, then. I'll have my secretary set it up. And, Danny?"

"Yes, sir."

"Please call me Hezekiah."

It happened exactly one week after the first day they met. Hezekiah and Danny stood on a corner in skid row talking to a homeless man.

"Hey, ain't you Pastor Hezekiah Cleaveland?" the man said, tucking a half-empty beer can in his coat pocket. "What are you doing out here on skid row?"

"I came out with Danny so I could talk to homeless people like you and ask what more my church can do to help."

The scraggly old man in dirty short pants struggled to his feet. "The first thing you can do is build more mother-fucking—excuse my French, Reverend—more affordable housing. They're always full, so me and my buddies have to sleep out here in the streets like dogs."

"When was the last time you stayed in a shelter?" Danny asked, goading the man to tell Hezekiah more.

"It's been months now. I gave up a long time ago. Every time I tried, some young son of a bitch would tell me they're all full. After a while you just get tired of trying."

"You know it's illegal to sleep on the streets, don't you?" Hezekiah said, restraining his irritation with the wobbling vagrant.

"Hell yeah, I know. The fucking cops won't let me forget it, but where the hell else am I supposed to go?"

Hezekiah looked to Danny. "Can't you get him into a program somewhere?"

"I can certainly try, but he's right. The shelters are usually full."

Hezekiah quickly grew impatient with the dirty man and his slurred speech.

"Danny, I should be getting back now," he said, dismissing the vagabond's observations. "Sir, it was nice meeting you. Good luck and keep trying to get into a shelter. I'm sure something will eventually open up for you."

As Danny and Hezekiah walked away and said, "That's my bus coming. I'm going to have to leave you now. I hope this has helped."

Hezekiah looked up and spoke quickly. "My car is around the corner. Let me give you a ride home."

Danny hesitated. "I'll be fine. I drove here too."

"Please, Danny, it's the least I can do. You've been very kind to me."

The ride to Danny's home was filled with animated conversation and laughter. Hezekiah sat cramped but inexplicably comfortable in the passenger seat of Danny's florescent orange 1973 Volkswagen Beetle as they hurled through the city streets. Danny skillfully shifted the grinding gears and the engine sputtered as Hezekiah's head jerked from side-to-side, back-and-forth with every shift of the transmission. After reaching Danny's apartment, they continued to talk for another fifteen minutes while the car engine was still running.

Danny finally said, "If we talk out here any longer I'm going to run out of gas. I'd better let you go."

Hezekiah looked at this watch. "I have two hours before my next appointment. Would you mind if I hung out with you for a while longer? I can have my driver pick me up here in an hour or so."

The floors of Danny's small apartment were covered with old rugs, dull from the afternoon sun. A burgundy couch from the local furniture outlet sat beneath arched windows looking onto the street. A computer sat on a large wooden desk which was covered with papers and open books. No art hung on the beige stucco walls.

A snow-white cat with one blue eye and one green greeted Danny as he and Hezekiah entered.

"This is Parker," Danny said as he stooped down to rub Parker's back.

"Why did you name him Parker?" Hezekiah asked.

"I was on my way to the market one day and I saw him walking down Park Street. It was a hot day and the pavement was burning his paws. I came back home and couldn't get the poor little guy out of my mind. He was so cute and he looked so helpless. So I got a bottle of water and a bowl and went to look for him. He was still there and he's been my best buddy ever since."

"From what I've seen today, that makes sense."

"What do you mean?"

"You've obviously dedicated your entire life to taking care of strays," Hezekiah said gently. "I feel like we have that in common."

"I would hardly call the members of your church 'strays.' From what I've heard, your church is full of celebrities, professional athletes, doctors, and lawyers."

"Some of them are, but not all. It doesn't matter how much money or education they have. That's not what I meant. People come to church because they are searching for something that money can't buy. Some are looking for peace, others for something larger than themselves to believe in. But the one thing they all have in common is they're looking for someone who cares about them, just like Parker and the homeless people you work with."

"The difference between you and me is that I don't charge these people for my services and I'm not paid nearly as much as I assume you are."

Hezekiah laughed. "Regardless of what you've heard, Danny, I don't charge either. People give to the church because the Bible instructs them to do so. I would still do exactly what I do even if no one ever gave me a dime." His tone turned somber as he continued. "For some reason it's very important to me that you understand that I do what I do because I believe deeply in the message and the good it does for so many lonely and lost people. It's not about money, Danny. In that way I think we are very much alike. Does that make sense to you?"

"I didn't mean to offend you but I'm glad to hear you say that. I'll be honest with you. The Hezekiah Cleaveland I saw today is nothing like what I expected."

Hezekiah laughed again. "I'm almost afraid to ask, but what were you expecting?"

"I thought you'd be the person I've seen on television.

All smiles and spewing a string of quotable quotes from the Bible. But, instead, I saw a very kind and vulnerable man. I think you're searching for something yourself."

"And what do you think that is?"

"I don't know yet. But I can see it in your eyes. I saw it the first day I met you on the street. There was something very sad about you that day. I kind of felt the same way about you as I did when I saw Parker for first time wandering the streets alone."

Hezekiah did not respond. He, instead, walked to the sofa and stared out the arched windows at the traffic passing below.

Danny changed the subject. "What do you think of my place? It's not much, but it's home," Danny said as he turned on the lights and laid his mail and keys on the cluttered but clean desk.

"It's very nice, Danny. It feels so comfortable and warm. It feels like a very loving and special person lives here."

"Would you like a cup of coffee?"

"That would be nice, if it's not too much trouble," Hezekiah replied.

Hezekiah felt strangely at ease in the little apartment, even though he had not been in a home that sparse in years. He sat down on the couch and thumbed through a magazine that lay on an old wooden coffee table.

"How do you take your coffee?" came a voice from the kitchen.

"Black is fine."

In a few moments Danny returned with two large mugs and set them on the coffee table. He flopped down on the sofa at a respectable distance from the pastor.

"Do you live here alone?" Hezekiah asked.

"Yes. I had a roommate but he moved in with his

boyfriend about a year ago." Danny chose this route of subtle disclosure rather than directly declaring that he was gay.

They talked and laughed for thirty minutes when Hezekiah said, "I hope I'm not keeping you from anything. I know you must be tired after such a long day."

"Not at all. I'm enjoying your company."

As they spoke, Hezekiah looked at his watch. "I should leave. I really enjoyed this afternoon. It was the most relaxed I've felt in years."

While saying the words, he squeezed Danny's hand tightly and looked intently into his eyes. They stood and studied each other's faces for silent moments. The exchange between their clasped hands and locked eyes spoke more than any words they could have spoke. For each, the extended gaze served as confirmation of their shared feelings. Then in a moment of mutual consent, they simultaneously pressed their bodies together and kissed long, deep, and hard. Hezekiah's soft, full lips enveloped Danny's mouth. The kiss was slow and passionate. Thoughts were shared with each breath they exchanged. Hezekiah took off his baseball cap and tossed it onto a nearby console without looking. His erection stretched the leg of his jeans as he probed the rear of Danny's faded army fatigues with one hand and pressed his face closer with the other.

They made love for the first time that afternoon. Hezekiah and Danny both knew that it would not be the last time they would be in each other's arms. Over the next year they had "coffee" together often.

9

Six Months Earlier

The alliance between Cynthia Pryce and Sandra Kelly had been forged six month earlier. Though their motivations for outing Hezekiah Cleaveland were different, the means served each of their purposes well. Sandra had introduced Cynthia to Phillip Thornton, the *Los Angeles Chronicle* publisher, after Cynthia told her about the e-mails between Hezekiah and Danny St. John during a dinner party at the Cleaveland estate.

The table in the dining room had been set to perfection. An elaborate floral arrangement in the center of the table was illuminated by the massive crystal chandelier above. Eight place settings held so many utensils, plates, bowls, and goblets that even the most sophisticated diner would have been at a loss determining what their specific uses were.

Four servers wearing black vests, dark pants and skirts, hovered unobtrusively near each guest. They poured wine and anticipated the needs of the guests before the diners had the chance to lift their hands or catch an eye for attention. Plates of ranch quail, grilled over vine cuttings, with red wine sauce, chanterelle mushrooms, potato cakes, and herb salad were placed before each guest.

Hezekiah sat at the head of the table. To his right and left were Hector Ramirez, the mayor of Los Angeles, and his wife, Miranda. Then came Percy and Cynthia Pryce, and next to them Sandra Kelly and Kenneth Davis. Samantha sat facing Hezekiah at the opposite end of the table.

"I've lived in Los Angeles my entire life and I've never seen as many homeless people living on the streets and in the parks as there are today," Cynthia said to the mayor. "Can't the city do more to help them?"

"I was downtown at a meeting yesterday and I was amazed at how aggressive panhandlers have become," Kenneth chimed in. "Two to three people on every block stopped me to ask for money. I like to think I'm a compassionate man, but that was a bit overwhelming for me."

"I don't feel that way at all," Percy said. "I always carry extra cash so I can give it to people when they ask."

"I think that does more harm than good, Reverend Pryce," Sandra said between sips of white wine. "Most homeless people are either addicted to drugs and alcohol or mentally ill. Giving them cash only perpetuates their addiction."

"Nonsense," Percy said defensively. "I'd rather give a dollar directly to a homeless person than to some of these so-called 'nonprofit agencies' that take forty cents off the top of every dollar they collect."

"That's a gross generalization," Hector said, leaning forward in his seat. "Many of the organizations that the city funds to serve the homeless are doing amazing work and are fiscally responsible."

Hezekiah finally spoke. "I agree. I know of an outreach worker who works for an agency downtown"—Hezekiah contained his passion and spoke cautiously—"He is a selfless and compassionate guy. He does amazing work with some of the most destitute people in this city."

Cynthia's ears perked up. She could not believe Hezekiah had the audacity to talk about his lover in such glowing terms in front of everyone. "He sounds like a wonderful person, Pastor. What's his name?" she asked slyly.

Hezekiah looked at her with an innocent expression and said, "I can't remember offhand, but I know he does good work."

"Don't get me wrong. I'm not saying there aren't any good social service agencies out there," Percy said before he could swallow his most recent bite of quail. "The point I'm trying to make is if I give the money myself, I know it won't end up in the pockets of some overpaid administrator."

"Since I've taken office, the city has doubled its budget for social service programs. We've built three new shelters and two new community clinics," Hector replied defensively. "But it's still not enough. The reality is governments can only do so much to address the social ills that face this city. We need to develop more public and private partnerships with the corporate and faith communities." Hector looked to Hezekiah. "We need churches like yours to step up to the plate and help us."

Hezekiah smiled and said, "Don't you start on me too. New Testament Cathedral has been on the front line in the fight against poverty. We have clothes and food drives. Our members volunteer at shelters, and we make generous contributions to several agencies around the city."

"That doesn't sound like the front to me," Sandra said.

"Sounds more like the tail." The table fell silent. "Homeless people don't need more hand-me-down clothes or dented cans of tuna. They need affordable housing. They need affordable health care and drug rehabilitation programs."

"Is that so?" Hezekiah asked. "Then why don't you tell us how much you give to the homeless? And I don't mean giving them your doggie bag after you've dined at Spago."

"Hezekiah, you shouldn't ask her a personal question like that," Samantha interjected. "Sandra, ignore him. He's just being provocative."

"No, I think it's a fair question," Sandra said, laying her fork gently on her plate. "First of all, I haven't eaten at Spago in years, Hezekiah," Sandra said, leaning back in her chair. "I didn't know anyone other than tourists still went there. And as for your second question, last year alone my law firm worked over one thousand hours pro bono on discrimination cases involving low-income housing. And, before you ask, I personally have donated a substantial portion of my own income to multiple charities in Los Angeles and New York."

Hezekiah looked coldly at Sandra and said, "That's admirable, Sandra, but I don't think that places you in a morally superior position, nor does it give you the right to criticize what we do at New Testament Cathedral."

"I hadn't intended for it to. I simply wanted to answer your question."

There was an uneasy tension at the table. The easy chatter that had preceded the most recent exchange was now replaced with awkward glances and a preoccupation with bread crumbs that had fallen on the table. The servers' pace slowed a notch as the tone of the party shifted.

There was a brief silence, and then Percy spoke. "Sandra,

Hezekiah is right. I don't think that is a thorough or fair depiction of the significant impact New Testament Cathedral has had on the lives of poor people in this city," he said diplomatically. "Hezekiah gives something more important than housing. He gives them hope with his message. He feeds their soul."

Sandra rolled her eyes but did not respond, and Cynthia coughed as if choking on the words her husband just spoke.

"That is very important," Miranda said, "but with all due respect to Hezekiah, and all other ministers in this city, a sermon doesn't keep a person warm and dry at night when they are sleeping under a bush in Griffith Park."

Hector looked at his wife sharply. "Miranda," he rebuked. "I'm sure Hezekiah is doing his best. As you can see, Miranda is very passionate about this issue."

"That's all right, Hector," Hezekiah said. "Miranda is right. The church should be doing more. Samantha and I have been thinking of ways we can get more involved in the issue."

Hezekiah looked to Samantha for support, but instead, she placed her napkin on the table and said, "Why don't we all go into the living room? We can have our coffee and after dinner liqueur, if you'd like, in there."

The guests filed in pairs from the dining room into the living room. They were greeted by the sound of a Mozart sonata played by a pianist on the baby grand in a corner of the room. A lavish silver coffee setting had been placed on a table behind the sofa, and a server stood near another table, which held a full brandy decanter and matching Baccarat glasses.

Miranda and Samantha sat chatting in chairs that faced

the floor-to-ceiling window overlooking the Pacific Ocean. "I hope I didn't offend you with my comment earlier," Miranda said. "I get so upset when people criticize Hector on his homeless policies."

"I wasn't offended. I'm glad you said it. Hezekiah needed to hear that," Samantha replied. "I tried to convince him that we should have built an affordable housing complex instead of the new cathedral, but you know how men are. It's all about ego and power."

"The same could be said about Hector. Sometimes I think if he could marry his ego, he would have no use for me at all."

The two women laughed in unison.

"Behind Hector's painted-on smiles and expensive suits, there really is a man who cares about people," Miranda continued. "It hurts him to see so many people living on the streets in this city. I think, if he could, he would build a shelter in every neighborhood, but people won't let him."

"I wish I could say the same for Hezekiah," Samantha said, "but he only has himself to blame for doing so little to help the homeless. It was his idea to build the cathedral, and once his mind is set, there is no changing it."

Hezekiah and Hector stood near the fireplace, sipping brandy. "I'm sorry about what Miranda said earlier," Hector said. "Sometimes she says things without thinking first."

"Not a problem, Hector. Samantha is the same way. I've had to apologize for inappropriate things she's said in public more times than I'd care to remember."

"The real problem this city faces in addressing homelessness is its lack of coordination of services," Hector continued. "There are five different departments that fund and monitor programs for the homeless and none of them know what the other is doing."

"You should hire Samantha," Hezekiah said with a smile. "She knows what every department in the church is doing and where every dime is spent."

Kenneth and Percy accepted cups of coffee from the server. "Sandra was completely out of line," Percy said quietly. "She took shots at Hezekiah every chance she got."

"I think the rumors are true about her," Kenneth said while stirring his coffee and clinking the inside of the cup with a silver spoon. "Did you notice the way she looks at Samantha?"

Cynthia and Sandra were huddled in a remote corner of the living room, having their own discussion.

"It's so sad how he cheats on her. I don't know why she puts up with it," Cynthia observed.

"I guess she loves him enough to ignore the other women," Sandra said in defense of her friend.

"All the other women he's had affairs with are bad enough, but . . ." Cynthia stopped midsentence.

"But what?" Sandra inquired.

Cynthia looked over her shoulder to ensure the other guests at the party were preoccupied and said, "Let's just say, I know for a fact that Hezekiah has recently expanded his horizons."

Sandra led Cynthia into the foyer. "You know something, don't you?" she inquired forcefully. "Spill it, girl. What's he done now?"

"I don't like to gossip, but I hate to see a wonderful woman like Samantha get hurt," Cynthia replied sheepishly. "I found out, purely by accident, mind you, that Hezekiah is having an affair. . . ." She paused, and then whispered quietly, "With a man this time."

Sandra quickly covered her mouth to prevent a gasp

from reverberating through the room. "Cynthia, you must be mistaken. Hezekiah is a lot of things but I don't think he's gay."

"I know, girl. I was just as shocked as you are."

On the last word Samantha walked up behind them. "There you two are. Why aren't you circulating? I'll be glad when this is over. I want to get this over with as soon as possible. What are you two talking about?"

Sandra was still in shock and could not respond, so Cynthia quickly interjected, "Sandra was telling me about the new case she's working on."

10

Tuesday

Cynthia Pryce greeted guests in the banquet hall of the Bonaventure Hotel. Her vanilla linen pantsuit followed perfectly each elegant gesture of her body.

It was the fifth annual Los Angeles Women in Business Awards Luncheon at the Bonaventure Hotel and Cynthia was the honorary chair. Due to time constraints Samantha Cleaveland had not been able to accept the honor, so the organizing committee viewed Cynthia as a suitable alternative.

Cynthia shook manicured hands and air kissed taut rosy cheeks as the powerful, the beautiful, and the well-heeled filed past her. The room was a sea of pinks and pastels, accented by sparkling china settings and crystal goblets. A string quartet played chamber music for those entering the room. Waiters mingled among the dense crowd as they balanced silver trays of shrimp, stuffed mushrooms, and cheeses skewered with colorful toothpicks. Large vases arranged with exotic bouquets dotted each table.

Sandra Kelly was the next in line to greet Cynthia.

"Cynthia," Sandra said, approaching with a glass of champagne in one hand and a cell phone in the other.

Sandra leaned in, kissed Cynthia on the cheek, and whispered, "These old divas look like they belong on a poster in a plastic surgeon's office."

"Sandra, you made it," said Cynthia. "I called your office but they said you'd be in Sacramento until this evening. How's your new case going? I hear the surrogate mother wants to claim her parental rights now."

"It's turning into a nightmare," said Sandra. "Never mind that. What's happening with the story?"

Cynthia took Sandra by the arm and led her to an unoccupied section of the ballroom in the Bonaventure. "Lance had to delay the story. He said he needed a quote from Hezekiah before the editor would approve it for publication."

"Has he got it yet?" Sandra asked.

"I don't know. He had a meeting with Hezekiah on Monday, but I haven't heard anything."

"I hope he didn't tell Hezekiah we're the source," Sandra said. "Our hands have to stay clean in order for this to work."

"He won't. Our agreement was that we anonymously provide him with the proof of the affair, and he keeps our names out of it." There was a long pause; then Cynthia said, "I hope Hezekiah's ego doesn't stop him from stepping down."

"Trust me, Cynthia, he'll resign," Sandra said, placing her now empty champagne glass on a vacant surface nearby. "Hezekiah's ego may be out of control, but he's not an idiot. Besides, if he doesn't, there is no way the board of trustees will accept a gay man as pastor, even if that man is the great Hezekiah Cleaveland."

Cynthia waved at an anonymous face across the room

and then continued, "Does Samantha know anything about this?"

"She knows Hezekiah is having an affair, but she didn't tell me it's with a man."

"Not that. I mean, does she know anything about the article Lance is writing?"

"I don't think so. If she did, she would have told me." Sandra waved off the question and continued. "I've set up a meeting tomorrow night at my home with Phillip Thornton. He wants to talk to you face-to-face."

"Why?" Cynthia asked nervously.

"He doesn't want to face Hezekiah's wrath if we get cold feet on this. He needs assurances that we'll stand behind the story in case Hezekiah pursues legal action against the *Los Angeles Chronicle*."

"Okay," Cynthia agreed hesitantly. "I'll be there, but I don't trust Phillip. He and Hezekiah go way back."

"I don't either, but it's a risk we have to take."

The two women embraced and walked arm in arm to the front of the ballroom.

It was three o'clock and Cynthia still had not heard from Lance. The luncheon at the Bonaventure Hotel had ended and throngs of admiring women had heaped praise upon her for hosting the successful event.

"Where is he? Why hasn't he called yet?" Cynthia said as she and Sandra Kelly drove out of the circular driveway of the hotel. "Hezekiah must have scared him off the story," Cynthia said. "We're screwed if he drops the ball on this."

Sandra veered her hunter green Jaguar into the flow of cars on the street and drove toward Cynthia's penthouse.

"Lance can take care of himself, Cynthia. This is the biggest story of his career. If he brings down Hezekiah, he'll be able to work for any major newspaper in the country. He won't screw this up."

"What if he buckled and told Hezekiah that we're the ones who leaked the story?"

"Cynthia, you're getting paranoid. Slow down, honey. Call Lance now, if it'll make you feel better." Sandra handed her a cell phone. "I'm sure he's at his dingy little desk at the *Chronicle* right now, finishing up the story."

Cynthia dialed Lance's number.

"Hello, this is Lance Savage," came the recorded message. "I'm not available to take your call. Please leave a message at the tone and I will contact you as soon as possible." The familiar *beep* sent a jolt through Cynthia's body.

"Damn it, Lance. This is Cynthia," she said into the wireless void. "Where are you? Have you interviewed Hezekiah yet? Call me as soon as you get this message." Cynthia disconnected the line and threw the sleek black telephone onto the seat of the car.

"Cynthia, you need to relax. We've come this far, right? This is no time to panic." While driving with one hand, Sandra reached into her pocket and handed Cynthia a vial filled with white pills. "Here, honey," she said, "take one of these. It'll calm you down."

"What are they?" Cynthia asked, reaching for the little brown bottle.

"It's Xanax. Just take one, honey. You'll feel better."

Cynthia eagerly consumed the tablet. "I could use a joint right now, too. This is driving me crazy."

Sandra looked cautiously in her rearview mirror, then reached into the glove compartment and produced the leafy prescription Cynthia had desired.

"I shouldn't be doing this but you look like you could

really use this right now," Sandra said nervously, looking in her rearview mirror and from side to side. The two women passed the joint between them as they drove along Wilshire Boulevard.

A woman driving beside them recognized Cynthia from the luncheon and waved while waiting at a red light. Cynthia clamped her smiling red lips shut to prevent a stream of smoke from escaping and dutifully waved back. Cynthia burst into a combination of laughter and coughs that filled the car with billowing white smoke after the woman had proceeded to a safe distance ahead.

"That bitch almost killed me." She laughed while coughing out more smoke. "I thought I was going to pass out." Cynthia considered what her next move would be as the Xanax and marijuana mixed in her brain. "I don't know what we're going to do if this doesn't work."

"It is going to work, and you're going to do just what we've planned for the last three months," Sandra said impatiently.

As Sandra turned the car into the covered carport of her high-rise building, Cynthia tossed the remains of the marijuana cigarette out the window of the rolling vehicle. The women embraced and an attendant rushed to open the car door for Cynthia.

"Good afternoon, Mrs. Pryce," a round-faced man, clad in a red uniform, said as Cynthia extended her leg to the pavement. "Reverend Pryce just arrived only a few minutes ago. He should be in your apartment by now."

Cynthia hesitated for a moment and looked to Sandra.

"Do you want me to come up with you? Are you going to be all right?" Sandra asked.

"I'm fine now. I'll call you as soon as I've heard from . . ."

Cynthia stopped when she realized the doorman was listening. "I'll call you."

Cynthia walked toward the double glass doors of the luxury building. Two rows of potted palm trees lining the carpeted path bristled from a slight breeze under the massive blue awning. The attendant sped past her to the glass doors and flung them open.

"Thank you," she said without looking at the man's anxious face.

The foyer sparkled from the afternoon sun. Classical music played as several residents retrieved mail from boxes partially hidden behind another cluster of potted plants. New overstuffed chairs and couches dotted the room. Two elderly ladies sat reading the afternoon newspaper in front of an oversized mahogany framed fireplace. From the lobby's cathedral ceiling, a massive chandelier glowed from internal and external light.

Cynthia walked quickly toward the elevator doors, hoping to avoid the inevitable greetings from omnipresent neighbors.

As she pressed the button, she heard, "Hello, Mrs. Pryce. The reverend went up a few minutes ago. You just missed him."

When she turned, she saw Carl, the building security guard. He moved toward her as he spoke.

"Seems like he's in a pretty bad mood today. Nearly bit the head off poor Mrs. Nussbaum, in 17D. She was complaining about the homeless guys who have been urinating behind the building. Said she walked up on one of them this morning as he was taking a leak. 'Nearly scared me to death,' she told the reverend, and before she could even finish her sentence, Reverend Pryce lit into her like there was no tomorrow."

Cynthia listened intently to the account from the overly familiar guard.

"He said to her, 'You wouldn't have seen him taking a piss if you weren't always lurking around the building. Maybe that'll teach you to mind your own business.' I thought she was going to cry after he got through with her."

"I'm sure he didn't mean to offend her," Cynthia said while pressing the elevator button again, hoping to speed its arrival. "He probably has a lot on his mind today. You know how he gets sometimes."

Carl gave her a knowing smile. "I sure do, ma'am. I've been on the receiving end of his sharp tongue a few times myself."

The elevator doors glided open.

"I will apologize to Mrs. Nussbaum the next time I see her," Cynthia said as the doors closed between them.

She pressed the button, causing the elevator to rise with a jerk.

The *ding* of the elevator alert told her it had reached its final destination and could ascend no farther through the artery of the building. As the doors slid open, Cynthia took a deep breath, then another, before stepping into the empty hallway. They shared the top floor with a reclusive tenant, a neighbor whom she had not seen or even heard through the walls in over five years. The double doors to her apartment seemed to throb as she walked toward them. She could hear footsteps from behind the doors when she turned the key.

"Percy," she called out, stepping into the empty foyer. "Honey, are you home?"

The two senior ministers of New Testament Cathedral sat around a large table in the conference room of the church. Hezekiah entered the room with his usual flare. "Good afternoon, Brothers," he said. "Let's get this meeting started."

Each man had his Bible placed on the table in front of him. Although no one wore black robes, the air still smacked of reverence and piety. Hezekiah sat at the head of the table with Rev. Percy Pryce to his right and Rev. Kenneth Davis to his left.

After a short prayer Hezekiah began the meeting. "The first thing on the agenda is the funeral for Mabel Smith. It's scheduled for this Friday and I'm going to be out of town for the weekend. Reverend Pryce, are you available that day?"

Percy retrieved his BlackBerry from his breast pocket. "Yes, I can officiate."

"Good. Next item."

Both men at the table shifted slightly in their seats and exchanged curious glances in response to the curt manner in which the pastor conducted the meeting.

"Someone needs to represent the church at the thirty-fifth anniversary of Mount Zion AME on the twenty-sixth," Hezekiah continued. "Neither Samantha nor I will be able to attend."

Reverend Pryce cleared his throat. "I can do it, Pastor. I'm very close to the pastor at Mount Zion."

Hezekiah looked up and said, "Thank you, Percy, but I was hoping Reverend Davis would cover this one."

"I can represent us. I had planned on attending, anyway," said Reverend Davis while looking sympathetically at Percy. "You can attend with me, if you'd like, Reverend Pryce."

Percy did not respond.

Hezekiah pressed forward. "I'll be here this Sunday, but Samantha will be preaching on the following Sunday. I won't be there, so I expect each of you to be present to support her."

The tension in the room grew thicker. The two men could sense Hezekiah was preoccupied. When the last agenda item had been discussed, Hezekiah placed his hands on the table and said, "Gentlemen, I have a question for you. What would the two of you do if I were no longer able to serve as pastor?"

The room was silent for a chilling moment as the question hung in the air. They all had thought about the possibility from time to time, but no one expected Hezekiah to raise that subject.

Confusion rushed through the head of Reverend Davis. He could not imagine New Testament Cathedral without Pastor Hezekiah T. Cleaveland.

Reverend Pryce spoke first. "Pastor, I'm not sure what you mean. Is something wrong?"

"No, but it is part of your responsibility as senior ministers of this church to think in these terms. I could die at any time and then what would you do? Who would replace me? How would you select him?"

Reverend Pryce leaned in closer. "Pastor, as you know, the decision of who will serve as pastor in the event of your departure does not fall within the authority of this body. It is the responsibility of the board of trustees to select your replacement, should the need arise."

Hezekiah gave him a sharp look. "I know what the bylaws say. I wrote them. But the trustees will look to you for counsel. They'll want to know what you recommend and you all need to be prepared to answer. Not as individuals but as the team of senior ministers."

The two men looked anxiously into each other's faces, searching for answers that they knew were not there.

Then in unison they returned their gaze to Hezekiah, and Kenneth spoke.

"What would you want to see happen?"

"The bylaws state that I cannot select my replacement, and I still think that is appropriate. You, meaning the members of the church, should have the right to select who your shepherd will be if I am forced to resign. The only thing I do want and expect from you is that you select someone who shares my vision for this ministry. And if you don't know what that is by now, you should not be here. I'd expect you to support whoever the new pastor would be in the same manner you have supported me. I also want you to make sure that he respects the heritage and traditions of this ministry and not allow him to make any sweeping changes to everything we've built over the years."

The clarity and force of Hezekiah's statements had a paralyzing effect on the ministers.

"This is your assignment, gentlemen," Hezekiah continued. "Think carefully on these questions and come to some definite conclusions. You don't have to share them with me, but make sure you have the answers if the situation should ever arise. I don't want my church to be left unprepared and end up like all those others, with bitter infighting that always leads to fracturing into smaller pathetic storefront ministries."

After a short pause Hezekiah said, "Good day, gentlemen. I'll see you on Sunday morning."

No further words were said. The two men gathered their belongings and left the room in silence. Hezekiah remained at the conference table with his hands clasped in his lap. He was too tired to think anymore and too afraid to cry. The swirl of the wood grain on the conference table occupied his thoughts for the next suspended moments. He then slowly picked up his belongings, turned out the light, and left the room.

Steel slammed against steel as men in shorts strained to complete their next set. Bodies stretched and treadmills churned from stationary workouts. Hezekiah started his next set of repetitions on the weight machine.

Hezekiah and Percy had met for their weekly workout. "Thirteen, fourteen, come on, Pastor, you can do it. Fifteen," Percy counted as he squatted at Hezekiah's side. "You still got it, old man. I think you should add another ten pounds next time."

Hezekiah lay panting on the bench, with his arms spread at his side. "You're trying to give me a heart attack."

He got up from the bench and wiped sweat from his brow. "Okay Rev., let's see what you got."

With that, Percy sat down and began his repetitions with the same weights. He gripped the steel rod above his head and lowered the weights to his chest.

"Push. Come on, man, push. Give me three more. Thirteen, fourteen, fifteen." Hezekiah helped Percy from the bench.

"That's it for me, man," Percy said between breaths. "I'm going to hit the showers. Are you coming?"

Hezekiah welcomed the words signaling the end of their workout. Percy led the way to the locker room. It was a large open space with orange lockers. Used towels were scattered on the floor and the doors of empty lockers hung open. The two men dialed the combinations to their locks and sat on a thin wooden bench to remove their shoes.

"What's going on with you, Hezekiah?" Percy asked as the two men stood naked under the steaming shower.

"What do you mean? I've never been in better shape."

"We've worked together for years now. Not only are you my pastor, but you're also my friend, and I'd like to think you feel the same. I know when something is troubling you. That whole thing about us thinking about your replacement—what's going on?"

"I can't talk about it right now, but I'm not sure if I'll be able to continue as pastor for much longer."

Percy stood naked and shocked before the pastor. "Are you sick?"

Hezekiah turned his back to Percy and continued to soap his body. He was not prepared to have this conversation. "No, it's nothing like that. I'm fine. I'll be honest with you, Percy. I'm struggling with a moral dilemma that I don't think I'll ever be able to resolve."

"Hezekiah, nothing could be that bad. Maybe you should talk about it with someone. Have you considered seeing a therapist? I know several ministers who are seeing a guy in Anaheim who's supposed to be excellent."

Hezekiah had never considered seeing a therapist, although he had made the recommendation to many members whose problems required more time than he was willing or able to give. "I don't think he could help me with this," Hezekiah said with a resolute expression on his face. "Everything is more complicated than you could ever imagine."

"No problem you could have on earth is too complicated for God. Let me get you the therapist's number. Give him a call. Whatever is going on might not be as bad as you think."

"Okay, Percy. I'll call him. But if I should leave, I want

you to take over as pastor. You're a good man and you're the only person I would trust with New Testament."

"Don't even think in those terms yet, Hezekiah. You know I'm honored, but I hope it doesn't come to that."

The two men showered in silence, only the sound of drops echoed through the tiled room.

11

Ten Months Earlier

The year of secrecy had been difficult for Danny. He wanted to tell someone, everyone, about his love for Hezekiah. However, the cost of such a revelation was too high. He had cursed himself on many occasions for loving a man who was a prisoner of public opinion. Why had he allowed himself to love a man whose existence, life, and livelihood depended on receiving daily approval from thousands of nameless, faceless people?

Hezekiah had warned him of the perils of their union on the day they first exchanged the words "I love you," exactly two months after they met.

"Are you sure you know what you're getting into?" Hezekiah questioned while they lay naked under the covers in Danny's bed. "I'm a pastor and I can't change that. It means a lot of sacrifice on both our parts."

"I didn't mean to fall in love with you, Hezekiah," Danny said as he laid his head on Hezekiah's chest, "but since I have, I'll have to live with the consequences."

"I didn't know I was going to fall in love with you, either, but I'm glad I did. I just don't want you to get hurt. I love you too much. If someone, anyone, finds out about us, your life will never be the same. You'll become a public figure. The media will be brutal. They'll try to destroy us both, and they'll probably succeed. I've seen it happen to other pastors."

"Then why are you willing to take that kind of a risk?"

Hezekiah answered without pause. He had asked himself the same question on many occasions. "Because I need you. I've never loved anyone, or even myself, as much as I love you. No one has ever forced me to look beyond myself and my own needs or my own ego." He sat up in the bed and placed Danny's head in his lap and looked earnestly into his deep brown eyes. "You've made me realize I've never really cared for anyone and didn't think I had the capacity to. My world has always been about me, and what I desired more than life itself. I wanted power and all that came with it—fame, wealth, and respect. It has consumed my every thought for as long as I can remember. Every word I spoke, and every step I took, was taken only to move me closer to my goals.

"Well, I've done it. I have it all, and when I got it, I began to hate myself more than I had ever hated my worst enemy. All I could see staring back at me in the mirror was a hollow, lonely man who had traded his soul just to be recognized when he walked down the street.

"I had actually thought about committing suicide on the day I first saw you helping that man downtown. I wanted to punish myself for being a fool, for forcing myself to waste an entire life chasing something that left me vacant and alone. And then I met you."

Hezekiah gently placed his hand on Danny's chest. "I don't know what happened, but when I first looked in your eyes, I had an overwhelming desire to have you know me deep down inside. I thought you might be able to understand me and maybe even help me understand myself. And you have."

The two then lay silently in bed, sharing hidden places in their hearts without words and with gentle, caring hands.

12

Tuesday

No response came to Etta's announcement of arrival at the Cleaveland estate. She called out again, "Pastor Cleaveland, Mrs. Cleaveland, are you home?"

Hezekiah's coat had been tossed over the back of a chair in the living room. This was the first clue that all was not well in the Cleaveland household. Hezekiah's fastidious and controlling nature had always prevented him from leaving clothes scattered about the house.

She began the long walk down the hallway toward Hezekiah's study. She could hear the telephone ringing in the room. Etta stood with her ear near the door. The ringing telephone went unanswered. Clue number two. Hezekiah never passed up the opportunity to talk on the telephone.

Etta tapped on the door and entered the dark room. The only light came from a glowing computer screen on the desk at which Hezekiah sat with his back to the door. Bookshelves filled with awards and mementos covered the walls of the study. Deep forest green carpet absorbed the remains of light that peeked through the drawn shades at the windows.

Etta could only see the back of Hezekiah's head above the high-backed leather chair.

"Aren't you going to answer the phone?" she asked softly. But there was no response. "Pastor Cleaveland, is everything all right?"

The leather chair spun around. From the computer light she could see his hollow eyes. A silk tie hung loosely from his neck and unfastened cuffs dangled around his wrists. His expressionless face peered through the darkness. He spoke after several agonizing seconds. "No, I'm afraid that everything isn't all right."

Etta's face contorted into an expression of concern as she approached the desk. "Pastor Cleaveland, you're scaring me. What's wrong?"

"Someone is trying to destroy everything I've . . ." He paused and swallowed deeply. "Everything Samantha and I have worked all these years for," he finished.

Etta sat slowly in a chair near the desk and asked, "Who?"

Hezekiah waved his hands in a sign of bewilderment and replied, "That's the problem. I don't know who it is. I only know it's someone intent on bringing down my ministry, and this time it just might work."

Etta looked puzzled as her heart pounded in her chest. She could clearly see the fear and despair on Hezekiah's face.

"What do you mean you don't know who?" she asked.

Hezekiah avoided her concerned gaze. He spun the chair around until his back faced her.

"I don't want to talk about it right now, Etta. I just need to think. Maybe I'm making too much out of this."

Etta stood and softly said, "All right, Pastor Cleaveland,

but you know we all love you, and no matter how bad this is, everyone will always stand behind you." She placed a hand on his shoulder. "I'm sure you'll figure something out. You always do. I'll be in the kitchen if you need me."

Chimes of the doorbell echoed through the house as she exited the room. Hezekiah turned his back to the door and said, "Whoever that is, tell them I'm not here."

Etta looked through the peephole and saw the head of Kenneth Davis.

"Pastor Cleaveland, it's me, Kenneth. Open the door. I need to talk to you," he said from the porch.

She opened the door. "Hello, Reverend Davis. Come in, but Pastor Cleaveland said he doesn't want to be disturbed."

"Hello, Etta," he said. "I'm sorry to come by unannounced, but I need to speak with Pastor Cleaveland. It's very important. Is he in his study?"

"Yes, but . . ."

Kenneth walked through the house toward the study before she could stop him. "This will take only a minute," he said over his shoulder.

Hezekiah heard the door open, and before he could see Kenneth, he shouted, "I said I don't want . . . Oh, it's you. What do you want?"

Kenneth entered and turned on the lights to reveal the crumpled man behind the desk. "Who is Danny St. John, and why didn't you tell me about him yourself?"

Hezekiah looked sternly at the towering man. "Because it's not your concern."

Kenneth closed the door and walked toward the desk. "When you talk about stepping down and ask me to think about who your replacement will be, it is my concern. Now, please tell me what is going on."

"It sounds like you've already heard everything. Who told you? Catherine?"

"Yes, she told me, but this isn't about Catherine."

"Yes, I know. Like everything else in this church, it's about me," Hezekiah said sternly. "Well, I wish I could tell you it's all a lie, but I can't. I've been with Danny for a year now and somehow Lance Savage found out about it."

"Who told him? Who else knows about this?"

"It looks like quite a few people know. Phillip, Hector, and Jonathon had a nice little surprise for me at lunch. Catherine, and now you."

Kenneth collapsed into a chair and threw his hands into the air.

"Do you realize how serious this is? If the public finds out, they're going to crucify you in the media."

"So that's your opinion? I pay you a fortune, and all you can do is predict my demise? That's the best you can come up with? Then maybe you should resign." Hezekiah waved his hands in disgust.

"This is just like you, Hezekiah. You screw up and then blame someone else. Well, this time you can't blame anyone but yourself. I hope he was worth it, because he is going to cost you your ministry."

Hezekiah jumped from behind the desk and stood directly in front of Kenneth, who bolted to his feet. The two men stood nose to nose.

"Who do you think you are speaking to?" Hezekiah said, poking a finger into Kenneth's chest. "I'm still the pastor, and you still work for me. No one talks to me that way."

Kenneth did not demur.

"You can get angry at me if you want, but that's not going to solve anything. I'm just being honest with you. You don't seem to realize the damage a story like this can do."

Hezekiah took a step backward.

"You're wrong. I do know the damage it can do. It's all I've been able to think about ever since I met him, and for some reason, I just couldn't stop seeing him."

The two men sat as the tension in the room slowly dissolved. "It wasn't just sex," Hezekiah said, looking into Kenneth's eyes. "I actually do love him." He placed his face in his hands and said, "Oh God. What am I going to do?"

Without pausing to ponder the question, Kenneth spoke authoritatively. "The first thing you're going to do is break it off with him. And then you're going to deny everything."

Hezekiah looked up. "I can't do that," he said with deep emotion. "It'll destroy him. You just don't understand."

Kenneth grabbed Hezekiah's shoulders. "No one in the world is that important. You've had your fun with this Danny kid. Now you've got to move on. It's either him or your ministry."

Etta stood silently outside the office door with her ear pressed against the wood. She prayed Hezekiah had finally found a love strong enough to draw him away from Samantha Cleaveland.

"What sides do you want with that? We've got macaroni and cheese, pinto beans, rice, cabbage, and candied yams. We're out of greens today," the waitress said, holding a pencil over a grease-stained order pad.

Rev. Willie Mitchell scowled. "You're always out of greens. I'll have the macaroni and cheese and cabbage. And give me a Diet Coke with that."

Willie sat in the soul food restaurant with Virgil Jackson. The slight smell of mildew filled the air of the crowded room. Momma Lee, the restaurant's owner, sat on a stool behind the cash register, where she pretended not to look at every bite each customer took. She never trusted anyone to run the register; so after twenty years of having sat on that stool, her stomach fit perfectly into the ninety-degree angle of the counter.

The waitress looked suspiciously at Reverend Mitchell's companion. "What will you have?" She knew a crack head when she saw one. The yellow on his fingertips and the pink scars on his lips from sucking a hot glass pipe were the first things she noticed about him.

"Get whatever you want. This is on me," Willie said.

"Then I'll have the short ribs with beans and candied yams and a Coke. Does corn bread come with that?"

The waitress nodded yes, took their menus, and abruptly left the table.

Patrons laughed and rubbed their bellies while Southern culinary delights paraded through the room in the hands of women wearing white blouses, black skirts, and comfortable shoes. Silk flowers with dirty edges and dusty plastic leaves sat on each table. Babies in high chairs wrestled with fried chicken bones, and hardworking men wolfed down barbecued ribs, so they could get back to work by one o'clock.

Willie rolled up the sleeves of his shirt. The paper napkin tucked into his collar was moist from the perspiration dripping down his neck. His cell phone sat on the table next to an arrangement of Louisiana hot sauce, ketchup, salt, pepper, and a jar of peppers in vinegar.

"I hear you just got out of jail. What were you in for?"

"Burglary, but I've been straight ever since."

"That's good. Where are you working at?"

Virgil knew the caliber of men like Reverend Willie Mitchell. A shallow facade of respectability and Southern charm, under which lay the heart of a man who would kill his brother, if there was something worthwhile to be gained. He played along, anyway. "Nobody's going to hire an ex-con these days. I've been looking for two months now."

"Where do you live? With your mother?"

"No. She put me out a month ago. I've been living here and there. I have a social worker at the Los Angeles Community Center. He's been trying to find a rehab program for me, but every place is full. I've been on a waiting list for over a month."

Willie snorted. "You need to get off that shit. Fucks up your brain, and then dumps you in the gutter. You're too smart for that. Man, all I need is plenty of tight pussy, a good suit, and new car every year, and I'm fine." He laughed out loud at his own wit. "Don't need no shit that's going to fuck me up and take all my money."

"I haven't had any pussy in almost a year. I almost forgot what it feels like."

"I got a job for you that'll pay enough to buy all the pussy you want."

Virgil could tell by the sudden change in the reverend's demeanor that the "job" entailed something illegal. But in his current state of desperation, he was willing to do anything.

"What kind of job?" he asked suspiciously.

"I'll get to that soon enough."

The waitress returned to the table with their orders balanced on her arms. "All right. Who had the fried chicken with cabbage and macaroni and cheese?"

"Right here." The reverend moved his cell phone to the side.

"And you had the short ribs, pinto beans, and candied yams." She placed the orders on the crammed little table. "I'll be back in a minute with your Cokes."

"Diet Coke," the reverend called out as she walked away. "And bring more butter with you."

The food required their full attention for the next few minutes. Hot sauce was sprinkled liberally over all of the reverend's food. Salt and pepper seasoned his meat and everything within six inches of his plate. His corn bread crumbled as he spread on a cold pat of butter.

The waitress returned with their sodas. Virgil immediately tore open six packets of sugar and poured them into his drink.

"What the hell are you doing?" the reverend asked, with the flesh of the chicken dangling from his slippery lips.

"I have a sweet tooth."

The conversation progressed too slowly for Virgil, so he decided to give the reverend a hand. "So what kind of work are you talking about? I'm desperate. I'll do fucking anything."

"I need someone taken care of."

"What do you mean, 'taken care of'?" Virgil asked, setting the fork on his plate.

"You know what the fuck I mean. Gotten rid of. Smoked. Eliminated."

"Hey, look, old man. I can't get involved in no shit like that. The next one is my third strike. My ass would be in jail for the rest of my fucking life."

Reverend Mitchell saw the fear in Virgil's eyes. He held up his grease-smeared hands and said, "Slow down, boy. Take it easy. I'm not talking about doing anything that's going to get you caught. I'm not as stupid as I look."

He didn't want to lose him and disappoint Samantha, so he quickly introduced what he hoped would be ample incentive. "You're a smart kid. I'm a smart man. You won't get caught. It pays ten thousand dollars. Part up front and the rest when the job is done."

Virgil heard the glass pipe calling his name. A familiar pang cramped his stomach. His lips became dry, and his eyes glazed over with a smoky film. He grabbed the Coke and took a long swallow. "It's not worth it," he said, nervously clutching the edges of the table.

Willie decided to up the ante. "All right. Twenty thousand and a plane ticket to anywhere in the fucking world you want to go."

"You're shit'n me, right? Who is it?"

"What difference does it make? Are you fucking in or not? Let me know so I can move on."

There was a long pause. Neither of the men ate. Virgil shifted from side to side in his chair while a fly buzzed over the corn bread. He pushed his plate away and asked, "When do you want it done?"

Reverend Mitchell started eating again. He felt he had regained control. Now it was just a matter of closing the deal. His stomach churned as he recalled the urgency in Samantha's voice earlier that day. "Sunday," he said in a whisper.

"This Sunday?"

Willie looked nervously over his shoulders and whispered, "Keep your voice down, boy. You want the whole fucking place to hear? Yes, this Sunday."

Virgil stared out the window at the cars moving past the restaurant. "When would I get the money?"

"Like I said. Part up front and the rest after it's done."

"I'd want half up front."

"You think I'm fucking stupid? You'd smoke it up before you got to the corner, and I'd never see your ass again. I'll give you one thousand on Sunday morning and then meet you somewhere later and give you the rest. So what's your answer? Are you in or not?"

Virgil thought of his mother, and what he could buy her

with $20,000. He also naively thought of how he could get his life on the right track with that kind of money.

"Do you have a gun?" he asked the reverend.

"Yes."

"You know if you don't pay me, I'll fucking kill you," Virgil said, looking directly into his eyes.

Under the tough, seasoned facade, Willie Mitchell was a coward. The stomach ulcer kicked with such force that the flow of sweat on his brow doubled. "You don't have to worry about that. You'll get your money."

"All right. I'm in. So who is it?"

"Hezekiah Cleaveland."

Virgil jumped up from the table and said, "You're fucking crazy. Do it yourself." He immediately walked to the door and left the restaurant.

Willie pulled the napkin from under his chin and bolted for the door past Momma Lee. She struggled to her feet and yelled, "Hey, wait a minute. You better pay for that."

Without slowing his stride, Willie shouted, "I'll be back. You'll get your fucking money."

By the time Reverend Mitchell reached the sidewalk, Virgil was a half block away and preparing to cross in the middle of the street. Traffic was heavy as he waited for a clearing. Willie caught up with him. He was winded and his shirt flap came out of his pants from the run. He grabbed Virgil's arm and said, "Wait a minute, Virgil. Hear me out. I know you need the money. What about your mother? I hear she's about to get evicted from her apartment. You don't give a shit about her?"

Virgil snatched his arm away. "Leave my mother out of this. I told you no. Now, get out of my fucking way, before I slam your fat ass into the fucking sidewalk."

Virgil had just started to step into the street when he heard Willie shout, "All right, thirty thousand dollars. Cash."

Even though the street was now clear, Virgil stopped with one foot still on the curb. He looked at Willie and asked, "Man, what is this all about? Why do you want this guy dead? What did he do to you?"

Reverend Mitchell caught his breath and said, "It's not for me. I've got a powerful associate whom he crossed and they asked me to take care of it."

"What are you getting out of it?"

Willie laughed nervously. "Nothing. At least not yet. If I do this for them, I'll get what I want soon enough."

Though he tried, Virgil could not turn away. The two men struck a deal and discussed the details as the cars whizzed by. Willie would pick up Virgil on Sunday morning in front of the Los Angeles Community Center. From there they would drive two blocks from the church, where Virgil would wait until exactly 11:30 A.M. The balcony of the church would be empty and all Virgil would have to do was get through the foyer of the church unnoticed, fire two shots, and escape as quickly as possible down Hezekiah T. Cleaveland Avenue.

"I'll meet you downtown that night with the rest of the money and drop you at the bus depot."

"Remember what I said, Reverend. If I don't get my money . . ."

"I know, I know. You don't have to say it again."

13

Eight Months Earlier

Patrons filled the lively restaurant on the waterfront in the marina. Men in light blue shirts and Bermuda shorts shared hearty laughs with their wives and companions. Casually dressed women with windblown hair chatted while sipping steaming flavored coffees.

"Good afternoon, gentlemen. Welcome to Shutters," said the maître d' through a studied French accent. "Table for two?"

"Yes, and somewhere quiet if you have it," Hezekiah replied.

"Would you prefer the deck? It is a lovely day for the sun."

Hezekiah looked at Danny, who nodded approval, and then said, "That would be fine."

The two men followed the maître d' to the sunny deck at the rear of the restaurant. It was the sixth month of their relationship. Danny's khaki pants and blue button-down shirt provided ample cover for the truth, that he was the younger man who held the heart of his elegant companion in his neatly pressed rear pocket. Together the couple struck the most innocent of poses. Maybe they were brothers, or mentor and protégé. Only one with the most sensitive radar could possibly have detected the truth about the two men.

Hezekiah hung his jacket on the back of his chair as they sat down.

"Enjoy your meal, gentlemen," said the maître d' as he bowed slightly and exited the deck.

Dark blue umbrellas shielded glass tables from the bright noonday sun. Polished silver utensils, lush linen napkins, and sparkling water goblets stood at the ready in their appointed places. Although the deck was filled with similar faces to those in the dining room, the tables were positioned farther apart, offering their occupants additional privacy. Large potted plants danced gently to music felt but not heard. The deck overlooked a glassy ocean, where sailboats drifted by lazily.

Hezekiah and Danny laughed together as they ate, obviously pleased to be in each other's company. They were not only lovers, but also the closest of friends. When they looked into each other's eyes, they saw themselves. Little lost boys searching for their reflection in the face of someone who cared.

They talked of politics, not religion. They talked about the Dodgers' chances at making it to the World Series. They talked about life, and they talked about love.

After lunch they walked along a boardwalk lined with shops selling souvenirs to the tourists that filled the cobbled path. Four pelicans lounged in the sun on a landing near the water.

After moments of silence Hezekiah said, "I want us to be together someday, Danny."

Not comprehending the gravity of the statement, Danny smiled and replied, "We are together."

"You know what I mean . . . permanently. I want us to live together. Meeting for a few hours here and there is so frustrating for me. I want us to build a life together."

"What about Samantha?"

"My relationship with Samantha is over. We're not in love, and if I stay around much longer, I'll end up hating her. I don't want that."

"So you want me to be the new Samantha? I'm sorry, Hezekiah, I can't fill those . . ."

Hezekiah moved in closer. "What are you talking about? My wanting to be with you has nothing to do with how I feel about her. Even if I did love her, I would still want us to be together."

"I don't want to be the person you run to because you suddenly realize who your wife really is. This may sound silly, but I want to be the person you come to because this is where you want to be, because it's right, not just convenient."

"I've called you a lot of things, sexy, smart, stubborn, even naive, but never convenient. Do you think these last six months have been 'convenient' for me—sneaking around, lying to cover up lies, juggling two relationships with two very demanding people? It's been hell for me, and you, of all people, should—"

"Should what? Be grateful that the great Hezekiah Cleaveland picked me. Well, I'm not grateful. You're not doing me a favor by being with me. If you're not with me because this is where you want to be, then we've both wasted our time."

"I was going to say, you of all people should understand. Why are you twisting my words around? I don't know how many other ways to say 'I love you.' If I did love Samantha, I would still love you. I've never felt about her, or anyone else, the way I feel about you. I wouldn't jeopardize my entire ministry if I didn't feel this way. You can twist my words, but I know exactly what I'm saying."

Danny stared out into the ocean. The wind gently propelled little boats past.

"I'm sorry. I've waited my whole life for someone like you, and now that you're here, I'm afraid I'll wake up one morning and you'll be gone. Sometimes I find myself pushing you away to keep from getting hurt."

Hezekiah smiled. "I thought I was the only one who felt that way."

"What about your church? Samantha will try to ruin you if she ever finds out. She'll never let you go. Her ego won't allow it."

"You let me worry about Samantha."

"This won't work, Hezekiah. You've got too much to lose."

"You don't want to be with me?"

"You know I do. It's all I ever think about. I just don't see how it could work."

At that moment walking in the sun with Danny made the risks seem worthwhile.

Their marriage had begun like so many others. Hezekiah met Samantha at the Bible Institute of Los Angeles. He was a senior and she a sophomore. He was the intense, smart boy on campus, president of the Black Student Union, number one on the dean's list, and editor of the school newspaper. She was the attractive and popular girl whom all the boys pursued, member of the debate team, the girls' track team, and volunteer tutor for the neighborhood children.

From the beginning they were a power couple, protesting at city hall when funds were cut for social services in poor neighborhoods. If there was a cause that affected disenfranchised people, of any race, Samantha and Hezekiah could be seen on the front lines of the struggle.

Ironically, the things that attracted Samantha to Hezekiah were the same that prevented her from ever feeling she truly knew him. There was always another mistress—not a woman, but his ferocious and insatiable ambition. Since their first year of marriage Hezekiah's obsessive and all-consuming desire to succeed in life was his first and only love. Yes, he showered her with outward affection, but still something was missing.

He skillfully concealed parts of himself from Samantha. She could see it simmering behind his smoldering brown eyes. She could hear it lurking just beneath the words he spoke, taunting her from behind his beguiling smile. Samantha didn't know what "it" was and couldn't be sure if he knew either. Hezekiah's secret gradually formed a chasm between them, which stretched wider as his ministry reached higher.

Samantha soon grew bitter and weary from years of foraging for the secret that Hezekiah hid so well. She began to sublimate her energy, instead, into regaining the goals she had abandoned on the day they married. Samantha completed her doctorate in theology, but only after much personal sacrifice and constant accusations of neglect from Hezekiah.

Still, their combined outward personas were dazzling and commanding. He, the handsome pastor who could do no wrong in the eyes of the public, and she, the strikingly beautiful wife who could sway and mesmerize even Hezekiah's most fanatic critics. Their smiling faces on the front page of any magazine would double its circulation. Their presence at a charity fund-raiser would guarantee its success. The Cleavelands were Los Angeles's cherished and much loved ecumenical dynasty.

However, in the sheltered darkness of their limousine, or in the cocoon of the gated mansion, their golden smiles turned to stone. Hezekiah's secret had eclipsed even the places in his heart that he had once shared with Samantha. The only part of him that remained for her to touch was the veneer that could be seen on the home page of their Web site, or in the pulpit of New Testament Cathedral every Sunday morning.

Rumors of Hezekiah's affairs with other women had haunted their marriage for years. The distance between them served as a sufficient buffer to protect Samantha's ego and heart. The influence and prestige she had accumulated over the years soon replaced the love Samantha once had for Hezekiah. It comforted her when she was lonely and held her at night, until she drifted into sleep. As Hezekiah withdrew deeper into his dark, veiled world, she relied more and more on public accolades and praise to fill the void created by their hollow union.

Dino had only seen Danny St. John once. Danny and Hezekiah had already been seeing each other for five months. It was well after 1:00 A.M. on a Thursday. Hezekiah had just completed an exceptionally long negotiation session with the building contractor. When Hezekiah settled into the rear of the car it was apparent he was emotionally spent. Dino instinctively headed toward the pastor's estate.

"I'm not going home yet, Dino," Hezekiah said as his blurry eyes adjusted to the street signs. "Take me to the Adams District. I'm going to have a cup of coffee with a friend."

Dino had heard the command on many occasions before that evening. Usually, the directive came late at night when no other engagements were scheduled. Dino came to assume that "having coffee with a friend" actually meant, "I'm going to get laid."

Dino drove to the familiar apartment on the corner of Adams Boulevard and Hillcrest Avenue. Until that night Dino had never seen its occupant, although he had been to the house on many occasions before. He parked in the red zone, knowing that no police officer would dare harass him, once they learned of his distinguished passenger.

It was a large faded beige Victorian-style house that had been divided into five smaller units. Perennials lined the brick walkway leading to a steep flight of stairs. Magnolia and pine trees illuminated by antique streetlamps bristled from a gentle breeze.

The front door of the first-floor unit swung open before Hezekiah could reach the top step. An attractive young black man in his twenties, wearing baggy green pants and no shirt, stepped from a pool of darkness in the threshold. The partially clad figure immediately embraced Hezekiah and kissed him directly on the lips.

Even through the heavy cashmere overcoat Hezekiah wore that evening, Dino could see Hezekiah's body stiffen. Hezekiah sternly, yet with gentle familiarity, pushed the young man away. As he did, he turned and looked Dino directly in the eyes. The message Hezekiah sent was very clear despite the distance between the car and the man's front door. This was an assignation that must be added to the already-lengthy list of those not to be discussed with anyone, including the pastor himself.

Four months after they met, Hezekiah flew Danny, in his private jet, to San Francisco for the opening night of *Porgy and Bess* at the War Memorial Opera House. The two arrived in San Francisco and rode in a waiting limousine to the Fairmont Hotel.

As the bellman placed their bags neatly in the parlor, he asked Hezekiah, "Will there be anything else, Mr. Radcliff?"

"No, thank you. We can take it from here," Hezekiah responded.

Their suite had breathtaking views of the city, framed by large picture windows that wrapped around the twenty-second floor. To the right they could see the pointed tip of the Transamerica Pyramid peeking through the fog and the sparkling towers of the Golden Gate Bridge. To the left were Grace Cathedral, the Flood Mansion, and Coit Tower, with the San Francisco Bay and Alcatraz Island as the backdrop. The suite had a parquet-floor entrance that led to a paneled parlor, cream-hued French Provincial furniture, a fireplace, and wet bar.

After unpacking their bags Hezekiah and Danny made love under cascading water in the marble shower.

"I love you, Danny," Hezekiah said as he caressed Danny's glistening body in the pulsating waterfall.

Through breathless panting Danny responded, "I love you too, Hezekiah."

They took a cab to the opera house. Ticket holders wearing their finest evening dresses and black suits were beginning to arrive. As the two men exited the cab, Hezekiah gave the driver an extra twenty dollars in appreciation for getting them there on time for their dinner reservations.

The hostess in the restaurant on the bottom floor of the opera house tried her best not to look impressed as the two handsome men walked toward her. "Good evening, Reverend Cleaveland. Welcome to Patina's Cafe," said the attractive woman standing behind a well-lit podium.

"Good evening," Hezekiah responded. "I'm afraid you've mistaken me for someone else. We have reservations for two."

"I'm sorry, but you look just like . . . Yes, sir. Under what name?" she asked apologetically.

"Radcliff. Michael Radcliff," Hezekiah said, smiling at Danny.

After scanning her list she replied, "Very good, sir. Please follow me."

At their table a flurry of waiters attended their needs in rapid succession. Waters, wines, breads, and appetizers were followed by their meals. A well-dressed couple approached the table as the two laughed and recalled previous performances of *Porgy and Bess* they each had seen before they met.

"Excuse me," said the man shyly, "we hate to interrupt your dinner, but aren't you Hezekiah Cleaveland? My wife and I watch you every Sunday. Would it be possible for us to take a picture with you? We're here visiting from Chicago."

Hezekiah looked up with a smile and said, "I'm sorry, I'm not Hezekiah Cleaveland, but whoever he is, he must be a very handsome guy."

The couple looked disappointed. "Are you sure?" the wife asked. "I would know that face anywhere. Is Samantha with you tonight? I love her. I've read her autobiography twice. She is such an inspiration."

Hezekiah kindly responded, "I really do hate to disappoint you, but—"

Danny looked up at the couple and interrupted, "This is Hezekiah Cleaveland. He's just feeling a little shy this evening. Give me your camera and I'll be happy to take the picture for you."

Hezekiah tensed. "Danny?" he said questioningly.

"It's all right, Hezekiah," Danny reassured him.

Hezekiah stood up and the couple flanked his sides. Danny took the picture, and the couple left smiling and apologizing profusely for disturbing their dinner, but only after asking Hezekiah to sign a menu they had taken from their table.

"Danny, I don't think that was a good idea. Pictures like that end up on the Internet."

"I realized that. That's why I took the picture so I wouldn't be in the photo. If you hadn't allowed them, they probably would have taken one of you from a distance and I would have been in it too."

"Sounds like you've done this before. Are you sure I'm the only famous person you've dated?"

They both laughed and Danny replied, "I'm sure. And, believe me, you'll also be the last."

In the grand gold-gilded theater a bronze diva on the stage passionately sang the aria to her man:

"I loves you, Porgy, don't let him take me. Don't let him handle me and drive me mad. If you can keep me, I wanna stay here with you forever, and I'll be glad."

She pleaded and wept to the rapt delight of the audience.

"Yes, I loves you, Porgy, don't let him take me. Don't let him handle me with his hot hands. If you can keep me, I wants to stay here with you forever. I've got my man."

Hezekiah affectionately brushed Danny's shoulder with his. Their knees touched as the songbird so graciously provided the prophetic soundtrack to their lives.

14

Wednesday

Catherine functioned as if it were a typical day at New Testament Cathedral. Telephone calls were returned, decisions made, and problems were solved.

Who could have leaked the story to the press? she thought while laboriously attending to the daily chores ascribed to a chief operations officer. Everyone was suspect. *Maybe it's the secretary who screens Hezekiah's calls, or maybe Dino Goodman, the pastor's driver. I've never trusted him. He must have known something was going on. Maybe he's being paid to sabotage Hezekiah.*

The list of suspects grew and rationales for betrayal abounded as five o'clock drew near.

"Ms. Birdsong," came a voice from the intercom in her office. "Reverend Pryce is here for your five-fifteen appointment."

"Give me two minutes and then tell him to come in," was the instruction that followed.

Catherine quickly looked into a mirror behind her desk to check the remains of makeup under her puffy eyes.

Once again she swallowed mouthwash and returned the little bottle to her purse under the desk.

"Hello, Catherine. Sorry I'm late."

From across the room Percy honed in on Catherine's troubled face.

"You look terrible. Is there something wrong? Have you been crying?" he asked, approaching her with an out-stretched hand. "What has Hezekiah done to you now?"

The comment was initially said in jest, but as he walked closer, he detected the faint remnant of a tear in the corner of her eye.

Catherine extended her hand and allowed it to be enveloped by Percy's hearty grip.

"I'm fine, Reverend Pryce," she said, pointing to the chair in front of her desk and inviting him to sit. "What did you want to see me about?"

"Catherine, you can't fool me. I know something is wrong. We've known each other a long time. I think of you as a friend, and I hope you feel the same about me. Has Hezekiah done something to upset you?"

Catherine looked away, avoiding his sympathetic gaze. There was silence for a moment and then she spoke, "Percy, something terrible has happened and I don't know what to do about it."

"Then tell me about it, maybe we can figure it out together."

"It's about Hezekiah, but he told me not to discuss it with anyone."

Percy threw his head back and laughed aloud.

"How many times have we both heard that over the years? We each know sometimes it's necessary to discuss our concerns with others we trust to make sure our perspectives are clear and unclouded by fear. Now tell me. What's going on? Maybe it's not as bad as you think."

Catherine proceeded to recount the antagonistic meeting with the reporter. It was a relief for her to tell the story to a man as wise as Percy. If anyone would know what to do, it would be Percy.

He listened attentively, shifting several times in the seat and occasionally interrupting to ask questions.

"What did Hezekiah say?" and "When is the story supposed to run?"

Catherine concluded her tale by saying, "I've never been this worried about anything in my life. I think I'm going to have a breakdown."

Percy's last question was "Who else knows about this?"

"I made the mistake of telling Kenneth. He's threatened to call Lance Savage and sue the *Chronicle.*"

"Don't worry, I'll talk to Kenneth." Percy then flashed a comforting smile and said, "Catherine, it doesn't sound all that bad. You know these crazies come out of the woodwork every few years. This St. John person is probably some nut who's obsessed with Hezekiah. I'll bet if I put a little scare into him, he'll stop spreading these lies."

"That's just it, Percy. I'm not convinced it's a lie. Hezekiah never denied it and swore me to secrecy. Why would he do that if it weren't true?"

"What kind of mood was Hezekiah in this afternoon?"

"I have no idea," she said fretfully. "He canceled all his appointments. I haven't seen or heard from him all day."

"That's not like him. I'll see if I can reach him on his cell later this evening."

"Please don't tell him you spoke to me. Tell him you ran into Lance in the hall and he told you."

"Don't worry about that. I won't even mention your

name. In the meantime we should meet with Naomi and Reverend Davis to see if we can come up with a plan for damage control, just in case the story does eventually run. Will you set that up?"

"Are you sure they can be trusted? How do we know one of them didn't leak the story in the first place?"

"Why would they do something as stupid as that? If Hezekiah is ousted, they'll both be out of a job."

"I know, but I just don't trust anyone," Catherine said.

"Right now we don't have a choice."

The two walked toward the door and embraced.

"Oh my God," Catherine said. "You wanted to talk to me about something. I'm sorry, Percy. This has got me so distracted."

"Don't worry about that. We can talk about it later. This is much more important."

Catherine had called together key staff members to decide how to address the impending scandal. Percy took the seat of power at the head of the table in the conference room. Catherine and Naomi sat to his left, with Rev. Kenneth Davis to his right.

Naomi broke the silence at the table and asked, "Where is Hezekiah? Shouldn't he be here to talk about this?"

"I thought the whole discussion might make him uncomfortable," Catherine replied. "He doesn't know we're meeting."

"I think that was a mistake," Naomi said nervously. "If he finds out we discussed this behind his back, he'll be furious." As she spoke, she began to gather her belongings from the floor. "I don't want any part of this."

Reverend Pryce leaned forward.

"Wait a minute, Naomi. There's no reason for him to

find out. I just wanted us to put our heads together and come up with a plan. This meeting never took place, as far as anyone outside this room is concerned."

Naomi searched the faces in the room for signs of agreement. Everyone signified yes by nodding.

"All right, I'll stay. But if he finds out about this meeting, I'll deny I was ever here."

"Good, then," Percy said with relief. "I tried to reach Hezekiah all last night, but he didn't answer his phone. Has anyone talked to him about the alleged affair?"

Kenneth Davis then spoke. "I spoke with Hezekiah, and it's not alleged. He confirmed the whole story. There is, in fact, a Danny St. John, and they are involved in a sexual relationship."

"How long has it been going on?" Percy asked.

"He said for about a year."

Percy threw his hands into the air in disbelief. "I don't believe this," he said. "If that story is printed, all hell is going to break loose."

"We're all aware of that, Percy, but there just might be some way to convince Lance Savage to kill the story." Kenneth looked at Naomi. "You know Lance better than all of us. What do you think? Can he be bribed, frightened off?"

Naomi shook her head. "I don't think there's any way he's going to let this slide. I've seen him in action. He's relentless once he gets his hands on anything sensational, and he stands to build a national reputation on this."

"Come on, there's got to be some way," Percy interjected. "Every man has a price. We just have to find out what his is."

"The construction budget has one million dollars in discretionary funds," Reverend Davis said to no one in particular. "I think we should offer to buy his silence. That's the only way."

Catherine sat silently while the three debated the plan's merits. The conversation progressed more rapidly than she had wished. She finally spoke. "I think we're getting ahead of ourselves here. What I'd like to know is who leaked the story in the first place. That's what's most important."

Naomi looked at her impatiently and said, "That's irrelevant. It's out, and now we have to deal with the consequences."

"I disagree," Catherine protested. "Let's say we are able to silence Lance. Whoever the source is could easily find another reporter to pick it up. We'll eventually have to buy off every reporter in the city."

Reverend Davis leaned back in his chair and said, "She's right. Whoever this person is, he or she is obviously very close to Hezekiah and has something to gain by him not being the pastor. Any ideas?"

"It could be anyone," Catherine said. "Even one of us."

Catherine's last words unleashed a flurry of retorts. Naomi bolted to her feet. "If you're suggesting I'm responsible, you're crazy. I'll be out of a job if this ever gets out."

Percy raised his voice. "I take personal offense at your accusations, Catherine. I've devoted the last five years of my life to this church and I deserve better than that."

Kenneth held up his hands in an appeal for calm. "Hold on, everybody. No one is accusing anyone, but we do have to look at every possibility. Who else could have got that close to Hezekiah to know about this?"

"How about Dino, his driver?" Catherine asked. "He must have known about it. Even though I don't trust him, I think he would rather take a bullet in the head than see any harm come to Pastor Cleaveland."

Everyone nodded in consensus. Puzzled expressions formed on their faces as they pondered who might be the Judas.

Catherine, with great caution, broke the silence.

"I know this might sound crazy, but I'm going to say it, anyway. What about Samantha?"

The puzzled looks quickly changed to shock and horror.

"Catherine, how could you even think something that horrible?" they all chanted. "Samantha worships the ground Hezekiah walks on. She would rather die than see him publicly humiliated."

Catherine recoiled into her chair.

"I know, you're right. I just wanted to put it out there."

"Well, please don't ever say anything like that again," Reverend Pryce said passionately tone. "She's going to be hurt enough when she learns about the affair. I'd hate to see her hurt even more if a rumor like that started circulating."

Catherine sat chastised. "I'm sorry. I'm not suggesting she did it, but we have to look at all possibilities."

"Look, this idle speculation isn't getting us anywhere," Kenneth said with his hands clasped in front of his face. "We could be here all day trying to figure out who did this. I say we go back to our original plan and offer Lance money. If the story resurfaces again later, then maybe we'll have more time to flush out the source. Not now, though. We don't have the time."

"Kenneth is right," said Naomi. "If we're going to act, we have to do it quickly."

"Are we all in agreement?" Kenneth asked.

Naomi and Percy both said yes, but Catherine simply stared out the window.

"Catherine, what about you? Do you agree or not?" Naomi asked.

"I don't think it's going to work, but if that's our only option, then yes, I agree."

Kenneth clapped his hands and said, "All right, then. I'll meet with Lance this afternoon and make the offer, and hopefully—"

"Wait a minute, Kenneth," Percy said. "I want to come with you. I'd like to have a few words with him myself."

"You don't want to upset Lance," Naomi said. "He's in control. If you threaten him, he'll turn you down flat."

"I won't threaten him. I just think we should hedge our bet with a little intimidation. Let him know if he reneges on the agreement, there will be serious consequences."

"It's risky, but it might help in the long run," said Kenneth. "Okay, Percy, as soon as I set up a time for the meeting, I'll call you." Kenneth stood and said, "Wish us luck, everybody. We're going to need it."

Hezekiah sat and read a magazine in the waiting room of Dr. Joseph Canton. The room was bright, and light reflected off the many chrome and glass surfaces. A piano concerto by Mozart played almost undetected in the background. Religious publications with the virtuous faces of the ecclesiastical elite on the covers were fanned neatly on the coffee table. A brass crucifix hung over the door leading to the doctor's office. A modern clock ticked on a console behind an unoccupied receptionist desk.

Hezekiah made the trip to the Anaheim therapist not for absolution but rather to somehow relieve his apprehension through an unorthodox form of confession. He did not expect to hear words of encouragement. No

Christian psychiatrist would condone his behavior, but maybe he could understand it.

Dr. Canton had served as psychiatrist and confidant to some of the most influential clergy in the country. When he explained to the receptionist that he was about to make a decision that would affect thousands of people and change his life drastically, Hezekiah was scheduled promptly for a session.

"Reverend Cleaveland," the receptionist said after returning from the doctor's inner chamber. "Dr. Canton is ready for you now."

Hezekiah entered the office and shut the door behind him before he focused on the figure standing behind the desk.

Dr. Canton was a tall, lean man with shiny white hair. His gray suit hung loosely on his body, and wire-rimmed glasses sat on the tip of his pointed nose. He walked toward Hezekiah, extended his hand, and said, "Hello, Pastor Cleaveland. I'm Dr. Joseph Canton. Please come in and sit down."

"Thank you for seeing me at such short notice. Your secretary was very kind."

"How can I help you? Of course everything we discuss within this room will be kept in the strictest of confidence."

The two men sat at angles to each other in slick leather chairs facing the front of the desk. The room did not reflect the modern style of the reception area. The walls were painted a forest green with a lighter shade as trim. Wood shelves filled with psychiatric journals, textbooks, and numerous versions of the Bible lined the walls. The carpet was a dark shade of burgundy bordered with a warm floral scroll. The same music from the waiting room played from sources unknown.

"Of course. That's why I selected a psychiatrist and not my gardener," Hezekiah replied with a smile.

Dr. Canton laughed as Hezekiah continued speaking. "I'm not sure where to start. By all outward appearances my life is perfect. My ministry is growing faster than I can keep up with. We're building a new state-of-the-art sanctuary and media center. I have a beautiful wife and daughter. It all looks great."

"Well, Hezekiah. May I call you Hezekiah? If everything is great, I can't imagine why you would be here today."

Hezekiah looked out the window and saw a sea of silver high-rise buildings. He felt like a child confessing to his father that he had stolen sweets from the cookie jar. A wave of shame and embarrassment filled his chest. "Maybe this wasn't a good idea."

"I'm not saying I can help you with whatever it is that's troubling you, but we'll never know unless you tell me what it is. There is nothing that you can tell me that will embarrass or shock me. Like you, I've pretty much heard it all."

Hezekiah took a deep breath and slouched in the chair. "Okay. To start with, my marriage is over."

The doctor nodded for him to continue.

"We've done and said things that we'll never be able to undo, and I'm not sure that I want to. When we first married and were building the ministry, I appreciated and even relied on her take-charge personality. Now I feel like it's choking the life out of me. She is a very beautiful woman—smart, creative—but she treats me like an employee. Telling me where I should go, whom I should talk to, what I should preach about."

"Have you talked to her about how you feel?"

"I've tried, but . . ."

"You've tried, but what?"

"She doesn't listen."

The doctor looked pensively at Hezekiah. "Is this about your wife or is this about you? What is really causing you to have such negative feelings toward her?"

"All right, Doctor, I'm just going to say it. The bottom line is I'm in love with someone else. I didn't mean for it to happen. It just . . ." Hezekiah clasped his hands together as if contemplating a difficult task. The doctor's face showed no sign of reaction.

Hezekiah continued to talk. "I've know him . . ." He paused and looked as though he had delivered a punch line to a joke. "Did I forget to mention it was a man?"

"Yes, you did. Have you always had homosexual tendencies?"

Hezekiah looked embarrassed. "I suppose maybe I have. But I never acted on them."

"Hezekiah, if you want me to help, you have to be honest with me. I'm not here to judge you. I'm here to listen and, if I can, to help you."

Hezekiah looked out the window and said softly, "There was another man a few years ago. He was a dancer I met in New York. I went to a play he was performing in on Broadway and a mutual friend introduced us backstage."

"Why did it end?"

"It was primarily a physical relationship. And the distance made it difficult for us to see each other that often. He eventually met someone else and we lost contact after a while."

"So now there's . . . What is the new person's name?"

"Danny."

"So now there is Danny. Tell me about him," Dr. Canton said as he removed his glasses and leaned farther back in his chair.

"He works with the homeless in downtown Los Angeles. I saw him on a corner about a year ago and asked him if he would speak to a homeless woman living near my church. When I approached him, my intention was only to help that woman."

"I don't doubt that. Please go on."

"But when I looked in his eyes, something just clicked in my brain. He was so handsome and his voice was so gentle. There was something so vulnerable about him. I still see that in him to this day."

"How else is this different from the man you were involved with in New York?"

"Like I said, that was just physical. With Danny it's . . ."

"It's what?" Dr. Canton prompted.

"It's more. Yes, it's physical, of course, but it's also emotional and even spiritual. Sometimes I feel like we are connected on a deeper level. It's very difficult to describe."

"Are you in love with him?" Dr. Canton asked delicately.

"Isn't that rather obvious?"

"Yes, but I didn't want to assume."

Hezekiah shrugged his shoulders. "I've known him for almost a year now, and I've decided to leave my wife to be with him."

Still no reaction from the doctor.

"He's the most beautiful person I have ever met. I've never been this happy before in my life. I know this sounds crazy. It sounds ridiculous to me every time I say it, but I've pretty much made up my mind. When I'm with him, nothing else in the world matters. He doesn't judge me. He doesn't expect anything from me. I can just relax and be myself."

"Hezekiah, that implies that you are not yourself at other times."

"Maybe that's true. Maybe everything else is just an act. Everyone around me has expectations of how I should behave, what I should wear, say, and think. But he doesn't. He accepts me for who I am at the moment. And to be honest, I think he's helped me to discover who I am for myself, for the first time in my life."

"He sounds perfect. So why have you come to me?"

"I really don't know. I think I wanted someone to hear me say the words, to see the reaction on someone's face so I could gauge what to expect from the rest of the world. I just needed to say it to someone."

"Have you told your wife?"

"I told her this week about Danny. She said she knew I was seeing someone, but she didn't know it was a man. I haven't told her about leaving yet."

"Why have you hesitated?"

"I just decided this week. I plan on telling her after this Sunday." Hezekiah went on to recount the inner struggles he faced.

Dr. Canton gave no indication of emotion. He only asked questions that he knew Hezekiah had already asked himself. The doctor was very familiar with the subject. Ministers from around the country had sat in the same chair and shared almost identical stories. Some spoke of female lovers. Others spoke of men. Regardless of the gender of the object of their affection, the pain was the same.

"Hezekiah," the doctor said after the details of the saga were exhausted. "I'm not here to judge you. I'm here to help you sort through your feelings. I would imagine they run very deep right now. You seem like an exposed bundle of nerves, sensitive to every word, every move, and every gesture, which is understandable under the circumstances."

Hezekiah rested his head on the back of the chair and spoke. "I don't expect you to understand, Doctor. I just needed you to listen, and you've done a good job. I'm very grateful. I've searched my heart and prayed more about this than anything in my life. I always end up at the same place."

"And where is that?"

"Back in a place where I'm happy, where I don't feel guilty, and where I'm not ashamed about who it is I love. It's a good place, and I don't want to leave."

The level of resolve in his voice surprised the doctor. "I'd like to help you with this problem," he said. "We, of course, won't be able to solve it today, but I would like for you to come back next week before you talk to your wife about it. I'd like to help you figure out how to save your marriage and your ministry. Would you allow me to do that?"

"I think it's too late, Doctor."

"It's never too late to do the right thing." They exchanged a few more words when a gentle reminder sounded on the desk. The two men stood and shook hands.

"I hope to see you next week, Hezekiah."

"I'll think about it. Thank you for listening."

As Hezekiah pressed the button summoning the elevator, he knew that this would be the last time he would ever see Dr. Joseph Canton again.

Danny sat alone as he sipped a frothy latte at the coffee shop a block from his home on Crenshaw Boulevard. The smell of freshly brewed coffee filled the space, and the compact disc "Pick of the Day" was playing over the shop's sound system. It was a funky little café with overstuffed secondhand sofas and chairs placed in positions that allowed customers varying degrees of privacy while they leisurely enjoyed exotic blends and overpriced pastries.

Customers stood three deep at the counter ordering subtly nuanced variations of the traditional steaming cup-a-joe. "Decaf caramel macchiato, with soy milk, extra hot, and no foam" was the order from one seasoned drinker. "Mint mocha chip macchiato, double shot, and chocolate whipped cream," another confidently requested of the barista.

Other patrons sat in chairs and sofas and read the morning newspaper, or busily tapped away on laptop computers. Danny was lucky enough to get his favorite table in an alcove at the front window. Here he could be assured that no one would sit close enough to subject him to an irritating one-sided cell phone conversation consisting of, "Who will be at the meeting today? Why was she invited?" or, "Where would you like to have dinner? I hear the food there is lousy. Okay, that sounds like a good idea."

Danny was reading the local section of the paper, when he felt the familiar vibration of his telephone in his pocket. The caller ID indicated it was his friend Kay Braisden, who had recently moved to Washington, DC.

"Hello, Kay," he said. "How are you?"

Danny and Kay had been friends since college. She was the same age as Danny, a devout Christian, and the daughter of a pastor. By all outward appearances they seemed an unlikely pair. But the reality was they were very much alike. She was pretty, prim, and proper, and he was the soulful poet who preferred staying home on Saturday night over dancing the night away out at the hottest new nightclub with the beautiful, young, and gay crowd.

"Don't 'how are you' me, Danny St. John," Kay answered snippily. "I've been trying to reach you for two weeks now. Why haven't you returned my calls?"

"I know. I'm sorry. I haven't been a very good friend to you lately, but I've been really busy here. What is going on with you in DC? Have you found an apartment yet?"

"I couldn't find one in Washington, but I finally got a cute brownstone just over the bridge in Virginia. I can't wait for you to see it. It has the coziest fireplace and original fixtures. It's two stories and I actually like my neighbors. It's a bit pricey, so I had to get two roommates. One is a writer and the other a buyer for a boutique in DC. You'll like them. When are you going to come and see me? I can't wait to show you around."

Danny hesitated. "I'm not sure when I'll be able to get away."

"All right, Danny. Who is he?"

"What do you mean?" Danny asked shyly.

"I know you very well. Whenever you disappear like this, I know you're seeing someone. Now tell me who it is this time."

Danny paused and then said, "You're right. I am seeing someone, but—"

"I knew it." Kay interjected and continued with a flurry of questions. "I want to know everything. Who is he? Where did you meet him? How old is he? What does he look like? What does he do for a living?"

"Slow down, Kay. I can't say who it is. You would know him."

"Why? Is he famous? Did you snag yourself one of the Lakers?"

"No, he's not an athlete," Danny replied with a hint of exasperation in his voice. "I really don't want to talk about it. Can we please change the subject? I saw your sister last week at the market. She said your father is thinking about retiring."

"Danny, I thought I was your best friend. Why are you

afraid to tell me his name? Do you think I'm going to blab it to the newspapers?"

"Don't be ridiculous. That never crossed my mind. To be honest, I'm concerned that you might judge me."

"I didn't overreact when you told me you were gay, did I?" she asked defensively.

"As a matter of fact, you did. You didn't speak to me for a week after I told you."

"I apologized for that. It just took me some time to get used to the idea."

"I know, and I accepted your apology. But for that whole week I thought I had lost my best friend. I don't want to go through that again. What you think of me is very important, and I don't want to risk our friendship."

"Why would you think this would upset me?"

"Because he's a married man." Danny took a deep breath and continued. "And a minister."

Kay did not respond. There was a long moment when no words were exchanged. Then Danny said, "You see. I knew this would upset you. That's why I haven't told you about him. I've never done anything like this before, but I love him."

To Danny's relief Kay finally spoke. "Who is he?" she asked with no expression in her tone.

"Hezekiah Cleaveland."

Danny could hear a slight gasp escape from her lips.

"Danny," she said with great hesitation in her voice, "I don't believe this. Honey, you know I love you, but this is wrong. He's a married man."

"I don't need you to tell me that. I've gone over this a thousand times in my head. I've wanted to break it off with him, but I just can't."

"Danny, I accepted the fact that you are gay, even though I never told you it broke my heart. I even held my tongue when you were dating that horrible egomaniac from San Francisco. But this . . ."

Danny did not interrupt, and allowed Kay's words to continue their painful course.

"Danny, I have to pray about this. I don't know what to say."

"I understand, Kay."

"I love you, Danny."

"I know you do."

"I'll call you in a few days."

"Good-bye, Kay."

Danny stared out the window of the café. The morning traffic had begun to subside, and the paper no longer held stories of interest to him. He knew this would be the last time he would receive a call from Kay Braisden.

15

Hattie had not slept well the night before. Exhausted and still a bit groggy, she made a strong pot of coffee, sat under the bird lamp, and turned her weathered brown leather Bible, with *King James Version* embossed in gold on the cover, to the Twenty-third Psalm. The dates of her mother's and father's births and deaths were recorded on the front pages of the Bible. The marriages, births, baptisms, and deaths of the Williams and Fisher, Hattie's maiden name, families were all chronicled within the pages of the Bible. Yellow highlighter striped passages on every page, and all the margins contained Hattie's handwritten notes in black, red, blue, and graphite.

Hezekiah had appeared in her dream again the night before. Hattie clearly saw Hezekiah's body falling through the sanctuary at New Testament Cathedral with a force that would ensure death. Members of the congregation scrambled frantically to clear a space on the sanctuary floor. Feathered and flowered hats scurried around the room like brightly colored marbles that had been spilled from a schoolgirl's sack onto the pavement. Choir members in flowing robes and sashes ran to safety and screamed, "Pastor Cleaveland is falling!"

Mothers shielded the eyes of their small children from the scene that would surely scar their young minds for life, while old ladies in sensible shoes hobbled away from the inevitable point of impact.

Hezekiah could see the look of horror and fear in the eyes of his beloved members even at the pace that his body fell. Women whose powdered cheeks he had kissed and men whose hands he had firmly shaken now ran with abandon from the one they once called pastor, shepherd, and friend.

The dream had faded as quickly as it had appeared. Hattie now pondered the scene that had played like a movie in her dream. Was the pedestal they had placed him on too high and unstable? Everyone knew a fall from so high was inevitable, but still they had insisted Hezekiah take the place of honor above their heads and beyond their reach. *What mortal could survive at such heights?* she thought. *How could his soul find peace at elevations so dangerously close to the sun?*

Hattie sat still under the glow of the lamp with her feet planted firmly on the floor and hands resting on the open pages of the Bible.

"Hold on, Pastor Cleaveland," she said softly. "I'm praying for you."

Samantha drove her car into the parking lot of the church. She retrieved her purse from the seat and walked briskly through the corridors toward Catherine's office.

Catherine Birdsong was sitting behind her desk. She wore a green skirt and a white ruffled blouse with a floral scarf around her neck. She looked like a woman who wrestled daily in front of her mirror to find a look befitting her station in life as chief operations officer to a prominent church.

A large, curved desk surrounded Catherine. The walls were covered with plaques that the church and pastor had received over the years. A fax machine and copier sat in the corner, and Catherine's desk held a computer, telephone, and pad.

"Good morning, Mrs. Cleaveland," she said to Samantha, who was standing in her doorway. "Pastor Cleaveland hasn't arrived yet. He called earlier and said he would be late."

"I'm not here to see Hezekiah. I'm here to see you."

Catherine saw the familiar hint of anger in Samantha's eyes. She adjusted her chair in preparation to stand. "Is there something I can do for you?"

"Yes." Her voice began to escalate. "You can tell me why you've been covering for Hezekiah when I call and he's not here. Why you've never mentioned to me that he's been unable to account for his whereabouts lately, and why do you think it's in your job description to interfere in my marriage?"

Catherine's eyes widened. Her knees shook as she braced herself on the desk and stood. "I'm not sure what you're talking about. I—"

Samantha cut her off. "Don't lie to me. You know exactly what I'm talking about. You are not to decide what information I should and should not have about my husband or this church. I knew this wasn't going to work out when I first met you. I knew you wouldn't fit in here."

Catherine could not speak. She found her throat was contracting as she tried to sputter out her defense. "I . . . I never . . ."

"Don't bother. I don't want to hear anything you have to

say. It's over. You're fired. I want you out of here by the end of the day, and you better leave every stapler, paper clip, and pen, or I'll have the police at your door to get them back."

Samantha clutched the purse under her arm and stormed out of the office.

Catherine sat down as the telephone rang. It was impossible for her to contain her tears. She felt as though breath had been snatched from her lungs by an incubus that had descended from the steeple of the church. The ringing of her unanswered telephone echoed through the empty halls of the building.

The *Los Angeles Chronicle* newsroom was busy as usual. Loud conversations mingled into an indecipherable buzz through the long, windowless room. Sounds of clanging computer keyboards, whirring copy machines, and ringing telephones flooded the space. The anonymous faces behind the stories that chronicled life in the city worked furiously to meet yet another deadline.

Lance Savage sat at a corner desk with his eyes on a glowing computer screen. His fingers tapped furiously at the keyboard, making the final revisions to the article he had toiled over for the last six months:

> *When confronted in his office at New Testament Cathedral, Pastor Cleaveland refused to comment on the allegations of the one-year affair with Mr. St. John.*
>
> *Sources close to Pastor Cleaveland have confirmed that he has been seen on numerous occasions going into St. John's home in the Adams District. St. John has not returned calls to the* Los Angeles Chronicle.

Lance paused as he read the last line on the computer screen. He had, in fact, never attempted to contact Danny. Hezekiah's shouting face flashed in his mind. He had denied the allegations so adamantly that a trace of doubt prevented Lance from further typing. *What if Cynthia is lying?* he thought. *What if this Danny person is just a cousin or a family friend?*

There had been no doubt concerning the relationship with the young outreach worker until the explosive confrontation with Hezekiah. But the look in Hezekiah's eyes, the indignation in his voice, caused Lance to hesitate. Had he overlooked some important piece of evidence?

Lance had questioned Cynthia Pryce's motives when she first contacted him with the unbelievable story six months earlier.

"Mrs. Pryce," he had asked when they spoke on the telephone months earlier. *"Why are you coming forward with this story? You know if this is true, Hezekiah will be forced to step down as pastor."*

"I know," she replied. *"But I can't sit by any longer and watch the Cleavelands waste so much of God's money building that horrible shrine to themselves. That money could be used to do so much good in the world. It's time someone exposed them for the immoral and greedy people they are."*

"So what is his alleged lover's name, and how did you find out about him?" Lance asked, making no attempt to conceal his skepticism.

"His name is Danny," she answered confidently. *"He's a homeless-outreach worker. I found out about it by accident."*

"By accident?" Lance asked.

"Yes, by accident. I was in a meeting with Hezekiah and several other people in the church conference room, and Hezekiah needed a document he had left on his desk and asked me if I wouldn't mind getting it for him. When I went into his office, his computer was on. There was a half-written love letter to Danny on the screen. I did a search for other e-mails sent to that address and found dozens of disgusting messages they had sent to each other. I printed as many as I could. I didn't have time to print them all because Hezekiah was waiting for me to return to the meeting. You can see them, if you don't believe me."

Lance had thoroughly investigated the story after the conversation with Cynthia. He reviewed all the e-mails between Hezekiah and Danny. Several telephone calls to agencies that serve the homeless in Los Angeles led him directly to Danny St. John. He even followed Hezekiah's limousine one evening to the house in the Adams District and saw Danny for the first time as he greeted his illustrious guest at the door.

Lance had also secretly followed Danny on his rounds for two weeks. Through the parks, under freeway passes, to homeless shelters, and to the emergency room at Los Angeles General Hospital, where the young man had accompanied a woman who later died from an overdose of heroin.

From a safe distance, ducking behind buildings, cars, and lurking in the shadows, Lance marveled at Danny's gentle manner. Without fail, he held the scab-covered hands and patted the weary backs of disheveled men and women whose singular existence was never acknowledged by housed residents of the city. They were simply called "the homeless," a lumbering beast roaming the city. Danny was the embodiment of the compassion that the creature craved so desperately.

Lance could not bring himself to confront Danny after all he had witnessed. He didn't want to disturb the gentle spirit he'd seen wandering the streets with the green backpack on his back, bending down to touch the weary shoulders of so many destitute people. Lance grew surprisingly fond and, against his better judgment, protective of the Danny he had come to know during those two weeks.

Moisture began to accumulate in the palms of his hands. The toxic words begged for closure as his eyes focused again on the computer screen. *I don't have a choice*, he thought. *I've got to interview Danny, or I don't have a story.*

Danny's weekly outreach schedule was predictable. He arrived at the homeless center on Central Avenue. There he would encourage members of the large crowd to visit the city's free clinic, where their myriad wounds and infections could be treated.

The large, open space was busy with activity. Men in tattered clothes and worn-out shoes sat transfixed in front of a large television screen, watching *The Today Show*. In the facility's shower area, women made futile attempts at washing away the streets' grime, while others slept in crumpled heaps on the floor, preparing for another night of aimless wandering through the city.

He walked through the room, searching for those in obvious need of medical attention: the man nursing a swollen foot, the woman cradling a bruised arm, or the old lady cowering in a corner with an open wound on her emaciated and frightened face. There was never a short-age of candidates for his services.

Danny spotted a man limping through the crowd. His pant leg was torn, exposing a deep gash on his right leg. "Excuse me, sir," Danny said, approaching the man. "That cut looks pretty bad. You should have a doctor look at it at the free clinic."

The man turned around slowly, attempting to maintain his balance. His white hair pointed in every direction from beneath a red bandanna. A scraggly yellow-stained mustache dipped in and out of his mouth as he spoke. "Who are you?" he asked in a raspy voice.

The smell of alcohol and stale breath met Danny's nose immediately. "My name is Danny." He smiled disarmingly. "I work for the Homeless-Outreach Team. I can make an appointment for you with a doctor, if you would like."

The man steadied himself on his good leg. "Some strung-out junkies jumped me last night. I was drinking with them out in Griffith Park and all of a sudden they just started beat'n the shit outta me. Took my last two dollars, too, fucking assholes." He leaned over to show Danny the wound on his leg.

"Cut me with a knife here," he said. Then, standing erect again, he raised his shirt to reveal yet another gash on the side of his torso. "And here," he said. "I'da gave 'em the fucking two dollars if they'd just asked for it."

Danny escorted the man to the only vacant seat in the lobby. "You really shouldn't be walking around with those wounds. You might have some internal damage. I'm going to have our outreach van come and pick you up and take you to the clinic. What's your name?"

"Nathanial Ford. Folks call me Nate."

"All right, Nate. Just wait here. I'll be back in a moment."

Danny made his way to the receptionist counter. "Hi, Chris," he said to an attractive Asian woman with wide brown eyes behind the counter. "Can I use your telephone? I have to call for a van to pick up Mr. Ford and take him to the clinic, and the battery on my cell phone is almost dead."

"Hello, Danny," she responded with a smile. "Looks like Nate got beat up pretty bad again last night."

Danny nodded in affirmation as the woman handed him the telephone.

"Hi, Emma. It's Danny. Could you send the van to the drop-in center on Central? I need to have someone transported to the clinic."

After completing the arrangement, Danny thanked the receptionist and headed back to the old man in the lobby. As he made his way through the crowd, he felt a light tap on his shoulder. When he turned, he saw the clean-shaven face of a man who looked out of place in the room filled with homeless people.

"Excuse me. May I speak with you for a moment?" he said. "My name is Lance Savage. I work for the *Los Angeles Chronicle*."

"I'm sorry. I'm not authorized to speak to the media," Danny said, turning to walk away. "It's against agency policy. You'll have to call my supervisor."

"This isn't about the homeless, Mr. St. John," Lance said with a hint of regret in his voice. "Is there somewhere we can speak in private?"

The sound of his name spoken by the stranger startled him.

"How do you know my name?" he asked.

"I know a lot about you, Danny. May I call you Danny? This is about Hezekiah Cleaveland."

Danny began to walk away.

"I've never met him."

"I know all about you two," Lance said as he followed Danny through the crowd. "And I've already spoken to Pastor Cleaveland."

Danny stopped in the center of the room when he heard the words. He fought off the urge to run to the nearest exit.

Lance stood behind Danny and spoke in a whisper. "If it's not true, Danny, you can deny it. This is the only chance I'm going to give you."

Danny did not respond. It was clear that the stranger in the wrinkled sport coat knew something of his relationship with Hezekiah. But how had he found out?

"This will only take a minute, Danny," Lance said in a soft and reassuring tone.

The sound of Lance's voice jarred Danny from his silent contemplation. His eyes focused again on the whirl of activity around him.

"Meet me in front of the building in five minutes," he said without looking at Lance. "I have to finish helping someone."

Lance stood on the busy street in front of the center and took the last puff from a cigarette. Noise from traffic streaming by drowned out the loud conversations and blaring television set from the room he had just left.

Through the windows he could see Danny bending over to speak to the weathered old man in the lobby. After a few moments Danny approached him on the street.

"Thanks for agreeing to talk with me, Danny. I know this is difficult for you."

Danny did not respond.

"Would you like to comment on your relationship with Pastor Cleaveland?"

"Who told you about that? Did Hezekiah say something?"

"I'll be honest with you, Danny. Hezekiah didn't confirm your relationship."

"Then what makes you think it's true?"

"I have a source who is very close to Hezekiah who can prove that you two are involved."

"Who?"

"I can't say. I can tell you, though, that I have been given a substantial amount of evidence that proves it."

"Why are you doing this to him? Do you hate him that much?"

"I'm not doing anything other than my job. This is a significant story, and people have a right to know about it."

"Why do they have a right to know something so private about him?" Danny asked. "He has rights too. He has the right to have some part of his life to keep to himself."

"I'm sorry, Danny, but he doesn't. When Hezekiah became a public figure, he gave up the right to privacy. Every part of his life is fair game and subject to public scrutiny. He must have told you that."

"He's told me a lot of things, but that doesn't make them right."

"So you admit that you do know him," Lance said gently, as though speaking to a small child.

Danny's eyes drifted wearily to the procession of cars that sped by. "Is there any way I can convince you not to pursue this? You're going to hurt a lot of innocent people."

"I'm not trying to hurt anyone. I just want the truth, and I want to give you a chance to tell your side of the story," Lance said innocently.

Danny looked sharply back at Lance. "You don't give a fuck about all the good Hezekiah has done for this city. What's important to you is furthering your career, and if someone gets hurt, or a few lives are ruined in the process, you justify it by saying, 'I'm just doing my job.' Well, you've come to the wrong person. I'm not going to help you do your job."

Danny peered deeply into Lance's widening eyes and continued his tirade. "For the record, Mr. Savage, I have never met Hezekiah Cleaveland. I have no desire to meet Hezekiah Cleaveland, and if my name appears in your paper in relation to this lie, I will contact my father's law firm in New York and they will be happy to sue the *Los Angeles Chronicle*, and you personally, for slander and defamation of character."

With these final words Danny adjusted the backpack on his shoulder, tipped his head in a gesture of farewell, and fell into step with the flow of pedestrians.

Lance stood astonished as Danny disappeared into the moving crowd. He had severely miscalculated the cunning of his prey.

Hezekiah has schooled him well, he thought while fumbling anxiously for the package of cigarettes. *Cynthia had better be right about this.*

16

Thursday

Samantha and Hezekiah still had an undeniable physical attraction, despite the chasm that had developed between them. Hezekiah was a man who found refuge and peace in the pleasure that physical contact gave him. Samantha, however, viewed erotic pleasure as simply another means by which to possess the body and soul of her prey, if only for a few brief moments.

The further apart they had grown over the years, the more intense their lovemaking had become. Hezekiah and Samantha woke together to find their bodies entwined, as they had on so many mornings before. As Hezekiah slowly emerged from his sleep, he felt his morning erection pressing against Samantha's soft thigh. Gentle brushing from the satin of Samantha's nightgown made her nipples stand firm.

By the time they had gained full consciousness, there was no turning back. Hezekiah grabbed the hair on the back of her head and pressed her lips to his. Their nightclothes provided ample shields for raw emotions, and their bodies did what seemed only natural. Hezekiah pinned her arms above her head as she twisted violently beneath the weight of his body. Her hands broke free and she plunged her fingernails into his back. He refused to allow her to squirm from beneath him, and she refused to be released.

"Fuck me. Hezekiah, please fuck me," Samantha whispered as she held him close.

Blankets and sheets lay in a bundle at the foot of the bed. Hezekiah entered her with such force that her head, cushioned only by the pillows, rocked the huge headboard. After moments of intense rhythmic pounding, Samantha forced her body on top, with Hezekiah still deep inside her. Her straddled legs held him like a vise beneath her silk nightgown. Her breast broke free from the garment as she moaned with each downward plunge. He slapped her face and grabbed her neck as if to choke her. In time he released her, not to spare her life but to slap her buttocks as though encouraging a horse to run faster.

Hezekiah groped for the side of the mattress when he knew the end was near. The edges of the large bed extended beyond his reach, so he gripped the sheets and braced himself for the reward of the pounding he had endured.

For the brief moments of climactic pleasure, the two could only hear, see, smell, and feel the overpowering sensations rushing through their bodies. There was no hate, no jealousy, and no remorse. There was only ecstasy.

Samantha collapsed, spent, on her side of the bed. She brushed the hair from her face with her last bit of energy. Hezekiah's chest continued to heave in attempts to regain the breath he had lost. Slowly their eyes focused on the light surrounding their bed. The feelings they had just shared began to dissolve and were replaced with remorse. Remorse for succumbing to desires they thought were no longer shared. Desires that only complicated their journey. The course of which was now irreversible.

No words were exchanged. They had none left. All that had to be said from that point on required no response. There were no more questions. There were only answers.

Hezekiah got out of bed, nightclothes still intact, and went into the bathroom. Samantha lay with her back to him, hoping he would be quick and leave her to wash from her body and memory what would be the last time he was in her, and she in him. Still in a daze she angrily kicked the bedcovers to the floor and checked the clock on her nightstand. Why had she done it? She searched for the answer in the light of the window and fought back tears when there was no response.

Danny stood at his living-room window looking out into the busy street below. The tidy apartment was filled with flea market and garage sale finds. His bare feet were planted firmly on an Asian-print rug he'd found abandoned at a curb, and a tea table bought at a thrift shop held his morning cup of coffee.

Female joggers, with ponytails bouncing behind, ran along the sidewalk. From his window he could see four homeless men bundled in sleeping bags at a bus stop across the street. He had never offered his services to the group of regulars, fearing that if he had, they would discover where he lived and return for additional kindness. The little apartment was his only refuge, and even he could not share it with the needy people to whom he had dedicated his life.

There had been no rest for him the night before. He tossed in bed and watched infomercials on television.

Twice during the course of the restless evening, Danny had picked up the telephone to dial Hezekiah's cell phone, but each time he resisted. The next conversation would surely mark the end of their relationship.

Through his twenties Danny had searched for the one man willing to look in his eyes and tell him honestly what he saw. Did he see a kind man with a loving heart, or a hideous monster intent on destroying all in its path? Was there a child playing behind his brown eyes, or a weary old man eager to share all that his life had taught?

But no one had stayed long enough or looked deeply enough to explore the depths of Danny's heart. No one, until Hezekiah.

Hezekiah offered himself as a mirror, reflecting images that Danny had never seen before. When they were together, Danny saw his own countenance for the first time in Hezekiah's comforting smile. He felt his own warmth in Hezekiah's embrace. He heard his joy in Hezekiah's laugh and tasted his fears in his kiss. Without him the light in his soul would be dim once again, and the Danny he had come to know would be lost forever.

Danny's cat, Parker, purred around his feet, waiting for the morning tummy rub that was long overdue. Footsteps from the neighbors above leaving for the day could be heard on the stairs near his door. Danny asked himself, over and over again, the same questions in his mind. *Is Lance Savage bluffing and really has no proof? How did he find me? Who could have known? How can I continue living in this city once everyone finds out?*

The questions were unending, and no answers came to provide refuge from his fears. Fear had prevented him from going to work that morning, and also from scratching Parker's fuzzy gray belly. His life was ending; yet the joggers continued to run, smiling news anchors continued reporting tragedy after tragedy on television, and steam continued to rise from his coffee cup.

As the cat's purring grew more insistent, Danny, without moving his feet, bent down and gently scratched his stomach. Parker rolled blissfully onto his back, and then the telephone rang.

It could only be Hezekiah at that hour of the morning. The ringing echoed through the room, but Danny could not move. After the fourth ring the answering machine on the table responded. "Hi. You've reached Danny. I'm not in right now. Please leave a message at the tone."

Hezekiah's strained voice came through the black box.

"Hello, Danny," Hezekiah said softly. "I called your cell, and I called your office this morning, but they said you were out sick. I hope it's nothing serious. Look, baby, something pretty serious is going on and I need to talk to you as soon as possible. You know I love you. I'll try again later."

A tear rolled down Danny's cheek as he continued to comfort the little rescued cat at his feet. There was no longer a need to remain at the window. There was no safe place for him to stand. The world had forced open his front door and barged in without invitation. The books on the shelves, magazines on the coffee table, and the chipped plates in the cupboard no longer belonged to him.

He looked around the room. The pale walls had lost their warm glow. The voices on television seemed louder than before. Had the walls inched in closer? Did someone rearrange the furniture? Were the leaves on the potted plants suddenly wilting, and had Parker stopped purring at his feet? Nothing in the room seemed familiar anymore.

On that morning Danny found the world to be lonelier and more frightening than he had ever imagined possible.

Hezekiah sat quietly in the rear of the limousine as Dino drove toward the church. He thought about how much he loved sex with Danny and compared it to the regrettable physical encounter he had just had with Samantha. They both were wildly passionate and tinged with the slightest hint of abuse. But at this point in Hezekiah's life, Danny was now his companion of choice.

Although Samantha had been silent for much of the previous evening and the morning, she seemed to handle his startling revelation with a surprising amount of restraint. They had exchanged no further words on the subject, which led him to believe she had resigned herself to the situation.

He thought of her beauty and knew she could have any man she selected. He would leave her wanting for nothing. *She can have that awful house.* He would continue to pay for her extravagant lifestyle. Samantha had never worked a day in her life and the only line on her résumé would read, "Dutifully served as the wife of Pastor Dr. Hezekiah T. Cleaveland."

She was nineteen years old when they met. Tall and skinny, but mature for her age. While other girls were throwing themselves at the feet of the handsome young man, Samantha ignored him. She considered him incapable of providing her with the life she knew she deserved. Nonetheless, he pursued her relentlessly, taking her for walks on campus and bringing her mother flowers every time he came to visit.

Samantha gradually began to see in him what he had always seen in himself. A man that could stir the souls of anyone he came in contact with. A man whose magnificent future was as apparent as his striking good looks. He knew he was handsome, but he had never relied on his looks to get ahead. He had something more important, sincerity. When he spoke to you, even if only to say hello, it was as though no one else in the world existed. You had his full attention, and whatever you had on your mind was important to him.

The limousine turned into the parking lot of the church. As he walked toward Catherine's office, he heard the telephone ringing. At the door he could see Catherine crying, with her head on the desk.

"Catherine," he shouted and entered the room. "Catherine, what's wrong?" He lifted her by the shoulders. "Stop crying and tell me what happened."

She looked as if she had been physically assaulted. Mascara ran down her cheeks and a scarf was twisted around her neck like a hangman's noose.

"Samantha was just here. She fired me."

"Fired you. Why? What did she say?"

"She accused me of covering for you. I didn't even have a chance to defend myself. She just stormed in, fired me, and left."

Hezekiah could hear his heart pounding in his ears. He had learned to tolerate the sometimes volatile behavior of his wife, but he could never stand by and allow her to attack innocent people. "She crossed the line this time. You didn't deserve to be treated that way."

"Now what am I going to do?" she asked through sobs.

"Come on, stop crying. This entire thing is my fault. You had nothing to do with it."

"Pastor Cleaveland, you've got to tell her. She wouldn't listen to me."

"Don't worry, Catherine. She can't fire you. I hired you

and I'm the only one who can fire you. Everything is going to be fine," he said, hugging her. She rested her head on his chest. "I'm so sorry you had to go through this, Catherine."

"I've never seen her that angry before. I thought she was going to throw something at me. I was frightened. Why does she treat people like that? She has no right."

When her sobs began to subside, Hezekiah said, "You let me worry about Samantha. Now go to the ladies' room and clean yourself up," he said, smiling. "Remember, we've got twenty million dollars to raise."

The intoxication from thoughts of Danny mingled in his head with rage at Samantha and pity for the trauma-stricken Catherine. He now knew what he had to do. Leave Samantha, move in with Danny, and accomplish this feat while maintaining the ministry he had dedicated his life to.

He could tell people that Danny was his housekeeper, or maybe the son of a dear friend in Texas. *There has to be a way to make this work*, he thought.

Particulars of the complicated process raced through his mind. The church was not big enough for the both of them. Samantha would have to leave it and join another one. There was no way he could look at her each Sunday in the audience with venom darting from her eyes. He could pay her to leave the church. Promise her something, anything she wanted, to let him go and allow him to start a new life.

Hezekiah, Samantha, and Jasmine sat at their dining-room table having dinner. Etta busily set platters and bowls of food around the well-appointed table. No one spoke and eye contact was avoided.

Over the years Etta had seen the Cleavelands at their

best and at their worst. This night was unprecedented, as far as she could recall. She could not begin to imagine how the evening would end, but she hoped she would have the opportunity to retire to her quarters before things got out of control. Her heart went out to Hezekiah as he sat at the head of the table with Jasmine to his right and Samantha to his left. She often wondered why he stayed with her. Why did he put up with her lavish spending and her often unpredictable temper?

"I hope the meat is cooked the way you like it, Pastor," she said as she placed the last dish on the table.

"I'm sure it's fine, Etta. Thank you."

"If you need anything else, I'll be in the kitchen." Etta said a silent prayer for the Cleavelands as she retreated from the room.

Jasmine shuffled food around her plate with her fork. She had grown to hate the dinner ritual. Her mind jumped from remembering the wild events of the previous evening to anticipating the ones scheduled for that night. She tried to ignore the tension between her parents as she prepared an excuse for leaving the house.

"Daddy," she said innocently, "I need a hundred dollars. I'm going out this evening."

Before Hezekiah could answer, Samantha stepped in. "Where are you going?"

"I was talking to Daddy."

Hezekiah sat and barely listened to the exchange. He had a rule not to get involved in arguments between his wife and daughter. He felt the relationship between a mother and daughter was far too complicated for any man to understand.

Samantha abruptly dropped her fork on the plate. "I don't care who you were talking to. I asked where you are planning on going."

Not wanting to tangle with her mother while she was teetering on one of her terrible moods, Jasmine snapped, "Never mind. Just drop it."

"Don't talk to your mother that way, young lady." Hezekiah finally spoke while reaching for his wallet. "Where are you going?"

Jasmine welcomed the intervention of her father. She could always count on him to look beyond her condition, regardless of how chaotic, and only see his bright-eyed little girl. "Kelly and I are going to a movie."

Hezekiah reached into his wallet and handed her a one-hundred-dollar bill. Whenever he looked at Jasmine, he could only see the little girl in a white lace dress with yellow ribbons in her hair who ran into his arms every time he entered a room. He couldn't see the rapidly deteriorating young woman who drank too much and had sex in the back of cars with men she barely knew.

"What are you doing, Hezekiah? She's lying. Don't give her that!" Samantha shrieked.

"Don't tell me what to do," Hezekiah said calmly.

"Why do you indulge her like this? It only makes things worse. Can't you see what's happening to her?"

"You're making things worse by blowing this out of proportion. If, for once in your life, you could stop and think of how your tantrums and manipulation affect others, maybe we wouldn't be in this mess."

"So it's my fault that you can't control yourself, and that our marriage is falling apart. The fact that you can't keep your . . ." Acknowledging Jasmine, Samantha had the presence of mind to censor her words.

"Yes, Samantha, much of this is your fault. You want to control everything and everyone around you. This is not the church, damn it. It's our home. You can't even tell the difference anymore. People have their own lives. People have a right to private thoughts—thoughts that even you can't control."

"Save your sermon for Sunday morning. I'm not one of your sheep that needs you to tell them when to sing and when to pray."

Samantha snatched the cloth napkin from her lap and threw it onto the table. The china shook as she stood and a glass of water almost tipped over.

"If you could pull your head out of the sand for once, you'd see that your daughter is killing herself and needs our help. But you've got more important people on your mind these days."

"Don't involve Jasmine in our problems. Jasmine, you should leave. Your mother and I have to talk."

Jasmine stood up from the table. "Are you going to be all right, Daddy?"

"I'll be fine, honey. Don't stay out too late. I want you home at a decent hour."

"I will be, Daddy." Jasmine kissed her father on the forehead and made a hasty exit.

From the kitchen Etta heard the loud voices and pressed her ear against the door.

Hezekiah waited to hear Jasmine close the front door before he spoke. "I want to talk to you about Catherine. You had no right to fire her. You crossed the line and you owe her an apology."

"Crossed the line? You must be joking. I'm not the one fucking men in alleys, or park bathrooms, or wherever the hell it is that you go."

Etta gasped behind the kitchen door.

Hezekiah stood up quickly and took a physically threatening stance. Samantha looked him in the eye and said, "What are you going to do, hit me?"

Hezekiah rushed toward her and slapped her hard on the cheek. Samantha's long hair swirled as she rebounded from the blow.

The force of the impact caused her to knock her plate off the table. After gaining her footing she stood upright and said, "So now you want to be a man. After seventeen fucking years, you want to be in charge now. I've got news for you, Reverend. It's too late! You never were a man and now you've proved it by letting some faggot fuck you in the ass."

Hezekiah slapped her again. This time, before his hand completely cleared her face, she lunged at him and wrestled him to the floor. Dishes and glasses crashed to the carpet. The flower centerpiece toppled over and water splashed against the wall.

"I'll kill you, you fucking bastard. I'll kill you." She pounded his head with her open palms. Hezekiah grabbed her neck and rolled her to her back. He straddled her chest while she continued to scream and claw at his face.

Etta burst through the kitchen door, screaming, "Pastor, no! Don't hit her." She ran behind him and tried to pull him away from Samantha's thrashing body. "Pastor, no. You're going to kill her."

When he heard Etta's voice, his hands froze. His eyes focused on Samantha's distorted face as she continued to spew obscenities. He pushed Etta aside and stood up.

Panting, Samantha moved away from him and scrambled to her knees, shouting through disheveled hair, "What's wrong—you not man enough to put me in my place?"

Hezekiah coldly stared at her and said nothing. He looked at Etta cowering next to the wall and yelled, "Don't just stand there. Clean this mess up!" He then gestured toward Samantha, still on her knees. "And get her out of here."

Hezekiah turned and walked out of the room. Etta bent down to Samantha and tried to help her up.

Samantha snapped, "Don't touch me. And if you ever mention this to anyone, I swear I'll kill you."

17

Danny St. John stood beneath the freeway overpass, next to a pile of clothes, soiled blankets, and soggy newspapers. He was one block from the sprawling construction site of New Testament Cathedral. The smell of urine and human waste assaulted his nose.

Sounds from cars speeding overhead filled the air. Remains of a campfire burned in the distance, and a mother with two small children gathered a large stuffed plastic bag and dashed from the area before he could approach. As Danny walked toward two men sitting next to a cement pillar, which vibrated from the traffic above, the mud squished beneath his feet. Their foggy eyes became alert as he approached. One man struggled to his feet and tried to walk away.

"Wait a minute, guys," Danny called out. "I'm not the police. My name is Danny. I'm an outreach worker."

The two men seemed to relax and turn themselves over once again to their alcohol-induced haze.

"Hey, man," one said, "you got any vitamins? I got a cold that I ain't been able to shake for weeks."

They each wore blue jeans covered with mud. One was a Native American, and the other's thick drawl told of his deep Southern roots. Their shirts were torn and missing several buttons. Hair that had once been their crowns was matted and covered with unidentifiable white flecks. Danny rustled through his backpack and found two small bottles of vitamin C. "Here you go, guys," he said, handing them the bottles. "I've also got clean socks if you need them."

The Indian's words were slurred from three days of nonstop drinking. "Man, I been trying to get an affordable apartment for three years now, but they always tell me there ain't none available."

"They told me I had to be sober before I could get an apartment," the Southerner chimed in. "What kinda shit is that? If I could get sober by myself, I wouldn't need their motherfucking charity."

Both men laughed in unison and leaned toward each other in a gesture of camaraderie. Danny had heard the story many times before.

"I know it's tough, guys, but if you come to my office, I can make a few calls for you and maybe get you in somewhere."

The two men seemed startled by Danny's proposal.

"Man, I got an appointment at the welfare office this afternoon. Can I come in some other time?" came the response from the Southerner.

The Native American held up his hand, signifying his rejection of the offer.

Danny handed them his business card.

"My office hours are on the back. You can come in anytime. If I don't hear from you by next week, I'll check back here, if that's okay."

"You guys oughta build more affordable housing," said the Indian. "Somebody should tell the fucking pastor of that church over there that instead of building that fucking forty-five-million-dollar piece of shit, he oughta be building housing for poor people."

As Danny walked to his car, he made a mental note of the conversation with the two men and the squalor in which they lived. He wanted to recount it to Hezekiah the next time he saw him.

Something was not quite right at New Testament Cathedral. Staff members speculated about the strange behavior of those closest to the pastor. Why had Hezekiah canceled all his afternoon appointments?

Why had Catherine barricaded herself in her office? "Hold all my calls" was the only instruction to the baffled secretary.

Why had Naomi suddenly dropped a wall of silence via an "urgent" e-mail sent to all department heads? It read:

> Until further notice, all communications with members of the press are to be cleared by me first. Violation of this directive will result in disciplinary actions by the pastor's office.

"I heard the pastor collapsed last night and had to be rushed to the hospital" was the rumor whirling through the carpeted cubicles of the finance office.

"Naomi finally stood up for herself and told the pastor to get off her back" emerged as the top theory with the maintenance crew.

"Hezekiah caught Percy Pryce in bed with Samantha. They had a fight and Percy punched Hezekiah in the jaw. Didn't you see the scar on his face this morning?" The scintillation of this rumor made it the top choice for staff in the cafeteria.

New Testament Cathedral still looked the same. The

grand main staircase continued to sweep elegantly to the main entrance. Sculpted white cherubs still dangled perilously from balconies. Mail room staff, on their usual morning rounds, delivered stacks of envelopes stuffed with cash and checks. This morning, however, the air was thick with a tension that caused conversations to halt suddenly when unfamiliar faces entered a room, or when a member of the pastor's inner circle walked by.

"Good morning, Naomi," a brave staff member said as Naomi passed her in the hall. "Is everything all right with Pastor Cleaveland?"

Naomi recognized the woman's face but couldn't remember her name. "Why? What have you heard?" Naomi asked, slowing her pace only slightly.

"Someone said that he looked sick."

Naomi turned her head to the woman, but her feet continued to move forward. "I just saw the pastor this morning. He looked fine to me. Only idiots believe the gossip they hear around here. What's your name?"

"Sarah," said the startled woman.

"Sarah," Naomi said, as if making a mental note. "I'll mention what you said to the pastor the next time I see him. I'm sure he'll want to know who said it."

"I didn't mean . . . It was just something I heard from someone," the panicked woman said to Naomi's back. "I would never gossip about the pastor."

Naomi said over her shoulder, "Have a nice day, Sarah."

Hattie Williams squirmed in her favorite chair as she dozed. An old gospel hymn crackled on the radio. She intermittently thrashed her head from side to side. "No, don't do it," she mumbled in her sleep. "Look out, Pastor. Don't listen to them."

The dream was so vivid, Hattie thought she was awake.

* * *

The church floor ripples to the rhythm of Hezekiah's beating heart as he falls in the sanctuary. From the top to the bottom, each pew ebbs and flows, mimicking the motion of an ocean wave.

Frightened people on the billowing pews ride the waves in horror as Hezekiah's body spirals downward. Women, wearing clothing inappropriate for such a turbulent sea, lose their footing as they look upward at the flying pastor. They tumble to the floor. Some hit the solid ground with a thud, while others scurry on hands and knees to avoid being crushed.

Chords of music screech from the pipe organ. The chandeliers flicker and shrieks of horror can be heard from every corner of the room. Suddenly the glass birds and cherubs in the stained-glass windows come to life and join Hezekiah in his flight. Beams of light reach through glass panels, trying to catch Hezekiah as he falls, but his twirling body eludes their grasp. He tumbles in the air like a leaf falling to the earth, which heralds the end of a long, hot summer, or a snowflake foretelling the cold winter to come. The fall seems endless. Laws of gravity have ceased and have left him suspended in air, unable to touch the ground below. He is a wounded bird in flight for all to see and pity.

Hezekiah looks down and suddenly sees the faces of his beloved members have contorted into hideous shapes, spewing bile and contempt.

"You lied to us, Hezekiah Cleaveland!" they shout.

"If God loved you so much, then why has he let you fall?" they challenge, mocking and laughing.

The chorus of truths causes Hezekiah's body to slow its descent. "Fall, Hezekiah Cleaveland," they chant. "Fall!"

"God doesn't love you anymore!"

The bulging eyes and distorted face of Samantha Cleaveland appears on the balcony of the auditorium. A diamond bracelet on her wrist sparkles as she extends her long, deformed hands toward the falling Hezekiah, not to break his fall, but to speed it.

Hezekiah's plunge continues mercilessly as familiar faces, dreaded confrontations, and painful events flash in rapid succession through his mind. This is it. His life has been condensed into the eight seconds it took to fall to the earth.

"Please tick faster." His eyes are pleading. "I don't want to see any more of my life. Please, God . . . let this end."

Hattie violently jerked her head one last time and bolted upright in the chair. She was shaking and her brow was doused with perspiration. She gasped for breath as she gripped the cushioned arms of the chair.

Through anguished gasps Hattie cried out loud, "She's going to do it. Lord, you've got to stop her."

Lance typed revisions to the article after his interview with Danny:

Pastor Hezekiah Cleaveland has been involved in a homosexual affair with Mr. Danny St. John, a resident of the Adams District. St. John is an employee of the Los Angeles Homeless-Outreach Team.

Cleaveland and St. John met for the first time in June of last year. It is not clear if they are still together, but e-mail messages obtained by this reporter show that their last correspondence occurred as recently as last week.

In one such e-mail Cleaveland wrote, "I can't

meet you tonight, baby, because there is a planning commission hearing I have to attend. They're finally deciding tonight whether to grant the conditional-use permit for the new sanctuary. Wish me luck. I am free tomorrow evening. I love you, Danny, and can't wait to hold you again. Love, Hezekiah." The e-mail was dated April 17.

Parties close to Cleaveland have confirmed that the relationship was sexual in nature, and that the two have met a minimum of once per week over the last twelve months. Our source, who requested anonymity, is quoted as saying, *"His driver takes him to Mr. St. John's house usually after dark. He stays there for at least two or three hours. I only know of one occasion when he actually spent the night."*

Colleagues at the Los Angeles Homeless-Outreach Team have confirmed that Cleaveland has called personally on many occasions inquiring as to the whereabouts of St. John.

A Los Angeles Homeless-Outreach Team employee is quoted as saying, *"We all thought it was strange that Hezekiah Cleaveland would call personally. He never said why he was looking for him, but just to tell him to call back as soon as he got the message."*

A total of 173 e-mail messages have been legally obtained by the Los Angeles Chronicle. The majority attests to both a physical and emotional bond between the two men. One such correspondence reads as follows:

"Dear Danny, Thank you for being in my life. You have given me more joy than I ever thought I deserved. My wife loves me, but I don't think she

*ever actually knew who I really am, or even wants
to. If only she had taken the time to look a little
deeper, she would have seen that I'm just a guy. A
guy that wants to be loved and cared for, just like
everybody else in this lonely world.*

*"I love you because I didn't have to tell you this.
Somehow you already knew. My biggest dream is
that someday you and I will live together. I often
think of what it will be like to wake up every morning with you in my arms. One day, Danny. One
day soon. Love you with all that I am, Hezekiah."*

*St. John has denied knowing or ever meeting
Cleaveland.*

The telephone rang as he typed the final line. "Lance,
I've been trying to reach you all week," Cynthia Pryce
said, sitting on her bed and removing her shoes. "What
happened in the interview with Hezekiah?"

"It went as expected. He denied the affair." Lance
pressed the save button on his computer and continued
speaking. "I talked to Danny St. John today."

"What did he have to say for himself?"

"He denied it all as well. Said he never met Hezekiah
Cleaveland. It was obvious he was lying, but it doesn't
matter. The e-mail messages are enough to nail them
both."

"So what's next? When does the story run?"

"I just finished the revisions. Now I have to get my editor's approval, and that's it. It should be on the stands this
Sunday morning." Lance paused for a moment and then
said, "I just have one more question for you, Cynthia."

"What's that?"

"Why are you doing this to Hezekiah and Samantha?"

"I've already told you. Someone has to hold the Cleavelands accountable for his actions."

"That is certainly understandable, but I feel like there's something you're not telling me. It's making me nervous about the whole story."

"Nervous?" Cynthia countered. "This is the biggest story of your career. How can you even think about passing it up?"

"This isn't just about my career, Mrs. Pryce," he said curtly. "It's about New Testament Cathedral, Hezekiah and Samantha Cleaveland, and Danny St John. It's about causing a lot of suffering for people in that church and around the country. It's about hurting a seemingly nice young guy who just got involved with the wrong person."

"You don't have to tell me what's at stake."

"That's what's confusing me. I get the feeling that you will actually gain more than anyone else if this story comes out."

"That's ridiculous," Cynthia said nervously. "What could I possibly gain from having my pastor exposed as a homosexual?"

"That's the exact question I need answered. And I think until I get that answer, I'm going to have to put the story on hold."

It was risky, but Lance felt it was necessary to ensure the information Cynthia had provided was legitimate.

Cynthia felt trapped by the reporter who, until then, had gobbled hungrily every morsel she had laid before him.

"All right, Lance. I'll be honest with you. I do have ambitions of my own."

"What does your ambition have to do with outing Hezekiah?"

"Come on. You can figure it out, can't you? What do you think will happen to my husband, Percy, if this comes out?"

"I don't know. What?" Lance asked.

"You're really going to make me say it, aren't you?" Cynthia paused in an agonizing plea for clemency, but there was no response.

She continued. "Hezekiah and Samantha are publicly humiliated and vanish into obscurity. My husband is second in command. He'll be called on to hold the church together through a devastating and embarrassing scandal, and then . . ."

The cloud lifted and all became suddenly clear. Lance snapped his fingers and said, "And then you and your husband take over New Testament Cathedral."

"Exactly."

"You must really hate them to do something like this."

"This isn't about hate or love—it's about power and doing God's work."

"Why did you pick me to do your dirty work? Any reporter in the city would have jumped at the chance to investigate a story this hot."

"I didn't pick you, Lance."

"What do you mean?"

"I mean that someone else selected you for the story."

"But I thought—"

Cynthia cut him off. "I know what you thought, but I didn't just call you out of the blue."

Sweat began to accumulate in the palm of Lance's hands. "Then who decided I would be the lucky guy?"

"Phillip Thornton selected you personally. He said you were the only one at his paper who had the balls to take on Hezekiah."

Lance stood up and nervously brushed the hair from

his face. "Phillip Thornton knew about this? He has nothing to do with the day-to-day running of this paper. I've never even met him."

"I had no idea you were so naive."

Lance calculated his next move as she spoke.

"Cynthia," he said with an exaggerated twang of ambivalence, "I'm suddenly not sure if I can go through with this. I don't like the idea of being a pawn in your little game."

Cynthia stood and began to pace the room. "Don't fuck with me, Lance. Just run the story and this will all be over."

Lance leaned on his desk and lowered his voice. "Now, now," he said teasingly, "let's not rush things. I think I'd like to see you in person before sending this to my editor."

"See me for what?"

"Oh, I don't know. Maybe you could be more persuasive in person. You're such a beautiful woman, Mrs. Pryce. Maybe seeing you would give me the extra push I need."

Cynthia writhed helplessly in the vulnerable position she now found herself: the woman possessing the final bargaining tool necessary to close a deal. She stepped back into her shoes while silently cursing her misguided candor.

"Where are you?" she asked. "Maybe a face-to-face meeting would be a good idea."

"I'm in my office."

"Meet me in front of the building. I'll pick you up in fifteen minutes," she instructed, and hung up the phone.

Cynthia left the condominium unnoticed and retrieved her car in the building's subterranean parking structure.

A loathing for Lance Savage, and what she was about to do, crept through her body as she drove toward the *Los Angeles Chronicle*'s building.

The sun had set, and the swarm of commuters had mercifully left the city virtually empty. She saw homeless men bedding down for the night in front of train entrances and at bus shelters as she drove. Steam rose from street grates at each intersection as she searched the sidewalks for Lance Savage.

Then she saw him. He paced at the entrance of the brick building, clutching a laptop computer case and waving to her as she approached.

"That was quick," he said, climbing breathlessly into the passenger seat. "Thanks for agreeing to meet me."

"I didn't know I had a choice," Cynthia said, restraining the anger she felt toward the unkempt man. "So why did you want to see me?"

Lance patted the computer carrier he held in his lap. "I've got the story right here, but I didn't want to send it until I had a few minutes alone with you."

Lance found it hard to resist the woman sitting next to him. She was more beautiful than he had imagined. A beauty most men found irresistible. Her hair seemed to glow in the moonlight. The silk of her stockings bristled as she manipulated the pedals of the car. In that moment her scent was enough to cause his sharp mind to drift in a haze of lust and desire.

Almost involuntarily Lance reached over and caressed her knee as she drove.

"I think you can guess what will . . . let's just say, inspire me to send this to my editor." The words surprised and embarrassed him as they escaped his lips.

Cynthia pushed the accelerator hard as they raced through downtown.

"I knew I couldn't trust you. This is extortion."

"Now hold on, Mrs. Pryce," he said playfully. "I wouldn't call it extortion. It's more like quid pro quo. You do something for me and . . . Well, I make you the first lady of New Testament Cathedral."

Cynthia turned the car onto Third Street. She silently reasoned, *A few minutes with this cretin is a small price to pay to get Hezekiah and Samantha out of the way, permanently.*

She looked Lance in the eye and said, "I'll do this on one condition."

Lance looked at her guardedly and asked, "What's that?"

"That when we're done, you'll let me send the article."

Lance laughed loudly. "Hell, when we're done, I'll probably be too tired to push the key myself. It's a deal."

"Where can we go? I, of course, can't be seen in public with you."

"We could go to my place. I live on the canals."

"That's too far. I don't have much time," she replied shortly.

Lance thought for a minute and then said, "The construction site is near here. We can park there and no one will disturb us. Turn left at the next light."

In a few short blocks Cynthia could see large mounds of dirt piled next to the skeletal structure of New Testament Cathedral. Lance instructed her to drive behind the building and turn off the car. He placed the computer in the rear seat and said, "Kind of poetic, don't you think?"

He removed his jacket and loosened his tie; Cynthia watched his every move.

Without hesitation Lance leaned toward Cynthia and kissed her hard on the lips. His breathing became intense as he kissed her neck and caressed her breasts. "Mrs. Pryce," he panted, "you are such a beautiful woman."

Cynthia saw flashes of herself standing behind her husband, Pastor Percy Pryce, on the television screen while Lance fumbled awkwardly to unbutton her blouse.

The intoxication of possible fame and power slowly overrode her initial feelings of repulsion for the man stroking her partially naked body. Cynthia felt Lance's lips gently circling her exposed nipples as the vision faded. The sounds of cold wind whirring at the base of the building and the distant hum of the freeway could be heard through the car's darkly tinted windows.

Cynthia lifted Lance's head to hers and kissed him passionately. Her panting now matched his, breath for breath. She skillfully undid his belt buckle and pants and firmly gripped his erect member.

"Fuck me," she moaned. "I want you to fuck me, Lance."

Lance fumbled with levers and pushed buttons until he found the one to recline the driver's seat. Their writhing bodies descended in unison into the depths of the vehicle as the seat glided into a fully prone position.

Lance lifted Cynthia's skirt, slid her panties around her ankles, and lowered his trousers. He then climbed on top of her to explore her waiting mouth once again.

"Hurry," she said in a whisper. "Fuck me and then we'll send it together."

Lance moaned as he thrust his hips against hers. "I'm going to fuck you first, and then we'll both fuck the Cleavelands."

Cynthia lifted her knees toward the roof of the car and in the process turned on the windshield wipers. Lance entered her with great force and pounded double time to the beat of the whooshing rubber blades. Cynthia held him tightly and raised her hips to meet each thrust. The two reveled in passion heightened by the euphoric prospect of the Cleavelands' demise. The car bounced uncontrollably until they reached a fevered climax, then lay spent and breathless in each other's arms.

Cynthia was the first to speak. "It's time. Get your computer."

Lance rolled, exhausted, back to the passenger seat.

"Wow," he panted. "You don't waste any time, do you?"

"That was the agreement, wasn't it? Are you planning to back out again?"

"No, no," he protested. "I'm a man of my word." With his trousers still around his ankles, Lance reached behind and retrieved the case. He turned on the computer and the glowing screen lit up the car. As he waited for the article to appear, he said, "You're quite a woman, Mrs. Pryce. New Testament is in for one hell of a ride."

The headline flashed onto the screen:

PASTOR HEZEKIAH T. CLEAVELAND
INVOLVED IN SECRET GAY AFFAIR

"There it is," Lance said. "This is what you've been waiting for."

"That's exactly what I've been waiting for," Cynthia said with a smile. "Now stop wasting time. Let's send it."

"Okay, Mrs. Pryce. Just press ENTER and you'll be one step closer to being queen of the empire."

Cynthia returned her seat to its upright position. She pressed the key without saying a word.

After a message appeared on the screen confirming that the article had been sent, Cynthia looked at Lance and firmly said, "Now, would you please pull your pants up and get the fuck out of my car?"

18

Friday

Richard Harrison, the editor of the *Los Angeles Chronicle*, stood behind his desk.

"Calm down, would you," he said as Lance Savage paced the floor. "Phillip thought it better that you not know. He felt the fewer people who knew about the arrangement with Cynthia, the better. He just didn't want to take any unnecessary chances."

"It's none of my business that he sold this paper's soul to Cynthia Pryce. It doesn't even bother me that you wasted six months of my life digging up information that you already had. What does piss me off is that you didn't trust me enough to tell me. I don't give a shit about Phillip Thornton or Hezekiah Cleaveland, but you, Richard. How could you have kept this from me?"

"I know, I know," Richard said with arms raised. "I wanted to tell you, but Phillip—"

"Fuck Phillip. This is about you and me."

"Whether you like it or not, Lance, Phillip owns this paper. He calls the shots."

"Why did he pick me? He's never met me."

"Because he knows your reputation. He knows that you are the only reporter on staff who's not impressed or intimidated by Hezekiah."

"But that doesn't explain why he's stabbing Hezekiah in the back. They've been friends for years."

"Don't be naive, Lance. Stories like this sell papers. We're facing layoffs, fighting off hostile takeovers. Papers all around the country are going under. This will save the *Chronicle*."

Lance prepared to ask another question, when the intercom buzzed.

"Sorry to interrupt, Mr. Harrison," came the secretary's voice, "but Reverend Hezekiah Cleaveland is on the line for you. He said it's important. Would you like to take the call?"

Richard looked into Lance's eyes and said, "Yes, Carol, I'll take it. Put him through."

Richard sat down at the desk and pushed the speaker button.

"Hello, Hezekiah. I was wondering when you were going to get around to calling me. How are you?"

The speakerphone made Hezekiah's voice sound as though he were calling from a barrel or a tunnel. "How do you think I am?" Hezekiah said bitterly. "Lance Savage has crossed the line with this one, Richard. I swear if—"

Richard cut him off. "Excuse me, Hezekiah. I think you should know that Lance is here with me now. You're on the speakerphone."

"Hello, Pastor. This is Lance Savage. Nice to hear your voice again."

Hezekiah's body shifted with each turn of the limousine. The city streets whizzed by as he spoke.

"Richard, if you believe him on this one, then that sad excuse for a reporter is going to cost you your paper."

"So, Reverend Cleaveland, you're saying this is all fabricated?" asked Richard.

"You're damn right that's what I'm saying."

"Then how do you explain the numerous e-mails between you and Mr. St. John that we now have in our possession?"

"How did you get those?" Hezekiah shouted. "That's invasion of my fucking privacy. I could have you both arrested for hacking into my computer." Hezekiah's hands began to shake uncontrollably. "Why do you need to make me look like a fool, Richard? I got you that job."

"It's about the news, and unfortunately for you, this is an incredibly important story. It's my responsibility to report relevant news that affects this city."

"Don't give me that bullshit, Richard. Nobody gives a damn about tabloid crap like this. You know you could bury this right now, if you wanted to."

Lance leaned anxiously forward in his chair to respond, but Richard held up his hand to silence him.

"You're right, I could," Richard replied. "But why should I? Why would anyone in my position suppress the fact that one of the most influential pastors in the country is a closeted homosexual?"

"Because it's not true, goddamn it," Hezekiah screeched. "I'm not gay!"

"Maybe that was a poor choice of words, Richard," Lance said. "Reverend Cleaveland, would it be more accurate if he had said, 'The pastor of New Testament Cathedral is on the down low'?"

Richard stifled a laugh. No response came from the speakerphone. "Reverend Cleaveland, would that be more accurate?" Richard asked cynically. "Hello, Hezekiah, are you still there?"

The last words Hezekiah could manage through his

rage were "Fuck both of you assholes!" He then slammed his cell phone shut.

Lance and Richard each flinched from the sound of the crash, followed by the dial tone. They sat breathless from the heated exchange.

"You did well, Lance," Richard finally said. "Phillip was right about you."

It was eleven o'clock when Danny locked his apartment door. A light fog met him on the porch and flowed between the cars and around the sycamore trees. He walked upstairs to his neighbor's front door, holding a note containing instructions for the care and feeding of Parker:

Dear Mr. and Mrs. Somner,

I will be away for a while and am not sure exactly how long. I know how much you both like Parker, and I ask that you will take him into your home until I return. I left a bag of dry cat food under the sink, along with several cans.

Thank you for watching him for me.

Sincerely,

Danny

Danny slipped the folded paper under the Somners' front door and proceeded back down the steps toward his car.

As he walked, he could not see the lush green grounds of the park across the street from his home. He didn't hear dogs barking as their masters threw tennis balls into the distance. The joggers with bouncing ponytails and aching muscles were mere dashes of color in the corner of his eye. Formerly fond images of rolling lawns and

trees gently quivering in the breeze now served only to remind him of the love and the city that had been snatched
from his tenuous grasp.

There were four messages on his answering machine
from Hezekiah that morning. The last came at 10:30 A.M.:
"Danny, baby, I'm so sorry," the trembling voice said.
"Since you haven't returned my calls, I assume Lance
Savage has found you. I never wanted you to get hurt,
and I did everything I could to protect you . . . to protect
us, but . . ." There was a long pause. "I guess I failed. I
know you're hurting right now. Believe me, this is eating
me up inside too, but they've got me trapped. They're determined to destroy me over this. I think it best that we . . ."
He stopped. An anguished sigh could be heard. "Danny, I
don't want to do this in a telephone message. Please call
me. I love you."

Rush hour traffic had given way to a light stream of mo-
torists attending to their midday errands. Danny drove
along Santa Monica Boulevard toward the Pacific Ocean.

The homeless shelter, where he spent every Thursday
afternoon giving out warm socks and medical referrals,
went by without a glance from Danny. The Department of
Motor Vehicles building, where he had recently paid fines
for a collection of overdue parking tickets, passed without Danny's usual sneer of disdain.

There was no longer a reason to look at the city he
loved. No reason to appreciate the rows of brightly
painted Victorian houses with neatly manicured lawns.
Two-story murals of brightly festooned Native Americans
and stern faces of the city's founding fathers no longer
held interest.

As Danny neared Ocean Park Boulevard, traffic began
to slow. A toothless man sat on a white plastic bucket in

the street's median. His left foot was wrapped in soiled gauze, while his other wiggled through a worn-out tennis shoe. Stains of dried blood dotted his ruddy cheeks, and his salty white hair whirled in the wind. He refused to make eye contact with drivers waiting at the red light. Instead, his tattered cardboard sign pleaded his case:

VIETNAM VETERAN WILL WORK FOR FOOD.
THANK YOU AND GOD BLESS.

When the light turned green, Danny removed the last twenty-seven dollars from his wallet. Driving forward slowly, he handed the man the wrinkled bills through the car window.

The man looked suspicious at first but then eagerly accepted the generous gift.

"God bless you, sir," he said with a toothless grin. "Thank you, sir. God bless you."

Danny merged his small car into the next lane and began the slow ascent up the winding ramp to the Santa Monica Pier. The lush green shrubbery along the side of the road was littered with the remains of human inhabitants. To his right he could see a bundle of blue blankets, soggy from water and mud. An abandoned shopping cart rested on its side, with the few remaining contents of plastic bags and newspapers scattered about. A poorly concealed man stood urinating behind a tree, while another searched the muddy ground for cigarette butts and a stray pebble of crack cocaine.

The pain that Danny had once felt upon viewing such human despair was nowhere to be found. There was no outrage toward an uncaring society. No sorrow for the discarded lives wallowing in the mud and debris. The numbing realization that his life would never be the same again was all that remained. He crept forward as if guided by fate.

The world had crossed an invisible line and boldly stepped into the space he had so carefully protected. He could have no more secrets. No more private moments.

His life would soon be on the front page of every newspaper in town. The sorrow that welled in his heart would serve as fodder for gossip at restaurant tables and park benches in every part of the city.

How could he mourn the loss of Hezekiah with the media exploring every pore of his existence under the microscope of public opinion? It would be impossible to start again without Hezekiah. Impossible to heal while his life was being delivered daily to front porches and sold for seventy-five cents on every corner.

The crush of traffic eased as he approached the parking lot for the Santa Monica Pier. Danny maneuvered the car into the lot and parked in the nearest available space. A cool sea breeze raced past him as he walked along the creaking wharf. Weathered wooden girders jutted from the side railing partially blocking the view of the turbulent waters below. Couples strolled by, hand in hand, and a massive Ferris wheel clanked and churned to the delight of a few small children as their parents waved from the dock below.

Once at the tip of the pier, Danny stood and stared out into the ocean. Waves crashed into the pylons below, causing sprays of mist to dampen his face and mingle with the tear that rolled down his cheek. Danny could hear the sea calling his name. He thought frantically for a reason not to respond.

Sympathetic tourists avoided eye contact with the

seemingly distraught young man as he inched closer to the railing. Danny looked out and could see the sprawling mountains of Malibu, the high-rise condominiums along Pacific Coast Highway, and the hills of Santa Monica. Without hesitation he hoisted his body onto the railing and dangled his legs over the edge. At that point the few pedestrians walking nearby began to watch him more attentively.

"Don't jump!" he heard a woman yell.

"Oh my God! Hey, wait, buddy, it can't be that bad!" came a husky, concerned cry.

"Go for it, guy! Fuck this place!" another man exclaimed.

Then Danny heard a little girl crying behind him. He looked over his shoulder and saw a little brown girl wearing a pink polka-dot bathing suit and holding a melting red snow cone. Danny climbed down and knelt beside her and asked, "Are you okay? Why are you crying?"

She looked up through her sobs and replied, "I can't find my mommy. She left me here. I want my mommy."

"Don't cry," Danny said, brushing a tear from her cheek. "I'm sure your mommy didn't leave you. Come on, let's go and find her together."

With that, Danny stood up and took the little girl by her sticky little hand and together they walked away from the edge of the pier to find the ones who could stop their tears from falling.

Hezekiah sat at his desk with pen in hand, suspended above the closing line of a form thank-you letter:

Yours Truly,
Pastor Hezekiah T. Cleaveland

A stack of white papers adorned with the embossed seal of the New Testament Cathedral lay before him. All were waiting for the ink from his pen to breathe life into the hollow words each contained.

Hezekiah didn't know the content of the official correspondence. Perhaps they were thank-you notes for $50,000 contributions toward the construction of the new cathedral or complimentary VIP tickets to the next big political fund-raiser. Their purpose and the protocol that dictated each line were of no interest to him.

He had dialed Danny's number four times that morning, but the only reply was the generic greeting on the answering machine.

Hezekiah had instinctively known when Danny was troubled throughout their year together. Days would pass without a word between them, when suddenly a "feeling" would come over him that something was wrong with the man he loved. Hezekiah would then call Danny, and inevitably he would be right. On one occasion Danny's mother had suffered a heart attack and died. Another time Danny's landlord had threatened to evict him.

Hezekiah was now having one such haunting premonition. As the pen, without prompting, glided across the first letter in the stack, a jolt suddenly kicked inside his stomach. He grabbed his belly and buckled from the pain. It was unbearable—what he imagined a heart attack must feel like. Droplets of perspiration formed on his brow, and the room began to spin around him. Then came another strike followed by yet another.

Hezekiah braced himself and stood with agonizing effort. He staggered toward the private bathroom at the rear of the office. Nausea overtook him as he stumbled across the floor. He gagged violently, clamping his lips shut to contain the bile that threatened to spew onto the freshly shampooed carpet.

An intangible yet familiar force was being yanked from the depths of his body. Hezekiah fought to maintain his grasp on the elusive energy that now thrashed violently for release. Without turning on the lights in the little bathroom, Hezekiah dropped to his knees and positioned his gaping mouth over the porcelain toilet. Vomit gushed out with each brutal contraction of his stomach. Troubling thoughts raced through his mind as his kneeling body heaved. *Something is happening to . . .* The thoughts stopped to accommodate yet another convulsion. Then again they came. *Danny. Where is Danny? Please don't do this. I won't leave you.*

After a series of painful spasms and agonizing groans, the heaving in his stomach gradually subsided, but feelings of fright and dread continued. "Danny, where are you?" he said out loud. "Don't leave me like this."

Hezekiah's body was drenched in sweat as he collapsed backward onto the tiled bathroom floor. He could hear his secretary pounding from outside the office door.

"Pastor Cleaveland!" came a panicked shout through the locked door. "Are you all right, sir? Pastor Cleaveland, please open the door!"

Hezekiah's white shirt clung to his body, wet and transparent from fluids he had released. His chest heaved up and down, gasping for air, and lifeless arms stretched at his sides.

He stared at the darkened light fixture above and surrendered to the overpowering need to cry, to mourn. His body convulsed again, not from the need to reject unwanted liquid, but to acknowledge the grief that flooded his heart. To mourn the loss of an essence that had been so painfully torn from his body. Hezekiah felt a familiar emptiness, which the last year with Danny had allowed him to forget. The void that Danny had so lovingly filled, the hollow that called for no one but him. At that moment Hezekiah felt that Danny was gone, and he was alone again.

Hezekiah stepped from the rear of the double-parked limousine. The curtains to Danny's apartment were open. He looked to the window for the familiar figure of Parker sitting on the sill. He was not there. Hezekiah rang the bell, then knocked loudly. There was no response. He leaned over the wrought-iron railing and peered into the window. The apartment was just as he had remembered, but Danny was nowhere to be seen.

Hezekiah walked to the car, when he heard, "Excuse me! Are you looking for Danny?"

Hezekiah looked up and saw an old man standing in the window above Danny's apartment. "Yes, I am. Have you seen him today?"

"Not today. But he . . . Hey, you're the pastor, Hezekiah Cleaveland." The man turned and yelled to someone in the apartment. "Norma, come here. Look, it's Hezekiah Cleaveland. I told you I saw him here the other week." Ray looked again to Hezekiah and said, "Norma watches you and your wife on TV all the time. She even sends you money."

An equally aged Norma joined her husband in the window to gawk at Hezekiah.

"I'm sorry. She didn't believe me when I told her that I saw you here before. I'm Ray Somner, and this is my wife, Norma."

Hezekiah smiled politely. "You were about to say something about Danny."

"Oh yeah. Strangest thing. He left a note under our door

this morning asking us to take care of his cat 'cause he wouldn't be coming back soon. I hope he's okay. He's a real nice kid. Works with the homeless, you know."

Hezekiah walked up the steps toward the couple. "Yes, I know. Would you mind if I saw the note? He's a friend, and I'm a little concerned about him."

"Sure. Norma, go get the note. It's over there on the table."

Hezekiah read the shaky print as Norma and Ray vowed their support for his new cathedral.

"Do you have Parker?"

"Yeah, we used our spare key to get him. He's in the kitchen right now, eating. Do you want to see him?"

"No. That won't be necessary. Will he be able to stay with you until Danny returns? He loves that cat."

"No problem. What's going on? Maybe we ought to call the police or something. This isn't like him to leave without telling us where he's going."

"Yes, that might be a good idea. If you hear from Danny, would you please tell him I came by?"

"Of course we will, sir. I hope nothing has happened to him."

"I hope not too. It was a pleasure meeting you both."

"Likewise, Pastor."

When Hezekiah reached the car, he heard one of the two shout from the window, "Good luck with the . . ." Dino slammed the car door before the final word could be heard.

Dino turned the car onto Crenshaw Boulevard. Hezekiah looked out the window through weary eyes and asked, "Where are you going? I just want to go home."

"Pastor Cleaveland," Dino said, holding up a sheet of paper, "your schedule says you have a meeting with a group of homeless advocates at the community center near the church in ten minutes. Would you like for me to call ahead and tell your advance man that you will not be coming?"

The muscles in Hezekiah's stomach churned again. "No. I should go. Take me there."

All heads in the room turned to the door when Hezekiah entered the community center in the South Central part of town. Folding chairs were placed auditorium-style in the center of the hall.

Clusters of people lined the perimeter walls, and the chairs were filled with a mix of homeless people and educated young men and women—many who had used their degrees from Brown and Harvard to advocate for the rights of the city's poor and disabled.

"Oh good, the pastor has arrived," a frail-looking man with thin hair said, addressing the audience. "Hello Reverend. For a moment there we thought you were going to be a no-show."

Hezekiah nodded his head in acknowledgment and moved toward the front of the room.

"Now that Pastor Cleaveland is here I think we'll hold our other agenda items until later and give him the opportunity to speak," the meeting facilitator continued. "I know you all have a lot to ask him, but please hold your questions until he has finished." With a grand sweep of his arm, he yielded the floor to Hezekiah.

"Good evening, everyone," Hezekiah said, standing before the crowd. "Thank you all for coming out to discuss this very important issue with me. As many of you may know, I have always been very concerned about the issues faced by homeless people in Los Angeles and in this country.

"New Testament Cathedral had spent the last ten years

giving money to local feeding programs and shelters. Members of my congregation volunteer their time at many social service programs around the city, and my wife and I sit on the board of several national programs whose missions are to serve homeless men, women, and children. We've held countless meetings with merchants, concerned citizens, and members of the faith community, listening to your concerns and—"

"We're tired of you just listening," a heavily bearded man interjected. "You're spending millions of dollars to build a shrine to yourself, and all you can do for the homeless is sponsor a food drive once a year so your members can drop dented cans of tuna in a box in your lobby. When are you going to do something that would help the homeless people that live on the streets all around your new church?"

The facilitator jumped to his feet. "Please, there will be plenty of time for questions after he's done."

Hezekiah proceeded with his speech. "There's no question that homelessness is a growing problem, not only here but all over the city. That is why I've recently instructed our accountants to increase the amount of money we donate annually to social service programs."

"We don't need your money. We need you to build more shelters and affordable housing instead of a massive glass church for rich people," came a shout from another part of the room.

An elderly woman near the front stood to her feet and said, "How can you justify spending forty-five million dollars on a building that will only be open on Sunday mornings when you know that every night, of every year, thousands of men, women, and children live and die on the streets of this city?"

Angry-faced people shook their heads and blurted out expressions of agreement.

Hezekiah raised his hands. "Please, please, everyone. I know this is a very difficult situation, but there are also factions in this city that believe the homeless have a constitutional right to live on the streets. You cannot force anyone to go into a shelter who does not want to go."

"That's bullshit and you know it!" shouted a homeless man near the rear. "You think I want to sleep under a bush and wash myself in park bathrooms? The problem is there's just not enough shelter beds in this city, and people like you, who could help to do something about it, prefer to ignore us and pretend it's our choice to live on the streets."

The crowd grew increasingly agitated. Random comments came from every direction:

"If you won't do anything about it, then maybe we should organize protests every Sunday morning on the steps of your church."

"You're a hypocrite. You claim to care about the homeless, but you only care about money."

"You could have built thousands of units of affordable housing with the money you're wasting on that church."

The effusive charm and quick wit that had served Hezekiah well his entire life now eluded him. He stood pummeled by the barrage of complaints and threats. Dino walked slowly toward the front of the room and positioned himself firmly a few feet from Hezekiah.

"Pastor Cleaveland," said the facilitator above the shouts. "Are you going to respond? These people are angry and frustrated. They deserve some answers."

The room fell silent. Hezekiah looked into the angry faces.

"I think I've heard enough," he said with a scowl. "For

some reason you people are under the misguided impression that I need your permission to build New Testament Cathedral. Well, for your information I don't. We have every permit required by law. We own the property, and at this point no one can stop the project. I came to meet with you as a courtesy, but I'm not in the mood to tolerate your abuse and misguided anger. You should direct it at the mayor and city council, not at me."

Gasps were heard throughout, but Hezekiah continued. "I don't pretend to have the solution to homelessness, and I don't know of anyone who does. I do know, however, that protesting and focusing your anger toward me is not the solution. It may get you on the six o'clock news, but it does nothing to help the people you claim to be advocating for."

Hezekiah turned to the stunned facilitator. "Mr. Facilitator," he said mockingly, "please do not invite me or anyone else from my church to these meetings again."

Hezekiah began to walk toward the exit. He stopped at the door and turned back to the stunned crowd and said, "Also, the next time I see any of you protesting on my property, I'm going the have the police throw you in jail for trespassing. Good night."

Hezekiah exited the room, with Dino walking protectively behind. A chorus of jeers and threats erupted.

"We're going to shut you down, Hezekiah Cleaveland."

"You've got no right to talk to us like that. We're good people."

"I've never been so insulted in my life."

The words of indignation were ignored. When they stepped into the cold night air, Dino asked, "Reverend, are you all right?"

"No, I'm not all right," Hezekiah said, turning up his collar. "Just take me back to the Adams District."

* * *

For the second time that day Dino stopped the car in front of Danny's home. Hezekiah could see Norma and Ray peeking through the curtains of their apartment. From the rear of the limousine Hezekiah stared into Danny's window. Nothing had changed. The lights had not been turned on. The day's mail was still in the box, and Parker was not on the sill.

Where is he? Hezekiah thought. *God, please let him be all right.*

The car was silent for several minutes, when Dino looked into the rearview mirror.

"Pastor Cleaveland, would you like me to knock on the door? Maybe he came back while we were away."

Hezekiah could see compassion and knowing in the reflection of Dino's eyes through the mirror. He simply responded, "No, Dino. I don't think he's coming back. I just want to sit here for a few more minutes. But thank you. Thank you very much."

Hezekiah's cell phone rang four times, but he did not answer it. The caller tried again. On the third ring Hezekiah picked it up. "Hello, what is it?"

"Hezekiah, it's Percy. Where are you? I've been trying to reach you all night. We have to talk."

"Now isn't a good time, Percy. Can I call you back in—"

"This will only take a minute. Now listen to me closely. I know about you and Danny St. John."

Hezekiah did not respond. He did not care.

"If that story appears in the paper, all hell is going to break loose," Percy continued. "You have to be prepared to respond. Have Naomi call a press conference for tomorrow afternoon so you can publicly deny everything. We can't afford to let this go without a statement from you. If you don't refute the accusations, everyone will assume they're true."

"I can't. I don't think I can face the public just yet. Danny is missing. No one seems to know where he is."

"You need to forget about him, Hezekiah. The rest of your career will depend on how you handle what's about to come your way over the next few days. If you mess this up, it's over. I'm going to try and talk some sense into Lance Savage. I don't know if he'll listen to reason. You should go home and get some rest. I'll call you in the morning. And by the way, make sure Samantha is standing with you in the pulpit on Sunday."

"I don't think she will, Percy."

"Why not?"

"Because she knows the story is true. What am I going to do, Percy? My life is falling apart. It's over. I don't think I can take any more."

"It's not over. We're going to fight this together, Hezekiah. It's going to be difficult, but we can get through this if you can just tough out the next few days."

Hezekiah did not hear the final words of encouragement. He looked for the last time into Danny's window and said, "I have to go now, Percy. Just do whatever you think is necessary. I'll talk to you tomorrow."

19

Kenneth Davis had tried, unsuccessfully, to reach Lance Savage all afternoon. He tried Lance's number again and was greeted with, "Lance Savage here. How can I help you?"

"Mr. Savage, this is Reverend Kenneth Davis. I'm an associate pastor at New Testament—"

Lance interrupted, "I know who you are Reverend Davis. What can I do for you?"

"I'd like to meet with you to discuss the article you're working on. Would that be possible sometime today?"

"There's nothing more to discuss. Besides, it's too late." Lance looked at his watch. "I've already submitted it to my editor."

"Now, we both know it's never too late to stop a story from going to press. I have a proposition for you that might convince you to put an end to this whole unfortunate misunderstanding."

"What kind of proposition?"

"A proposition that would be mutually beneficial to all parties involved, especially for you."

Lance was intrigued. He looked at his watch again and said, "All right, Reverend Davis."

"Please, Lance, call me Kenneth."

"Okay, Kenneth, I was just about to head home. You can meet me there in one hour."

Lance gave his home address and the two men exchanged civil good-byes.

After disconnecting, Kenneth immediately called Percy Pryce.

"Percy, I finally got us a face-to-face with Lance Savage. Meet me in front of the church in thirty minutes."

"What did he say? Is he going to take the money?"

"We didn't get that far. At least he's willing to listen to what we have to offer."

Lance lived in a 1920s bungalow on the canals in Venice. Cars sped along the narrow street within ten feet of his front door. It was a small house with a permanent dampness in the air.

Lance, wearing faded jogging shorts and a wrinkled T-shirt, answered the door. "Hello, Kenneth. You didn't say you were bringing Reverend Pryce with you. Is he here in an official capacity?"

"No, he's not," Kenneth said as the two men entered the cluttered bungalow. "And neither am I. We're not here to speak on behalf of the New Testament Cathedral, or Hezekiah. We only represent ourselves."

"Have a seat, gentlemen. Can I get you a beer, or maybe something stronger?"

"No, thank you," Kenneth said. "We don't plan on staying long."

Lance retrieved a beer he had already begun and sat on a leather sofa next to Percy. Kenneth lowered his body into a chair in front of them and laid a briefcase on the floor at his feet.

Kenneth calmly began to speak. "I think it goes without saying that we would appreciate it if whatever we discuss does not leave this room. As far as anyone is concerned, this meeting never took place, and if you ever repeat anything we say, we will deny it."

"Fair enough," Lance said, setting the beer bottle on a side table.

"First of all, we'd like for you to tell us exactly what it is that you know about this affair Hezekiah is allegedly involved in, and with whom," Kenneth stated.

"All right, it will soon be public information, anyway. Your pastor has been involved with a Mr. Danny St. John for the last year. They see each other no less than twice a week. Usually, they meet at Danny's apartment in the Adams District. They also have lunch together on occasions at various restaurants around the city. Danny is an outreach worker in downtown Los Angeles. He's twenty-eight, and quite a looker, if I might add. Is there anything else you would like to know?" Lance added smugly.

"Yes," Percy said. "Everything you've just told us sounds relatively innocent. But it doesn't prove that the relationship was sexual in nature?"

"I agree," Kenneth chimed in. "There's no law against Hezekiah having a male friend. He's been to my home dozens of times and we often dine out together. That doesn't make it sexual."

Lance stood up and walked to a desk under a window overlooking the canals. He opened a drawer and retrieved a stack of papers held together by a metal clasp. He then thumbed through the stack, pulled a sheet out and handed it to Percy.

Percy read the e-mail silently:

My Dearest Danny,

Last night with you was wonderful. I love holding you in my arms and tasting your soft lips. Each time I kiss you feels as sweet as my first kiss. Feeling your body against mine gives me more pleasure than I ever thought possible. Caressing your soft skin makes me feel like the luckiest man in the world. I am not a poet and I know it, but I want you to know that I love you with all of my heart.

I wish I could hold you in my arms forever.

Love you always,

Hezekiah

Percy handed the e-mail to Kenneth, who proceeded to read as well.

"Would you like to see more? That's one of the tamer ones. There's a few in there that give you the size of each of their members, and one in particular that goes into great detail about where Danny likes for Hezekiah to put his finger when he's about to come."

Percy quickly held up his hand and said, "No, that won't be necessary."

"One thing I can assure you is that none of the more graphic details of their relationship will be in the article. I don't think the public is ready to hear what Hezekiah does when he's about to come," Lance said with a sly smile.

"This is so unseemly," Percy said in disgust. "I can't believe the *Los Angeles Chronicle* would stoop to gutter journalism like this. It's no better than the supermarket tabloids."

"Pathetic, isn't it?" Lance agreed sarcastically. "It's a new day in journalism. The public craves shit like this, and if we want to stay in business, we've got to keep up with the times. No pun intended."

"I'm glad you think this is funny," Kenneth said angrily. "You don't seem to realize how many people will be hurt if this story is released. Hezekiah will be ruined. His wife and daughter will be devastated. The future of New Testament Cathedral will be placed in extreme jeopardy, and millions of people all over the country will lose a man they deeply love, and many will possibly also lose their faith in God."

"I'm sorry, gentlemen, but Hezekiah should have thought of all that before he, so indiscreetly, got involved with a man," Lance said as he sat back down. "I'm a reporter and I report the news. And this is definitely news."

Kenneth proceeded diplomatically with his appeal. "You are obviously aware that the story would cause immeasurable damage to Hezekiah and New Testament Cathedral."

"I am."

"Is there any way we can appeal to your moral consciousness?" Kenneth asked passionately. "Surely, you must feel some moral obligation to your fellow man. Hezekiah made a mistake, but who among us hasn't? I'm sure you've done many things that you're not proud of. How would you like it if they were splashed all over the front page?"

"I would hate that, but you fail to recognize a few significant differences between Hezekiah and myself. I don't claim any sort of moral authority. I'm not married. I'm not the head of a multimillion-dollar empire, and even more important, I am not on television twenty-four hours a day around the country preaching about the evils of sin."

"Point taken," Kenneth conceded. "Then, let's approach this from a different angle. Needless to say, we want to put this entire ugly situation behind us all as soon, and as quietly, as possible. To that end, we are prepared to offer you one hundred seventy-five thousand dollars to forget you ever heard the name of Danny St. John."

Kenneth retrieved the briefcase from the floor and placed it on the coffee table. He opened it to reveal stacks of one-hundred-dollar bills bound by white paper strips.

Lance sat erect. "You've got to be shit'n me," he said, laughing. "You think saving your boy's ass is only worth one hundred seventy-five thousand dollars?"

"That's all we are able to come up with."

Lance stood up and walked toward the door. "You and I both know that's not true. New Testament brings in more than that just from the interest you earn on money collected in the Sunday-morning offering plate. Gentlemen," he said, "I think you've wasted enough of my time. I would appreciate it if you'd leave my home."

Percy jumped from the sofa. "You fucking piece of shit," he said, pointing his finger. "Now it's clear to me what this is all about. You're trying to get rich off the backs of Hezekiah and New Testament Cathedral. That whole speech about 'the news' was a bunch of bullshit. You don't give a fuck about the news," he said angrily. "It's all about money."

"That's some strong language for a man of God," Lance said. "I'm impressed."

"Fuck you," Percy continued. "If you have half a brain, you'll take the money and forget about this whole thing."

"It'll take a lot more than that for me to forget Danny St. John. Try half a million, and then maybe we can talk."

"You're out of your fucking mind," Percy said, "if you think we're going to give you half a million."

"I think that's a fair price, Reverend Pryce, especially considering it was your wife who got you into this sordid mess," Lance replied as he opened the front door. "Now, if you don't mind."

Percy looked stunned and then slammed the door shut. "What are you saying? My wife isn't involved in this."

Lance walked away from the door to a nearby telephone. "Are you trying to tell me you didn't know she is the one who leaked the story?"

Percy bolted across the room and grabbed Lance by the shoulders. "My wife had nothing to do with this. You're lying. Don't listen to him, Reverend Davis. He's trying to get more money out of us."

Reverend Davis stood and said, "Let him go, Percy. Right now it doesn't matter who leaked the story." He then looked at Lance and said, "Five hundred thousand dollars is a lot of money. It'll take me some time to come up with it, but—"

"It matters to me," Percy interrupted. He then pushed the now-shaking reporter against the wall, causing a picture to crash to the floor. "I'm not going to let this little bastard extort that kind of money out of us."

"Reverend Pryce, you would be surprised at just how low your wife had to stoop to ensure that you become the next pastor of New Testament Cathedral. Take it from me, though. She knows her way around the front seat of a car."

Lance began to walk away, but Percy grabbed his neck. The two men struggled.

"Percy, stop it," Kenneth said, grabbing Percy by the shoulders. "Let him go. Let's go."

But their scuffle only escalated. A lamp fell from a table. Stereo equipment and CDs lurched from their shelves from bumps leveled by slamming bodies. Lance struggled for release as Percy pushed him to the ground.

When Lance fell, his head banged against the coffee

table, causing the briefcase, and all its contents, to topple
onto the floor. The reporter lay motionless, with bundles
of money scattered around his body.

"Oh God," Kenneth said, kneeling next to Lance's limp
body. "What have you done? He's not breathing."

Kenneth tried to revive the limp body of Lance Savage,
while Percy panted over his shoulder.

"Wake up," Percy said through deep, anguished breaths.
"He tripped. Make him get up, Kenneth."

Kenneth shook Lance's shoulders, causing his head to
flop from side to side. His arms hung limp and unrespon-
sive to the additional abuse at the hands of such a large
man.

"He's dead," Kenneth finally said. "You killed him."

"I barely touched him. You saw it. He must have
tripped. Oh shit. I don't believe this is happening. What
are we going to do?"

Without responding, Kenneth carelessly dropped the
mass of flesh and immediately began gathering the fallen
money, returning it to the case.

"Quick," he said, "get all the money, and let's get out of
here."

"We can't just leave him here. We should call the police."

"Are you crazy? You just killed a man for no reason.
They'll put you in jail for the rest of your life. Let's just get
out of here. Hopefully, no one saw us come in. They'll
think he was killed by a burglar. Now, pull yourself together and help me pick up this money."

Kenneth scanned the room, once the case was filled.
Much of its contents lay scattered on the floor, along with
the crumpled body. To his satisfaction it looked like the
classic botched robbery scene he had seen so often on the
evening news.

"If we pass anyone on the street, don't make eye contact with them, and try to look natural."

Percy looked again at the devastation his hands had wrought and cried out, "I don't believe this is happening!"

Kenneth ran to the kitchen at the rear of the house and retrieved a dish towel from the sink. He opened the back door of the house and stepped onto the wooden porch, wrapped his hand in the dish towel and smashed a pane of glass in the back door. With his hand still covered he closed the door and stuffed the towel into his pocket. The broken glass crackled under his feet as he quickly left the room.

The two men exited the apartment through the door they had entered. Cars raced down the busy street at speeds that permitted no more than cursory glances. No pedestrians were in sight as Kenneth drove away.

"This never happened, Percy," Kenneth said, looking directly ahead. "Do you understand? This never happened."

Percy was in shock and did not respond.

"You have to put this out of your head. We were never there."

"What if a neighbor saw us? What about Naomi and Catherine? They knew we were going to meet with him."

"No one saw us," Kenneth patiently said. "We were never in Venice. Don't ever mention this to anyone. Understand? I'll tell Naomi and Catherine that I wasn't able to contact him. If they question you, just tell them to talk to me."

"I won't mention it. I understand. I just can't get his face out of my head. Why did he make me do it? I just snapped. I don't know what happened. He shouldn't have said those lies about Cynthia. She would never do anything so cruel. She loves Hezekiah and Samantha. This would have never happened if he had just taken the money."

Kenneth deposited his shaken passenger at the main entrance of the church. It was 5:10 P.M., and a tide of fleeing employees streamed from the building.

"Are you going to be all right?" Kenneth asked as Percy exited the car. "Go directly to your office, get your things, and go home. And for God's sake, don't talk to anyone."

"I won't," Percy said, slamming the door. "But what about the story? If they don't hear from Lance, they'll just go ahead and run it."

"It's too late to worry about that now. It's out of our hands. We'll just have to brace ourselves for the worst."

Percy managed to choke out "Good night" to several familiar faces as he walked the halls to his office.

"Reverend Pryce!" came a shout from over his shoulder. "Wait a minute. So what happened? Did you talk to Lance Savage?"

When he turned, he saw Naomi's stiff hair progressing rapidly toward him. "Did you meet with Lance?" she asked again.

"No . . . we just . . . I mean, Kenneth wasn't able to reach him."

"That's just great," Naomi said bitterly. "He always has his cell phone on. Do you have the right number?"

"No, I . . . I don't know."

Naomi glanced at her watch. "Come with me to my office, and I'll give it to you."

"It is too late." Percy's voice began to tremble. "If you had done your job in the first place and kept tabs on what Hezekiah was doing, we wouldn't be dealing with this. All we can do now is prepare for the fallout. Now just leave me alone. I'm going home."

Percy darted away, leaving Naomi standing as stiff as her hair. When he reached his office, his secretary had already gone for the day. Waiting for him on her desk was a stack of messages, including four from Catherine marked "urgent" and three from Naomi. He tossed them into the trash bin.

He entered his office and put on his trench coat without turning on the light. He gathered stacks of paper from the desk and began stuffing them into a weathered briefcase, when Catherine appeared at the door.

"I just saw Naomi," she said frantically. "Why are you guys just giving up? This is our last hope. I thought we all agreed."

Percy continued shoveling papers into the case.

"It's over, Catherine. Face it. Hezekiah has screwed us all this time."

"How can you say that? I thought—"

"Well, you thought wrong. You can pretend that there's still some way to save him, but I won't. You were the closest person to him. How could you let him do this to us?"

"I didn't know anything about it. You know how secretive he can be," she said in the form of an apology. "Percy, please try to reach Lance at least one more time." Catherine held out a scrap of paper with numbers scribbled on it. "This is his cell phone number. I got it from Naomi."

Percy shuddered and threw the last handful of documents to the floor.

"I can't, all right? I can't call him," he said, dropping into the chair behind the desk.

"You can't fall apart now. Be a man and call him. Offer him the money, like we agreed. That's all you have to do. You owe it to the pastor."

Percy rocked his head in his hands.

"I can't call him. He's dead," he said, sobbing into his hands.

Catherine closed the office door and moved in closer.

She lifted his head and saw his red eyes and tear-smeared cheeks. "What do you mean 'he's dead'? What happened?"

"I don't know what happened. We were just talking to him. He said horrible things about Cyn . . ." Percy paused and looked away. "He demanded more money. Half a million. I just lost it. Before I knew what had happened, he was lying on the floor. He tripped. I don't know how, but . . . it was an accident."

"I don't believe this. You killed him." She moved backward toward the door. "I don't want any part of this, Percy. You and Kenneth did this without my knowledge."

"Catherine, please don't say that. We just wanted to talk to him."

Catherine opened the door. "I don't want to hear any more. Stop talking. Just stop."

As she vanished through the door, Percy heard her muttering, "Oh Christ. I don't believe this."

Percy entered the penthouse in a flurry. "Cynthia, where are you?" he shouted as he threw his briefcase to the floor. His trench coat flapped as he ran through the house calling her name.

Cynthia emerged from the kitchen. "Percy, I'm here. What's wrong?"

Percy darted across the living room to her. "I talked to Lance Savage today. Cynthia, what have you done?"

"I don't know what you're talking about."

"Did you leak the story about Hezekiah?"

Cynthia looked puzzled. "Stop yelling. Who is Lance Savage?"

Percy grabbed her shoulders tightly. "Don't play innocent with me."

"Percy, you're out of control. Let go of me. I didn't say anything to Savage about Hezekiah."

"Do you know what you've done?"

Cynthia's face turned hard. Her body tensed, and her face exploded in rage. "I know exactly what I've done. And I did it for us. You've slaved under him all these years, and we have nothing to show for it. Now it's our turn. Look at how he and Samantha lives. We deserve to live like that too."

Percy looked at her in surprise. "You're insane. You've ruined their lives. I knew you were jealous, but I never believed you would stoop this low."

She couldn't conceal her anger any longer. Years of bottled-up rage flooded to the surface.

"I've stood by and supported you all these years. If you think I'm going to watch you let this opportunity pass us by, you are mistaken. For once, you're going to take what should be ours, even if I have to take it for you."

"Listen to yourself. You haven't once thought of Pastor Cleaveland and what he must be going through. He's my friend and—"

"He throws you crumbs from the pulpit and you grovel around like a puppy licking them up. You call that a friend? I call it a user. Those two have exploited us from the beginning, and you're not smart enough to know it. Well, I'm sick of it. He only has himself to blame for everything that is happening to him," she said.

Percy turned to walk away. Cynthia grabbed his arm and swung him around. "This is what you always do when God places an opportunity right in your lap. You turn away. This time, Percy Pryce, I'm not going to let you turn away. You are going to be the next pastor of New Testament Cathedral, even if it kills you." She pushed him aside and stormed from the room.

Percy heard the door to their bedroom slam shut. He stood shocked and embarrassed that he had not realized, until now, that he was married to a woman whose ambition would drive her to destroy a man's life.

20

"Where have you been?" Hezekiah spoke softly into the phone. "I've been trying to reach you for two days. I've been going crazy worrying about you. I thought something terrible had happened to you. Are you all right?"

Danny came from behind his desk and closed the door to his office. The room was small and cluttered. Boxes of donated clothes were piled in the corner, and stacks of files and reports cluttered his desk. "Lance Savage found me. I know about the story. I know you have to leave me," he said as he settled behind his desk.

There was a long pause and then Hezekiah spoke. "I'm not leaving you, Danny. I'll never leave you. I don't care about the article. I don't care about anything but you. I'm going to leave Samantha. And before you ask, yes, I have thought it through. It's all I've been able to think about. I can't keep on living a double life. I know that I have to make a decision, and I've made it."

Hezekiah rested his head on the back of the chair. He nervously tugged on his necktie and continued. "I talked with a therapist. He tried to talk me out of it. He's a good man."

Danny sat at his desk. He only half listened to the voice on the phone. His computer screen went blank. Flying toasters suddenly appeared and began to dance across the screen. The words were ones he had dreamed of hearing, but something prevented him from having the anticipated response.

Danny finally spoke. "I think we should talk about this, Hezekiah. Are you sure you'll be able to forgive yourself if you split up your family? A year from now, you'll be miserable and blame me. Then what?"

Hezekiah smiled and spun semicircles in his chair. "I never thought it was your responsibility to make me happy. That's something I have to figure out for myself."

"Hezekiah, I don't ever want to feel like I made you do this. Being with you is the most important thing in the world to me, but it has to be your decision alone. Not in response to pressure from anyone. You've got to know in your heart that it is the right thing for you to do."

"I don't feel any pressure from you to leave Samantha. I know it sounds half-baked to you, but you can't imagine how much I've thought about this in the last year."

"You know that whatever you decide to do, I'm still going to love you. I'll accept whatever terms you decide to define our relationship by—friends, lovers, partners. I just want the best thing for you."

"I know, baby. That's why I love you. Now, get back to work. There are hungry people waiting for you."

Danny hung up the phone. Not wanting to be alone with his thoughts, he walked back to the lobby of the homeless drop-in center. The room was filled to capacity with street refugees. Virgil Jackson quickly approached him.

"Danny, when are you going to get me into a program? I

can't take this waiting any longer. You've got to get me in today, or I'm going to have to do something desperate."

Danny was startled by the aggressive tone in his voice and said, "I checked this morning and only three beds opened up. You are number eleven on the waiting list. You've got to be patient for a few more days."

Virgil's feet began to shuffle as if he were preparing to attack. He slammed his fist on the counter and shouted, "You've been saying that for over a month now!"

The reaction was to be expected from a man who had been living on the streets. It was the plea of a desperate man looking for a way out.

Danny's lips were moving, but Virgil could not hear the words. In his mind he began to rationalize what seemed to be his only option. The "system" had failed him. He had tried to do the right thing, but society wouldn't give him another chance. Who would blame him for doing what he felt he had to do to make his life better?

"There are only seven hundred detox beds in the city, and hundreds of people are waiting to get into them," Danny continued.

Before he could finish his explanation, Virgil hit the desk again, and suddenly ran out of the building.

Danny's eyes followed him as he wove through the folding chairs in the lobby and disappeared into the crowd on the street. His heart sank for the twentieth time that day. It never got easier for him to say, "Sorry, but there's just not enough for you today."

He knew that on the day he was able to utter the words without feeling a pang in his stomach, he would have to find a new line of work.

For the remainder of the day Danny forced himself not to think about the conversations with Hezekiah or with Virgil. He didn't want to allow himself to be elated by the prospect of having the man he loved all to himself. Something would not allow him that pleasure. Something would steal his joy.

Later that day Hezekiah and Danny lay, twisted and tangled, beneath the covers of the bed. The rough surface of Danny's tongue massaged Hezekiah's engorged shaft as his head thrashed on the pillow. His muscular chest heaved upward with each stroke of Danny's mouth.

Danny's hands probed the familiar smooth surface of Hezekiah's buttocks and found the spot that would take him to the height of ecstasy. Hezekiah grabbed the sides of the bed and violently jerked his head back as he neared climax. He moaned, "I'm going to come—you're going to make me come!"

With a violent jolt Hezekiah succumbed to the pleasure that Danny gave so unselfishly.

The two lay motionless with legs entwined after their needs had been met. Hezekiah stroked his lover's hair, kissed the top of his head, and softly said, "I stopped by the construction site this week. That crook Benny Winters is determined to get rich off my back. I have to watch his every move."

"Then why don't you fire him?"

"It would be impossible to find another contractor at this stage of the construction." Hezekiah pulled Danny closer and continued listing his concerns. "He told me the estimates were way off. Some are coming in lower than we budgeted but others are much higher than he expected."

"So what are you going to do?"

"I have no choice. I have to go back to my members and beg for more money."

"Don't worry about it too much, baby. You know you're

doing the right thing. Just think of all those people you'll be able to reach, once this is completed. I'm very proud of you."

Danny kissed Hezekiah's temples and nestled under his chin.

"Let's take a trip together next weekend," Hezekiah said without opening his eyes.

There was no response.

He tried again. "I said, let's take a trip together."

Danny leaned on his elbows and looked into Hezekiah's eyes. "Why are you fucking with me?" He rarely cursed around Hezekiah. He did it only on the occasions when he wanted to remind Hezekiah that the "holier than thou" facade had not clouded his thinking.

"I'm not. I mean it."

"Where?" Danny asked suspiciously.

"I don't care. We could go to Paris. Have you ever been to Paris?"

Danny adjusted his body and sat on the edge of the bed, turning away from Hezekiah. "Don't fuck with me, Hezekiah. If you can go, that's fine. If you can't, that's fine too. I don't want to make plans with you, and you back out at the last minute."

"Would you stop cursing at me," Hezekiah said with an understanding smile. "I said I want to go, so we'll go. I'll make the arrangements this week."

Hezekiah rubbed Danny's back. With each stroke he grew more pensive. "I told Samantha about us."

Danny jerked around to face Hezekiah. "Why?"

"She knew something was different about me and has been sensing it for weeks. She kept asking whom I was sleeping with," he said in a matter-of-fact tone.

"Did you tell her?"

Although Danny had never met Samantha, he was well

aware of her wrath. He'd heard from Hezekiah how she struck terror in those who dared to cross her. While watching her at Hezekiah's side on TV, he saw the sinister glimmer that hid behind her liquid brown eyes. If anyone could convince Hezekiah to leave him, she could. Through guilt, threats, extortion, and even violence, she could do it.

"No, I haven't told her who you are," Hezekiah replied. "And I won't. She doesn't need to know."

Danny was silent, but his eyes encouraged Hezekiah to say more.

"I'm not gay you know," Hezekiah continued. "I don't . . . I mean, I can't identify with the gay lifestyle. The banners, the bars, the parades."

"The people you see at parades in leather, drag, and feather boas don't represent or even look like most gay people," Danny responded. "Most gays and lesbians are just regular people living their lives. They go to work every day, buy homes, and raise families. They're proud men, women, mothers, fathers, sons, and daughters, first. After that, they define and express their sexuality."

Danny, without thinking, got up from the bed and paced the floor while he spoke.

Hezekiah loved watching Danny walk around in the nude, totally unself-conscious. He restrained a smile until he couldn't contain his amusement any longer and said, "Are you sure you're not a preacher? I thought you were me for a minute there."

Danny laughed and playfully jumped onto the bed. "Why do you tease me? I'm serious."

The two rolled around on the bed like puppies playing in a grassy field, and then Hezekiah gently replied, "I know you are, baby. I'm serious too."

* * *

Samantha Cleaveland sat alone in her living room and looked out the window. Muffled sounds from the city below served as background music to her racing thoughts. An antique grandfather clock chimed, alerting her that it was now 7:45 P.M. An ashtray filled with extinguished cigarettes sat on the table next to her. The house was dark and empty.

Samantha jumped when her cell phone rang. She extinguished her most recent cigarette. "Hello."

"Samantha, it's Willie."

"Where have you been? Did you talk to Virgil?"

Reverend Mitchell held his cell phone close to his ear to block the piercing siren of a passing ambulance.

"Yes," Willie said as though presenting a gift he had made in school to his mother. "He's going to do it. He's scared shitless, but he's going to do it Sunday."

A large smile appeared on Samantha's face. She held her head back and looked triumphantly up at the beamed ceiling. "Thank God," she whispered. "How much did you promise him?"

Willie had not been looking forward to delivering this bit of news. "He was getting ready to back out, so I had to offer him thirty thousand dollars. One thousand up front, and the rest after it's done."

"That's just what this city needs. A crackhead with thirty thousand dollars."

"No dealer in Los Angeles is going to see the money. Part of the deal is he's got to leave the city right after it's done."

"Good. Where did he say he was going?"

"He didn't say. I don't fucking care, and neither should you."

"I do care," she snapped. "What happens after he spends

the money? He might come back for more. I could end up paying him for the rest of my life."

"Why the hell didn't you think about that before now?"

A taxi swerved in front of Willie's car, forcing him to slam on the brakes. He removed the phone from his ear and shouted, "Watch out, you fucking foreigner!"

Samantha ignored him and continued. "I have thought about it, and I assumed you had too." Samantha had withheld the second phase of her plan, until she knew it would be too late for Willie to back out. "Willie, you can't let him leave town. After he's done the job, you're going to have to kill him."

There was silence on the phone. The realization of the depth of Samantha's evil unfolded before his eyes. He blinked uncontrollably as the picture came into focus. His hands shook and beads of sweat drenched his entire body. "Samantha, you're crazy. In a month he'll probably turn up dead from an overdose in some fucking alley, anyway. Why get ourselves in any deeper?"

"We can't count on that. I don't want any loose ends. You can make it look like a drug deal gone bad. They'll write him off as just another junkie that got in over his head. You've got to do this, Willie. There's no other way."

Willie tried for the next few moments to convince her that Virgil could be trusted. The woman whom he desired so deeply inspired fear in him now. "Samantha, you're asking me to kill someone. I can't do it."

"Think about it, Willie. With Hezekiah dead and Virgil out of the way, we'll be able to do anything we want. You and I can take over New Testament without interference. I thought you wanted this more than I do." Samantha had difficulty saying the next words. "I thought you wanted me."

Willie sighed as he turned the car. Hearing her say the words clouded his thinking. "You know I want you. But we never talked about me killing anyone."

"It's the only way."

Samantha's mind raced between persuading Willie to commit murder and manipulating the trustees to appoint her pastor of New Testament Cathedral. The reverend was talking rapidly, but she did not hear him.

She would have him introduce the idea immediately after Hezekiah was dead. Very few members of the board dared to stand up to Willie Mitchell.

Again she heard his panicked ramblings. "You wanted me to hire a hit man. I did it. You want me to convince the trustees to appoint you pastor. No problem. I said I'd fucking do it. But kill a man myself?"

She stopped him midsentence and asked, "Where are you? I want to talk with you in person."

"I'm almost at my house."

"Good. I'll be there in an hour."

Samantha parked her car in front of Reverend Mitchell's home. It was a large white house that was twice the size of every other house on the block. For Willie it represented his arrival as a successful black man from Texas. None of his family could have afforded a house like it, and he never passed up an opportunity to remind them.

Willie opened the door before Samantha pressed the bell. His face looked calmer than she had expected. His gray slacks formed a puddle at his shoes, and the ever-present beads of sweat were on his forehead.

He immediately offered her a drink when she entered the house. "I had to have one after I talked to you. My nerves are shot."

"You know I don't drink." She considered what she was

about to do and changed her mind. "On second thought, I will join you. This has me nervous too."

Willie left the room to prepare Samantha's drink. When he returned, she was sitting on the couch and had removed her shoes. Her jacket was lying neatly on the back of a chair.

Willie stopped in the doorway and admired her beauty. He handed her the drink and sat nervously beside her, causing the cushions to slant toward him. Samantha could smell his sweat-drenched body as his large stomach flopped over the gold belt buckle.

"Willie," she said before he could move closer, "have you thought any more about what I asked you to do?"

"It's all I've been able to think about. I'm glad you came. It'll help me make up my mind." A sly smile appeared on his face. "I always think clearer when a beautiful woman is nearby." He moved closer. "What are you going to do to help your daddy make the right decision?" he asked seductively.

Samantha took a sip of the drink and set it on the table. She untied the flowered scarf around her neck and let the ends drop seductively over her breasts. No sign of the revulsion she felt was apparent on her face.

"You know the only way I can do this is if I know you're willing to kill Virgil. Otherwise, the whole thing is off, and you and I will never be together."

Willie reached his arm around her.

She could see his erection stretching the thin fabric of his pants. Samantha quickly stood up. "I need to hear you say it, Willie. Before we do anything, you need to say you'll do it."

Willie struggled off the couch and walked toward her with his arms outstretched. "Baby, you know I can never say no to you. Come on. Don't tease me like this. Let Daddy have some of that."

Samantha allowed him to nuzzle her neck and nibble her earlobes. "Don't fuck with me, Willie. Let me hear you say it."

Willie moved his tongue up and down her neck while he whispered, "I'll do it for you, baby. I'll kill Virgil Jackson for you, and any other man you want me to. Just let me have some of that. . . ."

"What else, Willie? Tell me what else you're going to do."

He couldn't remember the second thing she wanted. "I don't know. Tell me," he purred while fumbling with the buttons of her blouse.

The growing mound in his pants pressed against her leg. His stomach felt like dough on her hip.

"The trustees, Willie. What are you going to do with the trustees?"

"Oh, that," he moaned. "Don't worry about them. You'll be the pastor of New Testament by this time next week."

Samantha took a deep breath and pulled Willie's lips to hers. She kissed him as passionately as she had ever kissed Hezekiah. She could taste the remnants of alcohol and cigarettes on his tongue. With Willie's final words of consent, she frantically unbuttoned his shirt and undid his pants. She wanted it to be over as soon as possible. She didn't want him to tear her clothes in his frenzied state, so she willingly undressed in the middle of his living room. Samantha stood naked as he groped her breasts.

As they lay on the couch, Willie's black nylon socks were the only items left on his body. Samantha flinched under the weight of his stomach. She had often wondered how men with such huge guts managed to reach a woman's vagina. She soon discovered it was at the agonizing expense of whoever was unfortunate enough to be under them. His belly flopped and slammed her stomach as he panted. Drops of sweat dripped from his brow onto her chest and neck as he pounded, oblivious to her discomfort.

For the first moments she tried to feign pleasure but quickly realized that he didn't even notice her efforts in his aroused state. The abuse went on for what seemed an eternity, until he collapsed full weight on top of her, panting to catch his breath.

"Phew! Baby, that was amazing. The pastor doesn't know how good he had it."

Samantha sat alone in the Polo Lounge in the Beverly Hills Hotel, one of her favorite restaurant. Waiters in black vests and pants appeared at her table in rapid intervals, filling her glass with water and offering her coffee and bread, while she waited for her lunch companion to arrive. A hazy yellow light that slightly altered the color of everything it touched consumed the room. The lunch crowd of men and women, dressed in the finest clothes available on either coast, quickly began pouring in.

She could still feel Willie Mitchell's gut pressing into her as she occasionally she waved across the lavish room at people she recognized but preferred to keep at a distance. She checked her watch when she heard, "Samantha, darling. Sorry I'm late. How are you?"

Samantha reached for the gloved hand of her best friend, Victoria Johnson. Victoria was the wife of Rev. Sylvester Johnson, the pastor of First Bethany Church of Los Angeles. She wore a pale peach pantsuit, which accented the beautiful curves of her body. A diamond-encrusted broach shaped like a butterfly twinkled on her lapel. Her hands were covered in sleek buttery cream-colored leather gloves. Victoria was the only other pastor's wife with whom Samantha never competed. The women were equals in every way, and both were more ambitious than their successful husbands.

Victoria sat down and removed her gloves. "Are you okay, Sam? You look like you've been crying."

Before Samantha could speak, a waiter appeared at the table. "Good afternoon, Mrs. Johnson. May I get you something from the bar?"

"I'll have a vodka martini, thank you." The waiter left the table and Victoria continued, "Now tell me, honey, what has that bastard done this time?"

"Just more of the usual. He's having another affair. He came right out and admitted it."

"I'm so sorry. You must be devastated. Did he tell you who she is?"

Samantha picked up her napkin and caught a tear running down her cheek. Even though she shared her most intimate secrets with Victoria, she could not bring herself to confess that Hezekiah was sleeping with a man. "No, he said I didn't know her. I don't really care who it is this time."

"What do you mean you don't care? You're not going to leave him, are you?"

"No, I'm not going to leave him, but there's more. She's been calling the house at all hours and hanging up the phone. This morning I saw a car with a woman in it sitting outside the house. When he left, she followed him down the hill." Samantha dabbed her eye with the napkin and continued. "Yesterday I got a call . . . a call saying if he did not leave me, she would kill us both."

"Oh my God, Sammy. You must be frightened out of your mind." Victoria took a long swallow from the drink the waiter had delivered. "The bitch sounds crazy. Have you called the police?"

"No, I can't. I don't want to get the police involved."

"You have to. She's a psycho. I don't mean to scare you, but this is serious. What does Hezekiah have to say about it?"

"He says she's harmless. He's going to break it off with her today. Victoria, I'm so frightened." Samantha prayed Victoria's brain was not too clouded from the vodka to recall their conversation later. She had to have someone vouch for her innocence in court if the need ever arose.

Victoria drank down the remainder of her second drink and ordered another from a passing waiter. "Who cares what he thinks."

"It's not his fault, he—"

Victoria grabbed her hand across the table. "Samantha Monique Cleaveland, don't you dare defend that bastard. He doesn't deserve it. You have stood in his shadow all these years, put up with his ego, made him look better than he really is, and this is how he repays you. I swear, all men should be lined up against a wall, have their dicks cut off and shoved down their throats."

Samantha forced a laugh through her tears. "Victoria, you should do something about that mouth of yours."

"You know I'm right, girl. Sylvester has cheated on me so many times, I get suspicious when he's around too much. If he didn't have so goddamned much money, and that fucking prenup, I'd have left his ass years ago."

Samantha laughed freely. "Girl, you ought to quit."

"You're different, Sam. You could take his church and his money. Everyone knows you're a much better preacher than he is. I bet if he wasn't around, those tight-ass Holy Rollers would still follow you around like you had gold on your ass."

Samantha suppressed a hearty laugh and hoped no one could hear their conversation. "Don't say that, Victoria. I still love him. I just hope this woman doesn't hurt him."

"I hope she does, and if she doesn't, I know some guys that'll break both his and that bitch's legs for fifty dollars and a carton of Newports. You give me the word, and I'll show him just how much you love him."

"I think Hezekiah will learn his lesson this time. He'll never do this to me again."

After lunch the two women embraced on the busy street in front of the restaurant. Samantha had ended the lunch abruptly after Victoria's fourth vodka martini. She feared Victoria would get too drunk to remember they had even met that day.

"Sammy, you call me if you need anything, honey. And don't let that bitch frighten you."

They laughed and embraced one last time as the valet brought Samantha's car and held open the door.

"I just might take you up on that broken-leg offer," Samantha said as she climbed into the driver's seat. "I'll call you next week and let you know how things turn out."

As she drove away, she heard Victoria yelling to the parking attendant, "Where's my car? I've been standing on this curb so long, people are going to think I'm a hooker."

21

Saturday

Hezekiah and Danny dodged rollerbladers and couples jogging on the bike path at Santa Monica Beach. They had met earlier for breakfast at a sidewalk café, and decided to take a walk afterward. It was a beautiful morning, and the beach was already filled with tourists wearing Venice Beach T-shirts and Bermuda shorts. Children were jumping waves and sun worshippers were lying prone on colorful towels. Waves slammed against the weathered remains of the pier, which reached into the horizon.

"Heads up!" yelled a man behind them, wearing black biking shorts and a helmet. Danny and Hezekiah separated to opposite sides of the path and returned to the center when the biker had passed. Danny's shoulder brushed the arm of Hezekiah's gray jogging suit in the closest display of affection they dared in such a public place.

"I promise I'll never let a man in tight biking shorts come between us again." They both laughed as Hezekiah led the way off the paved path toward the ocean.

"I made arrangements for us to fly to Paris next weekend," Hezekiah said as he stumbled over tracks left behind by a lifeguard truck.

"I hadn't thought about that since you mentioned it. I assumed you had forgotten."

"I remember everything we've ever said to each other. Just like I've memorized every inch of your beautiful body. I know you didn't believe me. Now you can see I'm serious about this and about us."

Danny tried to switch the topic. "How did your session go with the therapist?"

"Exactly the way I expected it to. He said I should leave you and let him 'help me' save my marriage and church."

"Maybe he's right."

"Maybe. Or maybe not. It doesn't matter, though. I'm not leaving you. Sorry, but you're stuck with me. And stop trying to change the subject. My plane will be at LAX on next Friday afternoon, and a driver will be waiting for us in Paris."

Hezekiah looked at his watch. It was 11:00 A.M. "We'd better head back. I've got some work to do on my sermon for Sunday."

They walked back to the restaurant with a comfortable silence shared between them. Seagulls hunted for sand crabs while the waves erased the footprints they left behind.

Danny interrupted the silence. "Can I tell you something?"

"You can tell me anything."

"I'm afraid."

"Of what?"

"Of what I think Samantha will do if you ever leave her."

"What do you think she'll do? Kill me?" Hezekiah said with a smile.

"I'm serious, Hezekiah. I think she's capable of doing something that . . . I know you love her, but I can't shake this feeling I have about her."

"I do still have feelings for her, but not in the same way I feel about you. Yes, she has a mean streak, but she's also very pragmatic and a survivor. She'll adjust just like millions of other women do when they divorce. It's going to be difficult, but I'm sure she'll be fine."

"Just be careful, Hezekiah. I don't want anything to happen to you."

The Harbor Freeway was bumper to bumper as Samantha drove her car toward the church. Chamber music hummed from her CD. Dark sunglasses protected her eyes from the afternoon sun. As she exited onto Hezekiah Cleaveland Avenue, she saw Willie Mitchell leaning against his car in the church parking lot. Samantha pulled in next to him and got out. He looked at her silky legs as they extended from the car, and he immediately remembered why he subjected himself to the whims of the woman.

"Where's Catherine?" Samantha asked.

"She must be at lunch." He leaned in to kiss her.

Samantha pushed him away and said, "Not here, you idiot."

Samantha reached into her purse and handed Willie the gun wrapped in one of Hezekiah's handkerchiefs. She already had carefully wiped her fingerprints from it. "Put it in your pocket and give me back the handkerchief. Before you give it to Virgil, make sure you wipe your prints off, and don't let him have it until Sunday morning."

"I'm not stupid. Where'd you get this?"

"It belonged to my mother. I don't know where she got it but I found it under her mattress when I was clearing out her house after she died. What's important is it's not registered and can't be traced back to either of us."

Willie placed the bundle into the breast pocket of his coat and removed the cloth.

"Where is Virgil?" Samantha asked in a half whisper.

"I think he's at the mission downtown. He goes there every day," he answered nervously.

"Just make sure he doesn't back out at the last minute."

"He won't." Willie looked around the parking lot and then whispered, "When am I going to get some more of that good loving?"

Samantha's eyes glazed over with disgust. "Just take care of this, and you'll get more than you can handle."

Samantha turned and walked quickly toward the church entrance. Willie rubbed his gut as he watched her legs and muttered, "Damn, that woman is fine." He then bounced into his car and drove away.

Samantha entered the church. Although no one was in sight, she could hear footsteps in the distance. As she neared the glass office, her heart began to race. It was bright from fluorescent lights, and the telephone was ringing. She fumbled trying to put her key in the door as she heard the footsteps growing nearer.

"Good afternoon, Mrs. Cleaveland."

The voice startled her, and she dropped the keys. When she turned around, she saw Rauly Jenkins, the facility manager.

"Rauly, you scared me," she said. "I wish you wouldn't sneak up on me like that."

"I'm sorry, ma'am. I was up in the baptismal pit. I don't think they've cleaned it since I left for vacation two weeks ago."

As Rauly spoke, Samantha became concerned that he

had witnessed the exchange between her and Willie Mitchell. "Have you seen Reverend Mitchell? I thought I saw him on the street when I drove up."

"No, ma'am, I haven't seen him all day."

"I guess it's time to get my eyes checked. Rauly, please make sure the lectern is polished before this Sunday. And the stained-glass window behind the pulpit needs to be cleaned. It looked murky last Sunday morning."

"Yes, ma'am."

"Also, Pastor Cleaveland doesn't like the looks of one of the support beams under the balcony. He's concerned it could collapse if there is too much weight on it. He wants you to post CLOSED signs at the balcony entrances and set up the television monitors in Fellowship Hall for this Sunday's service," Samantha said, hoping Rauly and Hezekiah would not cross paths before the end of the day.

"That's funny. He didn't mention it earlier, when I saw him. I'll get my men on that right away. It'll be done before I leave for the weekend."

"Thank you."

Rauly returned the way he came, and Samantha entered the office. She picked up a pad from the desk and was beginning to write a note when she saw Catherine approaching.

"Hello, Catherine. I was just writing you a note. I hope you're not too upset with me about the other day. There was just so much on my mind, and I got carried away. I was completely out of line, and I hope you can forgive me."

Catherine stared at her cautiously and said, "That's all right, Mrs. Cleaveland. I understand. Pastor Cleaveland explained it to me."

A flush of blood rushed into Samantha's head. She wondered what horrible thing Hezekiah had said to the girl. "I hope he didn't say anything too terrible about me. Whatever it was, I'm sure I deserved it."

Catherine did not respond.

"Well, anyway, if there is anything I can do to make it up to you," Samantha continued, "please let me know." Samantha had already decided that after Hezekiah was dead, the first thing she would do was fire Catherine Birdsong, again.

"Please, I just want to forget about it."

As Samantha approached the door, she turned and said, "I almost forgot. Could you order lilies, white lilies, and birds-of-paradise for the pulpit this Sunday? They're Hezekiah's favorites."

"Yes, ma'am," Catherine responded coldly. "Will there be anything else?"

"No, that's all. I'll see you on Sunday morning."

22

An attractive woman with too much makeup stood behind the counter of the beauty spa. "Mrs. Cleaveland, how nice to see you again. Andre is in with a client right now. He'll be with you in a few minutes. He asked that we start your manicure first."

The smell of chemicals and freshly shampooed hair filled the waiting area of the salon. A haunting song by Nina Simone played over the speakers as customers, in overstuffed chairs, sipped champagne and lemon-garnished drinks while catching up on the latest gossip. The sound of falling water came from a marble fountain surrounded by lush green plants and exotic flowers.

"Please follow me to the changing room, and we'll get you started."

Samantha followed the young woman through white doors surrounded by carvings of grapevines and puffy-faced cherubs.

Inside, women were leisurely milling around, wearing thin blue robes with towels covering their wet hair. Some wore mint clay masks, while others had cellophane dangling from limp hair.

The buzz of hair dryers could be heard coming from an adjoining room. Samantha exchanged greetings with several women as she passed through the crowd.

"Are you having your hair colored today, Mrs. Cleaveland?" the young woman asked.

"No, just a facial and manicure."

Monique held open the door of a small dressing room for Samantha. "When you're done disrobing, Frances will start your manicure. Would you like an espresso or mineral water?"

Samantha disliked the vapid smile of the woman, and she had always refused to address her by name. "Mineral water. Thank you."

After having her hands massaged, nails treated and painted a classic clear, Samantha lay vulnerable on a padded table, with the hands of Andre gently massaging her face. A bright light pointed directly at her face, and steam sprayed to open pores. Samantha had grown fond of Andre, despite the fact that he was obviously gay. How could she not like someone that made her look five years younger than her age?

"I don't think you need a peel today. I'm just going to give you a good cleansing and facial."

Andre was a well-built man with thick dreadlocked hair, which went in every direction. He wore an African-print shirt with tight black pants and boots.

The music played softly as Andre gossiped. "Victoria was in yesterday. She nearly drank a whole bottle of champagne, and then got an attitude when we refused to serve her more. She was so drunk we had to call a cab to take her home."

Samantha smiled through the steam. "You're lucky that

didn't happen five years ago. You would have had to call the police. Victoria is a lot calmer than she used to be."

"How's that gorgeous husband of yours? I saw him on television the other day. Something about a new building."

Samantha's body tensed. She instinctively reacted to a man referring to her husband as "gorgeous." She looked up at Andre standing behind her and asked, "Do you think he's gorgeous? I didn't think men noticed that kind of thing."

"Samantha, when a man looks that good, it's hard not to notice. I hope I didn't offend you."

"Not at all. Andre, may I ask you a personal question?" she inquired as he applied a gooey substance to her face.

"You can ask me anything, sweetheart. You know you're my favorite client."

"Why do you prefer men over women? We've never discussed it, but I assume you're gay."

Andre's hands froze in place for a moment, then resumed. "Why do you ask?"

"No particular reason. A friend's husband recently told her he was gay, and I guess I'm curious."

"I knew it," Andre blurted. "It's Victoria's husband, isn't it? I can tell a gay man from a mile away. The first time I saw Sylvester, I knew he was family."

"It's not Sylvester. You think he's gay? That's ridiculous. What man in his right mind would want him? He looks like a buffalo in a bad toupee. Anyway, it's not him. It's no one you would know. So tell me. What attracts a man to other men?"

"I've been attracted to men as far back as I can remember. Beyond the obvious physical stuff I guess I would say it's because a man can understand me better than any woman ever has."

"Why does that necessarily lead to sex?"

"For me they're one and the same. I can't separate my mind from my body. If I like a man, I mean his mind and how he thinks, then the physical attraction comes naturally, and that's when the fun . . ."

Andre had drifted easily into the usual salon chatter, when he suddenly remembered to whom he was talking.

"Samantha, darling. I really don't feel comfortable talking about this with you. My God, you're a minister's wife." He laughed nervously.

Samantha reacted sternly. "What does the man I'm married to have to do with anything? You think just because I'm married to Hezekiah, I wouldn't understand."

"No, I'm not saying that. I just meant I don't want to offend you."

"Never mind. Just change the subject." Samantha sat through the rest of the facial in silence. Andre made several unsuccessful attempts to resuscitate their exchange, but Samantha would not participate beyond a curt "yes" and "no."

As he walked her to the lobby, he said, "Samantha, I'm sorry if I said something to upset you. The next time you come in, your facial will be on the house."

Without looking at him she curtly said, "That won't be necessary. I won't be back. I don't approve of your lifestyle."

Samantha quickly paid her bill and left Andre and the salon in her past.

Samantha opened the door to her closet. The lights came on automatically. Bulbs lit up around a mirror that stretched the length of the wall in the closet, which was at least half the size of her bedroom. Clothes she had acquired over the years of her marriage lined the walls. A stepladder leaned against shelves filled with cashmere sweaters and silk scarves stacked neatly according to color.

The pride of her collection was the hundreds of shoes displayed on racks that ran along the base of the room. Each had been carefully selected to accompany a new suit or special event she had attended. Many of the shoes could only be distinguished from others by a fraction of an inch on the heel or a bow instead of a buckle. Rows of round boxes held the hats that served to accentuate the face that so many admired.

Samantha stood in the door and marveled at the items that meant so much to her. Rarely had she given any of her clothes to charity. She felt she gave enough of her life to others and drew the line at her cherished belongings. Garments and shoes that had not been worn in years, and would probably never be worn again, stood waiting for their chance in the sunlight.

It usually took Samantha only a few hours to prepare for church, but this was going to be a special Sunday. She needed at least a day. Samantha wanted to look her most radiant, yet wear something practical that could be easily cleaned in the event it got spattered with blood. Her heels had to be just the right height for the inevitable rapid climb up the pulpit steps to cradle the body of her dead husband.

She had to select an ensemble that would not inadvertently rise and reveal too much leg if she decided to perform the "Jackie O" lunge to dodge stray bullets.

After an extended search Samantha pulled four outfits from the racks and displayed them on hooks like suits of armor in a medieval castle corridor. They all had one thing in common; they would not fly any higher than her thigh in case strenuous maneuvers were required. Two of the outfits selected were made of vibrant floral-print fabric. One was a peach suit with a skirt designed to obediently follow the lines of her well-shaped lower half. The fourth was her favorite. She had purchased it a month earlier on a shopping trip on Rodeo Drive. It was a simple cream-colored sleeveless dress by Givenchy, and it perfectly mimicked the contours of her body. The accompanying jacket helped to partially conceal the low-cut neckline.

Over the next hour she tried on each of the dresses several times. She put each outfit through a sequence of tests that included kneeling down in front of the large mirror, walking at a quick pace across the length of the dressing-room floor, and a series of abrupt twists and turns.

She decided on the cream dress and jacket at the conclusion of the high-fashion aerobic session. The shape, and easy movement suited her purposes well And the color would serve as the perfect backdrop for his blood.

The shoes she selected were not the pair originally purchased for the ensemble. Instead, she chose a pair with a slightly lower heel and a shade darker than the dress. She did not want to risk tripping or snagging her shoe on the carpet. The accessories were the easy part. The dress would only tolerate pearls, a single strand that stopped just short of the neckline, and a matching bracelet.

Samantha stood in front of the mirror to examine her choice and was pleased. She looked like a magazine's cover model, an image that most women would never dare to try and emulate.

Hezekiah had already begun eating his dinner on Saturday evening when Jasmine rushed in and kissed him on the forehead. The smell of mouthwash surrounded her head. "Hi, Daddy. Where's Mommy?"

"She's around here somewhere. I think in her study. Where have you been all day?"

"Daddy, I'm not a little girl. I wish you would stop asking me that every time I come into the house."

Etta emerged from the kitchen and set a clean plate in front of the breathless girl. "Hello, Jasmine. I hope you're hungry."

"Not really, Etta. I think I'll just have salad tonight."

Samantha suddenly appeared below the arched entry to the dining room. "Hello. Why didn't you tell me dinner was ready?"

Hezekiah continued eating and said, "Etta knocked on your door, but you didn't answer."

"I was on the telephone."

Samantha joined them at the table. To watch the three, one would not have known what lay ahead. The conversation was polite. No mention was made of men, alcohol, or murder. Hezekiah and Samantha never made eye contact, but they did direct several inconsequential comments to each other.

The dinner went on without an argument. Etta frequently entered the room to remove dishes and fill empty glasses. She was pleased that the pastor was able to enjoy in peace the food she had prepared for him.

Before finishing her salad, Jasmine stood. "I'm going to Shelly's." She braced herself for her mother's response. There was none.

Hezekiah broke the silence. "Honey, I expect to see you at church tomorrow."

"I'll be there, Daddy." Before reaching the door, she looked over her shoulder and said, "Good-bye, Mommy."

Samantha set her fork on her plate and said, "Good-bye, Jasmine. I love you, honey."

Samantha waited until she heard the roar of Jasmine's car passing the window. Then she looked at Hezekiah and said, "I think you should sleep in the guest room tonight."

Samantha retreated to the bedroom and was not seen again that evening.

The doorbell in Sandra's condominium rang. Cynthia walked from the kitchen, holding a fresh tray of cheeses and crackers. Lavender-scented candles had been extinguished, but remnants of their bouquet lingered in the air. Sandra quickly turned off a languid tune sung by Nina Simone.

"Are you ready, girl?" Sandra asked, adjusting the shoulders on her black suit. "That's Phillip now."

"I'm as ready as I'll ever be. Let him in."

Sandra opened the door.

"Phillip," she said to the man at the threshold. "Thank you for coming. I know this is awkward for you. Please let me take your coat. Would you like a glass of wine?"

Phillip Thornton graciously accepted the wine and walked tentatively into the living room.

Sandra and Cynthia sat down on the couch and Phillip sat in an overstuffed chair directly in front of them. He was a handsome man with a hint of gray at each temple. He wore a navy blue sport coat and tan khaki pants.

Sandra was the first to speak. "Let me start by saying, Phillip, that we appreciate and understand the risks you are taking by being here tonight," she said, leaning forward on the sofa. "I know that you and Hezekiah have been friends for years, and this whole ordeal must be very difficult for you."

"That's a nice speech, Sandra," said Phillip, placing his glass on the table. "You seem to be under the misguided impression that I have some reservations about running the story. Let's be clear about this. I don't. Yes, Hezekiah and I are friends, but this isn't about friendship. It's about business. This has the potential to be the biggest story in the country.

"Last year alone my paper lost fifty million dollars. I've got the unions on my ass. The fucking Internet is drawing away my readers by the thousands, and on top of that, advertisers are dropping like flies. I stand to make millions if the *Los Angeles Chronicle* breaks this story. For me it comes down to either running the story or filing bankruptcy and shutting down the entire newspaper, and shutting down is not an option I want to entertain. This paper has been in my family for three generations. My great-grandfather started it in his father's garage when he was a teenager. I don't want to be the Thornton who ran my family's legacy into the ground. I'll leave that honor to my sons."

Cynthia sat silent as Phillip continued. "Hezekiah is going to come after us with an army of lawyers when this story breaks. Cynthia, I need some assurances that you'll stand behind your story. We'll protect your identity as long as possible, but I can't make any guarantees that at some point a judge won't insist that we reveal our source."

The room fell silent for a moment, and then Cynthia asked, "Will *Chronicle* attorneys represent me if a judge forces you to reveal who I am?"

"Yes. You will have full access to our legal department. I need to be honest with you about the risks. This story will be national and international news. You will be hounded by reporters for months, and possibly years, if your identity is made public. You'll also be setting yourself up for a potential civil lawsuit from Hezekiah."

"You're scaring her, Phillip," Sandra chimed in. "Cynthia, I think Phillip is overestimating the public's interest in Hezekiah. I personally think it will make a big splash in the headlines for a few weeks, and then some politician will get caught with a hooker and the public will lose interest in this. Plus, there is a strong possibility that the public will never find out who the source is."

"That is true, but she still needs to be prepared. You each know Hezekiah is loved by a lot of people. Cynthia, you will not be very popular with people who think Hezekiah walks on water. Can you handle that?"

Sandra jumped in again. "Hezekiah is also hated by just as many, if not more, people. They will see you as a hero, a woman who exposed hypocrisy at the highest level of the church."

Cynthia listened intently as the two continued to present her with the pros and cons of her actions. However, none that were mentioned came close to her own reason for outing Hezekiah.

As they talked, she saw images of her husband standing center stage at New Testament Cathedral and saying, "I am proud to be your new pastor."

She saw herself standing next him and smiling lovingly at him as cameras beamed their images to televisions all over the country. She could feel the buttery leather of the limousine caressing her body as she was being driven to luncheons, parties, and banquets in her honor. She could hear the roar of the Learjet engine as it whisked her and Percy off to the East Coast to meet with the president or some other very important person.

"All right, you two," she said. "I've heard enough. I

refuse to back down because of fear. This isn't about me. It's about doing the right thing. Phillip, don't worry. I'll stand behind the story."

"Good. Then I'll give it the green light," Phillip said, clapping his hands together.

"I've told you why I'm doing this. I'm curious, ladies, why are you so eager to out Hezekiah?"

Cynthia spoke first. "This has been so difficult for me. I love Hezekiah and Samantha deeply. I would give my life for them. They've done so much for Percy and me. We wouldn't be where we are today if it weren't for them."

Both Phillip and Sandra looked skeptically at Cynthia as she continued. "I just can't sit by and not expose such a horrible abomination. Hezekiah has sinned, and it must be brought to light. It's for his own good. He has to repent before God and man and beg for forgiveness. I'm doing this to save his soul from eternal damnation."

"That is very Christian of you, Mrs. Pryce," Phillip said with a smirk. "I suppose the fact that your husband is the heir apparent to the New Testament Cathedral dynasty has had no impact on your decision."

"That never crossed my mind. This is about exposing sin and—"

Phillip interrupted, "So what about you, Sandra? Hezekiah got you your first job out of law school."

Sandra crossed her legs and said, "That's simple. I'm doing it for Samantha. She deserves better. She's too blinded by love to see how Hezekiah is destroying her life. She would never leave him. She would never do anything to hurt him, so I'm helping him leave her."

Phillip showed little interest in what he considered half-truths from the women. He could clearly see that whatever the true reasons for their betrayal, they were strong enough to ensure their full commitment to the story.

"All right, then, ladies. It looks like we're in business," he said. "The story is scheduled to run in this Sunday's paper. You had better brace yourselves because it's going to be a hell of a ride."

23

Sunday Morning

It was 1:00 A.M. Hattie Williams lay awake in her bed, staring at the ceiling. A sheer curtain quivered gently from the breeze through the open window. She hadn't slept well since viewing the images in her kitchen window days earlier. Concern for Pastor Cleaveland consumed her thoughts.

If he were already dead, someone would have called her by now. She had called Etta the day before, and everything seemed normal. Hattie prayed that the pastor would make it through the night so she could see him at least one last time. She felt helpless because there was nothing she could do to prevent it.

A tear trailed down her temple to her nightcap. "Jesus, you know what's best for the pastor. Thy will be done on earth as it is in heaven. But, Lord, let his passage be easy. Let him be surrounded by people who love him. Let him be in the place that he loves so much when you call him home."

* * *

Hezekiah's legs jerked and his hands swatted at imaginary demons as he slept. The dream that caused his brow to sweat, and his body to toss and turn, was so vivid, it felt as if he were actually awake. Hezekiah tossed in his sleep as he wrestled within the grips of another nightmare.

New Testament Cathedral is in a state of turmoil. The church grounds are filled with religious-right protesters waving placards, and gay activists demanding a full confession from Hezekiah. A squadron of broadcast news vans clogs the streets.

Hezekiah is riding in the rear of the limousine. A swarm of men and women toting cameras, lights, and microphones rush toward the car as it approaches. Dino drives slowly, and police officers clear his path. Protesters shout louder as cameras deliver their images live to homes throughout the country. Hezekiah then sees an anchorwoman standing at the foot of the church steps.

"This is Wendy Chung, with ABC News," she says crisply into the camera. "We have interrupted your regularly scheduled programming to bring you live coverage of a dramatic story unfolding in the city of Los Angeles. Pastor Hezekiah Cleaveland's car has just arrived here at New Testament Cathedral. We will try to get a statement from him on a story that broke this morning, which claims that he has been involved in a long-standing homosexual affair, but as you can see, it's a mob scene here this morning.

"Pastor Cleaveland," she shouts as Hezekiah sees himself stepping from the car. "Would you comment on the allegations of a homosexual affair that was reported in this morning's Los Angeles Chronicle*?"*

Dino steps in front of the woman as Hezekiah walks to the stairs.

*"Sir, these are startling claims and the American peo-
ple would like to hear your response."*

*The reporter's pleas for attention are replaced by those
of others.*

*"Pastor Cleaveland, over here," shouts a man in the
crowd. "Is it true that you refurbished a live/work loft
for Danny St. John using church funds?"*

*Hezekiah proceeds up the stairs, but the questions
continue.*

*"Where is Mr. St. John this morning, sir? Has he gone
into hiding?"*

*"Are you going to divorce your wife, sir, and live
openly as a same-sex couple?"*

*"How is this revelation going to affect your plans for
the new cathedral? Will you halt construction?"*

*When Hezekiah reaches the top landing, the doors
fling open, and Percy Pryce walks out.*

*"The pastor has no comment at this time," he says,
reaching for Hezekiah's arm. "He will make a full statement today, after this morning's church service. Now,
please, let him through."*

*Police officers block the doors to prevent the reporters
from rushing into the building.*

*Wendy Chung faces the camera again. "Well, you
heard it. Pastor Hezekiah Cleaveland has refused to
comment, but his spokesperson states that he will make
a statement later today.*

*"As a result of this extramarital homosexual affair,
some pundits are suggesting that Cleaveland should resign as pastor of one of the largest churches in the country. They say that his credibility as a spiritual leader
has suffered irreparable damage. Believed by many to
be one of the most powerful ministers in the United
States, Pastor Hezekiah Cleaveland has served as spiri-*

tual confidant to two presidents. His future now seems to be in ruins if these startling allegations prove to be true. Also, sources close to the family have informed us that Mrs. Cleaveland intends to file for divorce and possibly mount her own campaign to replace her husband as pastor of New Testament Cathedral. We will bring you live coverage of the press conference later today. Now back to your regularly scheduled programming."

Hezekiah's body twisted and turned in bed. His legs and arms became tangled in the sheets as he fought to emerge from the dream. His mind raced forward at an alarming speed.

Hezekiah is standing on the roof of the church above the stained-glass window, looking down on the throngs of protesters and reporters. In the distance he can see the construction site of the new cathedral. It is covered in a smoky gray haze, and steel beams are falling off and crashing to the ground, causing huge plumes of dust to envelop the crowd below.

He then hears a booming voice from the clouds over his head. "Good morning, ladies and gentlemen of the press," the voice says. "Pastor Hezekiah Cleaveland has called this press conference to respond to the article that appeared in this morning's edition of the Los Angeles Chronicle. *He will first make a brief statement, after which we will have a few minutes for questions. Please hold your questions until he has finished."*

Hezekiah steps forward to the edge of the roof. A bright light forms a halo around him.

"Good morning," Hezekiah says solemnly. His booming voice echoes like thunder in clouds. "I am here to ad-

dress what I consider to be a very sad day for Los Angeles and for the country.

"It is a tragic commentary on the state of American journalism when a member of the media is permitted to fabricate the news without benefit of facts, truth, or credible evidence. It is a crime against the American people when a once-trusted publication appoints itself judge, juror, and executioner in matters pertaining to the lives of private citizens of this country.

"Let me say, in the most emphatic terms possible, that I have never had a sexual relationship with a man. I have never met Mr. Danny St. John in person, and I have never sent the collection of e-mail correspondence that has been falsely attributed to me. Yes, I have spoken to Mr. St. John on the telephone, but only as a citizen who is concerned about homeless people in this city. Mr. St. John has on numerous occasions responded to my requests to assist homeless people whom I encounter on a daily basis. The calls that Mr. Savage referred to were nothing more than my acting not only as a pastor but also as a citizen who is concerned about the plight of homeless women, men, and children.

"Now, as for the e-mail messages, it pains me to say that yes, the e-mails were, in fact, generated from my home computer."

Hezekiah takes another step closer to the edge. "I am sad to report to you that all the messages were written by my wife, Samantha Cleaveland."

Gasps erupt from the crowd. Cameras flash throughout, and reporters grab for cell phones.

Hezekiah continues his statement. "She wrote and sent the letters in an attempt to further her own ambitions. Mrs. Cleaveland conspired with Mr. Danny St.

John, Lance Savage, and other unscrupulous individuals."

Reporters immediately begin shouting questions, but Hezekiah holds up his hand.

"Please let me continue," he says. "I wish Mr. Savage were here so that I could ask him why he wrote a story that is based solely on lies, innuendo, and unfounded rumors, but I do not see him among you today.

"Finally let me say to the citizens of this great city that this entire ordeal has only served to make me a better and stronger pastor. I will work even harder to earn your trust and support of my efforts to build the church of the future. Thank you."

A jumble of questions fills the air and buzzes around Hezekiah's head.

"Pastor Cleaveland, how do you account for the fact that you were seen entering Mr. St. John's apartment on numerous occasions by his upstairs neighbors, Mr. and Mrs. Somner?"

"I'm sure that the Somners are a very nice and well-intentioned couple, but I have no idea where they live, nor have I ever met them."

"Pastor Cleaveland," calls out another reporter. "Why do you think Mrs. Cleaveland did this? What did she have to gain?"

"I would imagine that some misguided person, possibly Sandra Kelly, convinced her that I was the only thing preventing her from being pastor of New Testament Cathedral. It is unfortunate. I loved, and still do love, my wife with all my heart and soul, and have dedicated my life to making her happy."

"So what's next? Are you going to file for divorce?"

"I would never divorce Samantha. She is obviously suffering through some sort of emotional crisis because

that's the only way she could have been convinced to do something this horrible. Even what she did is not enough to make me leave her. I will, instead, stand by her and make sure that she receives the best psychiatric care possible."

"Did you use church funds to renovate a loft for Mr. St. John?"

"I won't even dignify that with a response," Hezekiah says sharply. "Next question, please."

"Sir, has this in any way changed your mind about building the new cathedral?"

"As I said in my statement, it has only invigorated me. My commitment to serving the people of this city is stronger than ever."

Then Hezekiah sees a woman begin to levitate above the crowd. Her lips do not move, but he can hear her speak. "Pastor Cleaveland, Sandy Gingham, from the Los Angeles Chronicle," *she calls out. "The body of Mr. Danny St. John has been recovered from the ocean off Santa Monica. He apparently committed suicide by jumping from the Santa Monica Pier. Do you have any words of condolence for his family and friends?"*

The mob falls silent. Hezekiah stands motionless and stares into the flashing lights. Moments pass before the reporter speaks again.

"Pastor Cleaveland, would you like to comment?"

Hezekiah does not respond, still frozen in a wash of flashing lights. Instead, he takes another step closer to the ledge.

Hezekiah puts his foot forward into the air and begins to fall. Pandemonium ensues. Reporters and cameramen begin to float up to Hezekiah and continue the line of questioning that caused him to step over the edge of the building.

"*Pastor Cleaveland, would you like to comment on the apparent suicide of Mr. St. John?*"

"*Pastor Cleaveland, were you aware of his death prior to the press conference?*"

"*Sir, do you suspect foul play in the death of Mr. St. John?*"

Will this fall never end? *he thinks.* Will God have mercy and release me from this torment? Can the earth stop spinning for one moment and allow me to leave this body, which is Hezekiah T. Cleaveland?

Hezekiah's plunge continues as familiar faces, dreaded confrontations, and painful events flash in rapid succession through his mind. This is it. His life condenses into the few seconds it takes to fall to the earth. It took a lifetime for Hezekiah to reach the heights of power and prestige, but only seconds to fall to the ground. When his body crashes onto the polished stone, the screaming stops and the glass birds stop flapping their wings.

The impact caused Hezekiah to bolt upright in the bed. His chest heaved as he searched the room frantically to assure himself that it was only a dream.

24

Around the city merchants jostled sleeping men in doorways.

"Wake up, you bum!" they said. "It's time for me to open my shop."

The morning sun readied for its first appearance over the horizon as the city grudgingly came to life. Compact cars, with headlights piercing the remains of night, scurried through neighborhoods delivering bundles of information, while vans stopped on every corner, filling news receptacles with the Sunday paper.

In the dim morning light the headline read: OUTSPOKEN NEWSMAN FOUND DEAD, SLAIN IN HOME.

The paper landed with a thud on the front porch of Kenneth Davis's home. Still in his bathrobe, he retrieved the paper and stood in his foyer in shock. He froze when he read the headline, and then quickly read the first paragraph:

Lance Savage was found murdered late Saturday evening in his home in Venice, California. Police confirm that the cause of death was blunt trauma to the head.

Kenneth dropped the paper to the floor and poured a glass of bourbon. His hands shook as he swallowed, but the liquid offered no escape from the bold print that stared up from the carpet.

A gentle tap on Cynthia's bedroom door drew her from a fitful sleep. "Reverend and Mrs. Pryce, are you awake?"

"Come in, Carmen. What is it?" Percy responded.

A dark-haired housekeeper wearing a white apron entered. "I've brought your coffee and the morning paper," she said with a Spanish accent.

Cynthia sat up and probed the nightstand for her reading glasses. The words assaulted her eyes, causing them to blink in disbelief. She covered her mouth with a trembling hand as Percy read over her shoulder.

"Oh my God," he said, sitting upright.

"I don't believe this. It says they think he was killed by a burglar." Cynthia continued reading:

Savage was found by Richard Harrison, the editor of the Los Angeles Chronicle. *According to Harrison, at the time of his death Savage was working on a very controversial story that many powerful people did not want to see printed. Harrison declined to give any details.*

"In these kinds of cases we look for possible motives, financial, family, or work related," said Assistant Police Chief Michael Pincus. "We believe this was not a random killing. All indications at the crime scene are that he was targeted."

Percy got out of bed and began to pace the floor. "You see what you've done, Cynthia. If you hadn't given him those e-mails, he would still be alive."

Cynthia slammed the paper onto the bed and said, "What are you talking about? This has nothing to do with me. The article says he was being robbed. Oh God, Percy. They must have killed him shortly after you spoke with him."

Carmen spoke again. "Reverend Pryce, is there something I can do? Your hands are shaking. Can I bring you more coffee? I can put something in it to calm you."

Percy stopped pacing and sat back down on the bed and said, "No, thank you, Carmen. There's nothing anyone can do now."

The smell of coffee filled Naomi's kitchen as she summoned the courage to open the front door and retrieve the morning paper. She prayed there would be no mention of Hezekiah or New Testament Cathedral. When she opened the door, the headline greeted her as she looked down at the paper on the porch.

Naomi sat at the kitchen table with her favorite coffee mug and read:

> *Richard Harrison said that even though they have delayed Lance's most recent story, the* Chronicle *fully intends to run it at a later date. According to Harrison, the story was scheduled to run in today's edition, but out of respect for Lance and his family, "we have decided to publish it at a later date." He declined to elaborate further.*

Naomi placed the paper facedown on the table and cradled the coffee mug.

"Thank God," she said out loud. "At least we have a few more days to figure out what to do about Hezekiah."

Sandra Kelly was already dressed for the day when the paper arrived.

"What the fuck?" she said after reading the headline. "Lance, you idiot. How could you do this to me?"

"We are grief stricken," said Los Angeles Chronicle *publisher and owner Phillip Thornton. "We've lost a family member."*

Longtime associate Edward Wieland called Savage a great reporter and very controversial. "He was persistent and would not let people off the hook, whether he was reporting on corruption in government, the entertainment business, or anyone else. He ruffled a lot of feathers because of it."

Pincus said police had no motive for the killing, but that it did not appear random. Pincus said investigators would look into every possible connection with Savage's work.

Savage, who had been a reporter for the Los Angeles Chronicle *for the past three years, was killed around 8:00 P.M., Los Angeles assistant police chief Pincus said. He said witnesses told police they saw two men leaving the house earlier that evening.*

Thornton reiterated the fact that the most recent story Savage was working on would eventually be published. He stated that he didn't know if the tragedy was related to it, but if it was, "those responsible for his death should know that they cannot stop the truth from coming out."

Sandra dropped the paper to the floor and thought, *Fortunately, Phillip's greed is more powerful than his conscience.*

It was a beautiful Sunday morning at New Testament Cathedral. The parking lot was already filled with freshly washed cars. Members were soon required to park along Cleaveland Avenue. Children played on the lawn in front of the church, carefully trying to keep their flowered white dresses and little tan suits clean for as long as possible. Women rushed their husbands up the stairs to the church to get a good seat. The lobby was filled with members waiting to be seated by the ushers. White gloves handed neatly folded powder blue bulletins to each person who entered the sanctuary.

Rauly Jenkins had dutifully placed CLOSED signs at each balcony entrance. Worshippers were directed to Fellowship Hall, where folding chairs had been assembled auditorium-style, when the sanctuary had reached capacity. No one liked viewing the service over the television monitors, but they could not refuse the only remaining option.

At 10:50 A.M. the choir lined up behind the now-closed double doors to the sanctuary. Except for choir members waiting to enter the sanctuary, the lobby was empty. They waited patiently for the first chords from the organ. Singers nervously fastened buttons on their robes and adjusted the sashes embroidered with the name of the church.

The doors flew open and the procession began when the chord was finally struck. Parishioners stood to welcome the jubilant march.

In the quiet of his office, Pastor Cleaveland retrieved

the vibrating telephone in his pocket. "I'm glad you called. I thought you had forgotten me."

"I could never forget you. How are you?" Danny asked.

I'm okay, baby." Hezekiah spoke like a teenager in love. "I've got you. What else could I ask for? How are you?"

"I didn't sleep too well last night. I'm still worrying about you."

"I wish I were there with you now. Maybe I should come by later and give you a back rub."

Danny smiled. "I'd like that. I'm going to the gym, but I should be back by two o'clock."

Hezekiah stood from his desk and stretched. "I'll see you then. I love you, Danny."

"I love you too, Hezekiah."

Although he was within the safe confines of his office, Hezekiah felt exposed and vulnerable to the world. A cold resolve showed in the lines of his face. His yellow necktie was neatly in place, and the pin-striped suit hung elegantly from his shoulders.

As he reached for the door, the telephone rang again. It was Percy Pryce.

"Have you read this morning's newspaper?" Percy asked.

"I never read the paper on Sunday morning. You know that," Hezekiah responded with a hint of irritation.

Percy dropped his head and propped his forehead up with his palm. "Lance Savage is . . ." There was a pause. "He's dead, Hezekiah. They found him yesterday in his home."

Hezekiah froze in place. "What happened to him?"

"The police don't know. From what I read, it sounded like a robbery."

"God rest his soul," Hezekiah said softly. "Did the article mention the story he was working on?"

"It did, but no details were given."

"Well, at least we can be thankful for that."

"Yes, but this is not over yet, Hezekiah. Phillip Thornton said they will run the story eventually." Percy began to sob into the telephone. "You know I would do anything for you, Hezekiah. I'm so sorry. I am so very sorry."

"This isn't your fault, Percy. You're a good friend. I know I can count on you and Cynthia."

Percy dropped his head to the dining-room table in front of his penthouse window and continued to cry as Hezekiah said, "I'll see you in the pulpit in a few minutes, my friend."

Willie Mitchell dropped Virgil three blocks away from the church. He then double-parked his car in the parking lot of the church and ran up the stairs. His seat was waiting for him in the pulpit. As he passed Samantha on the front row, he bent over to kiss her cheek and whispered, "Everything is set."

Samantha had decided against pearls for her wrist and instead chose a diamond bracelet that Hezekiah had bought her for Christmas. She listened attentively as the church secretary read announcements from the morning bulletin.

The woman at the podium had a sultry voice better suited for radio. Her glasses rested on the tip of her nose as she read, "Please mark you calendars for the first Sunday evening of next month. As you know, that is the kick off of our tenth anniversary at New Testament Cathedral."

Everyone applauded. The worship service proceeded as it had for the past ten years. The choir sang, the people rejoiced, and the cameras rolled. Pastor Cleaveland entered the sanctuary on cue. The cameras followed the precisely sculpted black suit as it floated up the steps to the pulpit. He nodded good morning to the choir as they continued their song. When the song ended, all cameras focused once again on Hezekiah. The applause subsided and Hezekiah spoke his first words of the morning.

"I know a lot of you are not going to want to hear what I have to say this morning, but, praise God, I'm going to say it, anyway.

"Brothers and Sisters, it's time for us to stop lying to ourselves. It's time we stop lying to each other, and, most important, it's time we stop lying to God. He already knows our hearts, so who is it we think we're fooling? Now, please understand, I'm preaching to myself just as much as I'm preaching to you."

A mixture of laughter and "Go ahead, Preacher" came from the far reaches of the sanctuary.

"Now, one lie is only the tip of the iceberg. Once you tell one lie, you've got to tell ten more to cover it up. Pretty soon we don't even know what the truth is ourselves. We lie about our hair color. We lie about our jobs. We stretch the truth about our income." Hezekiah extended his arms to illustrate his point. "And some of us even lie about whom we love."

Samantha looked nervously over her shoulder to the balcony. She hoped Virgil would act before Hezekiah said something that would destroy the rest of her life. She wanted to be remembered as the wife Pastor Cleaveland loved, not as the woman he had planned to divorce for a man.

Virgil Jackson entered the now-empty lobby unnoticed and quietly climbed the side stairs of the balcony. The double doors of the sanctuary were closed, and all eyes and ears were focused on Hezekiah and his cryptic sermon. When he reached the landing at the top of the stairs, Virgil knelt down and crawled along the side aisle of the balcony. He could not see the pastor, but he heard his familiar baritone voice.

On his knees Virgil turned into the second row of pews and crawled toward the center of the gallery. He tensed as the uncarpeted floorboards creaked from his weight. The gun in his pocket accidentally banged against the leg of a pew, and Virgil froze on the wooden floor. No one seemed to have heard the noise, so he raised his head. Pastor Cleaveland was now in clear view. The tall man in the black suit was standing behind the podium. Virgil waited patiently, hoping Hezekiah would move from behind the oak structure.

Hezekiah continued his sermon. "I will be the first one to say before God and all of you that I've told my share of lies. I'm just a man, a man who must humble himself daily before God to confess my sins and to plead His forgiveness." Hezekiah picked up the handheld microphone and walked away from the podium. "I, like you, have done some things in my life that I am not proud of."

No amens were uttered. Hattie Williams sat rocking with her Bible open and reading the Lord's Prayer. A quiet confusion began to work its way through the pews. This was a sermon like none they had ever heard from the pastor. He had lowered himself to the level of mortal. The faces became troubled by his descent, because they needed him to be better than themselves.

Hezekiah put one foot on the steps, preparing to walk down, when two loud shots reverberated over the sanctuary. The first shriek came from someone in the center of the church as Hezekiah fell backward into the pulpit. Everyone was paralyzed for what seemed like minutes. Women began ducking behind pews, while men shielded them. Screams were heard now from every part of the auditorium. Hezekiah Cleaveland lay bleeding from bullet wounds to the head and chest. The members in Fellowship Hall gasped as they watched the mayhem on the massive flat screen unfold.

Virgil stood erect and ran, stumbling up the center aisle of the balcony. The shadow of a man running out of the dark balcony was the only thing that could be seen from the choir stand. He charged down the stairs, partially covering his face with a denim jacket, and pushed aside two small boys at the base. The foyer was still empty as he crossed to the exit of the church.

Virgil tripped on the cement steps and rolled to the ground. After regaining his footing he ran to Hezekiah Cleaveland Avenue and vanished among the houses and cars on a quiet side street.

Samantha broke free from Dino, who was trying to protect her body from danger. She ran up the steps to her husband. Some members of the choir had dashed from the stand, while others crouched and wept behind seats. The organist sat frozen in fear on the bench as several people ran, overwhelmed and screaming, out the double doors.

Samantha dropped and cradled Hezekiah's head on the arm of her suit. Her bracelet sparkled from the light in the church's stained glass. She screamed hysterically. "Hezekiah, baby. Hezekiah, don't die! I need you." She lovingly placed her head on his chest which caused blood to smear on the collar she had so carefully selected. "Hezekiah! Please, God, don't take him from me!"

After a respectable moment Willie Mitchell and Rev. Percy Pryce gently separated Samantha from Hezekiah's body and briskly escorted her, crying and thrashing, out the side door. Hezekiah's lifeless body lay at the top of the steps, clutching the microphone, while Dino tried unsuccessfully to resuscitate him.

Jasmine had not attended church that morning. Samantha had instructed Etta to let her sleep in. She did not want Jasmine to witness her father's assassination.

By two o'clock the church grounds were teeming with police cars and news vans. Satellite dishes pointed to the heavens, and high heels stumbled over electrical cords crisscrossing the parking lot. The police had emptied the sanctuary of parishioners, and the double doors were cordoned off with yellow tape. Members were now milling in the halls and outside the church, giving and receiving comfort. The final word had already spread that the pastor was dead.

Cynthia Pryce retreated to a far corner of the parking lot. Her hands shook as she dialed Phillip Thornton's number.

"Hello, this is Phillip. I'm not available right now. Please leave your name, number, and the reason for your call, and I'll call you back as soon as I can." Then came the beep.

"Phillip, this is Cynthia," she whispered through tears. "Call me as soon as you get this message. Hezekiah is dead. Someone shot him this morning. I want you to stop the story. Do you understand? Do not print that story. If you print it, I'll deny I ever talked to you."

Several reporters for the local and national news networks, with microphones and cameras in tow, cornered members for their reaction to the tragedy. Television programming around the country had been interrupted to report on the assassination of Pastor Hezekiah T. Cleaveland. The hats, fresh haircuts, and pain of New Testament Cathedral were beamed live to televisions throughout the country.

The television monitors in Fellowship Hall had been

turned off by the time the police had arrived. Folding chairs were clustered in small groups to accommodate mourners around the room. By then, most of the tears had turned to sobs of disbelief and an occasional outburst of anguish.

Scarlet Shackelford took the news of the pastor's death especially hard. The hat she wore that morning was now bouncing on the table she pounded with an open palm as she cried inconsolably. The paramedics were summoned from the parking lot and gave her a sedative to relieve the shock. Her thoughts were of her daughter, who never knew the identity of her father, and the father, who never knew his child. That morning the astonishing realization that she actually still loved him took her fragile world by surprise.

Hattie sat nearby as the paramedics checked Scarlet's blood pressure. "That's all right, Scarlet. Let it out. It's going to be all right," she said, rubbing her back. Hattie was unable to block the emotions of the crying woman in her arms. After a while she stopped trying. The pain Scarlet Shackelford felt now was very appropriate.

The covered body of Hezekiah was quickly removed from the church. Cameramen scrambled to get a shot of the gurney being lifted into the rear of the van. Women crying, with children clinging to their thighs, provided a dramatic backdrop for the parting shots of the vehicle.

On the sofa inside Hezekiah's office, Samantha sobbed into a crumpled tissue. The suit jacket Hezekiah had worn that morning was draped over her lap, and blood from his head had dried on her sleeve. Reverend Pryce and Cynthia sat on either side of her. Somewhere in the corridor between the sanctuary and the office, Samantha's tears had become real. Yes, she wanted him dead, but they had shared many years together, and he was the father of her daughter.

Samantha had called home shortly after being taken to the church office.

"Jasmine, honey," she said. "This is Mommy. Something terrible has happened."

At that moment Jasmine looked out her bedroom window and saw three police cars, with red and blue lights flashing, roll up the long driveway toward the house.

She jumped from the bed and cried into the phone, "Mommy, the police are here! What's going on? I'm afraid."

"There's nothing to be afraid of, darling. Everything is going to be all right," Samantha said gently.

"Where's Daddy? I want to talk to my daddy."

Samantha paused before responding. For the first time she questioned her decision. "You can't talk to Daddy right now, honey."

Jasmine's voice began to tremble. "Why not? Something has happened. Why won't you tell me what is happening?"

"I'll be home as soon as I can, honey, and I'll tell you everything."

"Tell me now. Is Daddy all right? Tell Daddy I need him to come home to me now."

Samantha took a deep breath before she spoke. "Daddy has been shot, Jasmine. He's dead."

Jasmine dropped the phone and fell to the floor, screaming. Etta heard her from downstairs and immediately ran to her room. Samantha then broke the news to Etta and instructed her not to turn on any television in the house. "I'll be home as soon as possible. Don't leave Jasmine alone."

A police officer was stationed at the door leading to

Hezekiah's office with instructions not to let anyone in, especially the media. Willie Mitchell, Reverend Pryce, and Cynthia remained in the room the entire time. The full weight of what had just occurred kept Reverend Mitchell pacing the floor. Samantha had requested that he stay with her. She wanted to keep a watchful eye on him. She didn't want him to panic and speak to the ravenous reporters around the scene. He tried to remain calm, but all could see that he was rapidly losing control. Samantha told him to sit down and drink a glass of water.

Reverend Pryce did not speak while in the office. His thoughts flashed to the words of his wife, Cynthia. This could not be a coincidence. He lamented the plight of the beautiful woman on the couch. Percy periodically gave Samantha a tissue, then retreated to the opposite side of the room. With what he knew, he could not look her in the eye.

Danny St. John watched the news coverage on the television in his living room. He stared blankly at the footage of Hezekiah's body being placed in the van. Danny was empty. His soul had left his body and hovered above the room to protect him from the horror of the images on the screen. He understood why sleep had evaded him for so many days.

Nina Simone was playing on the CD: "Someday I know he's coming to call me. He's going to handle me and hold me. So, it's going to be like dying, Porgy, when he calls me. But when he comes, I know I'll have to go."

Danny wanted to cry, but he couldn't. He could not find the tears. He could not feel his soul. All he could feel was a familiar emptiness that had been a part of his life for as long as he could remember. It was a void he had not felt for the last year.

* * *

Reverend Pryce and Cynthia had offered to go home with Samantha, but she graciously refused their company. "I'll be all right. Etta is there, and I have to spend time alone with Jasmine."

Samantha rode home in the rear of a police car. When they arrived in front of the house, she saw the three police cars. Two officers stood at the ready at the entrance.

A strong-looking female officer walked Samantha to her front door and asked, "Mrs. Cleaveland, would you like me to come in with you for a while? I can stay as long as you need me."

Samantha still held Hezekiah's jacket. "No, thank you. My housekeeper is here. I need to be alone with my daughter."

"Ma'am, I am very sorry about what happened. Two officers will be stationed here as long as you think it necessary. Please call me if you have any problems or questions about the investigation."

"Thank you, Officer. You've been very kind. Good night."

Etta ran down the foyer stairs, clutching a tissue, when Samantha entered the house. "Oh Lord, Mrs. Cleaveland. This is terrible. Just terrible. Are you all right?"

"No, Etta, I'm not all right. How are you?" The two women hugged. "Is Jasmine in her room?"

"Yes, ma'am. There wasn't much I could do for her. She's been hysterical since you called."

When Samantha entered her room, Jasmine was sitting on the floor beside her bed. A blanket was wrapped around her shoulders. She didn't look up. Samantha sat down on the floor and put her arms around her crying daughter. "It's okay, honey. Mommy's here."

"I should have been there. Why didn't you wake me this morning? I could have helped him."

"No, honey, there was nothing anyone could have done. It all happened too fast. He didn't feel any pain."

"Why? I can't understand. Everybody loved Daddy. What kind of monster would do something like this?"

"I don't know, baby, but I'm sure the police will find whoever did this."

They stayed together for most of the night, until Jasmine cried herself to sleep. Samantha pulled the covers over her chest and kissed her forehead. When she went downstairs, Etta was reading a Bible at the kitchen table.

"Thank you for staying tonight, Etta. You should get some rest. Jasmine is asleep now, and I'm going to my room."

Etta was silent for a moment; then she looked suspiciously at Samantha. "Mrs. Cleaveland, who could have hated the pastor so much that they wanted him dead? I can't understand that kind of hate. Whoever did this must've come straight from hell."

"Try to get some rest. I'll see you in the morning."

Samantha didn't trouble herself with the ramblings of the housekeeper. At the moment hell was the least of her concerns. She undressed, neatly placing the bloodstained dress on the hanger. She sat at the vanity mirror and began to remove her makeup. A smile emerged from under the mask she had worn all day. She took a deep breath and thought, *It's over. I'm finally free. No one can get in my way now.*

It was 11:00 P.M. The streets of downtown were empty, except for encampments of homeless people under cardboard boxes. Willie Mitchell was driving to the Los Angeles Community Center, where he saw the figure of Virgil Jackson pacing in front of the building. Virgil opened the door of the car and jumped in before Willie could stop completely.

"Where the fuck have you been? I've been waiting here for five hours," Virgil said before closing the door.

"I had to lock up the church. You did a good job, boy. I'm proud of you."

"Fuck that. Where's my money? I'm getting out of here tonight. It seems like the fucking police are everywhere I look."

"It's in the trunk. I'll get it when I drop you near the bus station. Relax, boy. It's over. No one will ever find you. Give me the gun so I can get rid of it."

Virgil anxiously removed the gun from his waist and handed it to the reverend. "Here. I never want to see the fucking thing again."

Willie parked the car two blocks from the bus station.

"Why are we stopping here?" Virgil asked, looking over his shoulder.

"I don't want to be seen with you in front of the depot. You can walk from here."

Both men exited the car. Reverend Mitchell opened the trunk and handed Virgil a brown paper bag. As Virgil opened it to inspect the contents, the reverend quickly removed the gun from his coat pocket and shot him in the chest. His body lay half in the street, and half on the sidewalk, holding a bag filled with folded pages of the Sunday paper.

25

Once again, Samantha stood before five outfits hanging in her closet. It was the night before Hezekiah's funeral. She searched her collection for the perfect black dress, shoes, and accessories. *No need to buy anything new for this*, she thought. *I'll only be able to wear it once.*

She took special care in selecting each piece. *After all*, she thought, *this is a special occasion. Hezekiah would want me to look my best.* Samantha was a firm believer that women never looked more beautiful than on their wedding days and on the days they lowered their husbands into the ground. Samantha wanted to look stunning for the many mourners who would see her in person and on television. She felt she owed it to the memory of Hezekiah.

She needed an outfit that prompted such observations as "Even on the most difficult day of her life, Mrs. Cleaveland looked radiant" and "The brave widow of the slain minister, Hezekiah T. Cleaveland, looked more glamorous than ever." Even more important, "So young, beautiful, and dignified. Samantha Cleaveland should be the next pastor of New Testament Cathedral."

No acrobatics would be required on this occasion. She simply needed to convey dignity, class, and strength. Samantha selected three outfits from the section of black dresses in her closet and hung them in a row. The first was a simple black linen suit with a tuxedo-cut jacket that had pearl buttons down the front and on the cuffs. Next to it hung a silk dress she had purchased in Paris earlier that year, with an intricately laced gold collar. The third was a black dress with a halter neckline accented by a band of crystal beads. She particularly liked this choice because it accented beautifully the curves of her hips.

Samantha modeled each of the outfits in front of her floor-to-ceiling mirrors. She tried on a series of leather, plain, beaded, and buckled shoes with each.

She ultimately selected the black suit and a pair of black Italian leather pumps. She felt it was elegant, yet dignified. She decided no jewelry would be necessary. The pearls on the front and cuffs were enough.

Samantha viewed her selection from every angle. She sat in a chair and crossed her ankles and placed her gloved hands gently into her lap and struck a pose. She leaned over a table in the center of the room to emulate the move she would make when leaning in to kiss Hezekiah's cheek. *Perfect*, she thought. *There's just enough leg to give the cameras something to look at.*

Hezekiah T. Cleaveland Avenue was lined with a row of six black Rolls-Royce limousines, filled with family members and friends, in front of New Testament Cathedral. Streets were cordoned off within a two-block radius of the church due to the massive crowd attending the funeral. At the foot of the church steps was a black hearse containing Hezekiah's body.

An army of television and newspaper reporters provided blow-by-blow coverage of the events that were unfolding in front of the church. News vans sent live footage from satellite dishes to stations around the world, and six helicopters buzzed overhead waiting for the perfect shot of Samantha walking behind the casket into the church.

Dino exited the driver's seat from the limousine that sat directly behind the hearse. The gun was tucked discreetly in a shoulder holster under his jacket. Six additional armed bodyguards stood around the limo as Dino opened the rear door.

Samantha extended her sleek black-leather-clad foot to the sidewalk and paused for a brief moment. Dino took her arm as she exited the car. The helicopters zoomed in, causing her silky hair to blow gently in the breeze. She brushed the stray strands away from her dark-tinted sunglasses.

Jasmine Cleaveland emerged next from the rear seat. She wore a black suit that mirrored her mother's. Jasmine chose to wear a hat to cover her puffy eyes and tear-stained cheeks.

Everyone in the room stood as Samantha and Jasmine walked in, hand in hand, behind the mahogany casket, down the center aisle, and to the front row of the sanctuary. Their movement was accompanied by a hymn played by the orchestra. Samantha clutched a handkerchief in her left hand and placed her right arm around the shoulders of her sobbing daughter.

Cynthia Pryce sat quietly in the second row. The brim on the black hat she wore was so wide that it blocked the views of two mourners in the seats behind her. It cast a shadow over her eyes and nose. Only the red of her lips could be seen, except on the rare occasions that she lifted her head. She stood when Cynthia, Jasmine, and Hezekiah's coffin entered the sanctuary. *Leave it to Samantha to wear something that flashy to her husband's funeral.*

Cynthia reached out and embraced Samantha when she reached the front row, whispering, "I'm so sorry, Samantha. He was such a good man."

"Yes, he was," Samantha responded. "Thank you, Cynthia."

"You know Percy and I are here for you," Cynthia continued.

Samantha pulled away when she heard the last words. She looked Cynthia directly in the eyes and whispered, "I know you are, dear. Just make sure that you keep out of my way."

Cynthia flinched at the words and clutched her handbag tightly under her arm and breast. She looked up and saw Percy peering down from the stage at her. He looked intently at the exchange and then quickly averted his eyes away from her glance.

Percy's heart pounded in his chest as the coffin was positioned at the foot of the steps. Waves of guilt caused his shoulders to tense. He felt like he was going to pass out. *I'm going to leave her,* he thought while the women embraced. *I'm going to leave her penniless.*

He looked down again in Cynthia's direction and saw her red lips peeking from beneath the brim of the hat. They were full, and the gloss seemed to shimmer like a drop of dew on the petal of a lily. *God, she's beautiful,* he thought as his mind wandered. *I'm sure she loves me. I know she thought she was doing the right thing. Maybe . . .* The sweet and pungent smell of the flowers on Hezekiah's coffin summoned him painfully back to the somber occasion, which was unfolding at his feet. The tension in his shoulders returned.

Victoria and her husband, Rev. Sylvester Johnson, sat in the seats behind Samantha. Beads of perspiration formed puddles under Sylvester's toupee. The off-kilter hairpiece sat atop his scalp and shifted with every turn of his head.

Victoria's head was floating from a mix of gin and the little white pills she had consumed during the car ride to the church. "Don't tell me what to do," she had chided her husband. "There's no way I can get through this funeral without something to calm my nerves."

Victoria leaned forward and placed her gloved hand on Samantha's shoulder and whispered, "Don't worry, Sammy. We're going to get that bitch. She'll wish she were in that coffin when we get finished with her."

Samantha placed her hand on Victoria's and said, "Thanks, honey. You are such a dear friend."

A slight smile appeared on Samantha's face as she thought, *Thank God she remembered. I knew I could count on Victoria.*

The funeral attendants removed a heavy spray of yellow, white, and red roses from the coffin and lifted the lid to reveal Hezekiah's serene body lying in state.

Hattie Williams sat in her usual seat on the center aisle, third row. She wore the dress that she had worn to her husband's funeral years earlier. She did not stand when Samantha walked past her, but she could feel Samantha approaching from behind. *She's more concerned about which direction the cameras are pointing than about her dead husband, or Jasmine.*

A string of dignitaries paraded across the stage and expressed their sorrow over the loss of such a great man. Sandra Kelly blended into the crowd. On the surface she was just another somber face. Another black suit and one more handkerchief poised to catch a tear. But beneath the grieving facade, her dark heart distinguished her from most others in the room.

I wish I had been the one who pulled the trigger, she thought as she dabbed her eye to wipe away the tear that wasn't there. *Now it's Samantha's turn, and I'm going to make sure she gets everything she deserves.*

Renowned gospel artists serenaded the body and the distraught family. The JumboTron flashed images of Hezekiah in various incarnations of his life. Then the crowd heard, "Ladies and gentlemen, the president of the United States."

The somber face of the commander in chief appeared on the twenty-foot screen and said, "Hezekiah was not only a great man, a shepherd to millions of people around the world, and the pastor of New Testament Cathedral, but also he was my friend and confidant. He will be missed by all of us. To Samantha and Jasmine, please know that you can call on Megan and me anytime for support, and if you just need a friend to talk to. We love you. You will always be in our hearts and prayers."

Samantha pressed her gloved fingers to her lips and directed a heartfelt kiss toward the twenty-foot head on the screen.

For the mourners in the back row of the sanctuary, Hezekiah's coffin on the floor below looked like a postage stamp with a red dot in the center. They were so close to the ceiling of the building, they could feel the heat from the bright lights. Danny St. John sat quietly in the most extreme corner seat of the last row. He felt dead inside. *It might as well be me in the coffin,* he thought as the president spoke.

She's done it. A single tear broke free from a dark place

in his heart and fell to his shoulder. It was over. Hezekiah was at peace, and he was alone again.

I never thought I would live to see this day," Reverend Davis said. "I think the pastor must have known something was going to happen to him."

Cynthia, Percy, and Reverend Davis walked slowly away from the grave site. Hezekiah had been laid to rest on a quiet hill in Inglewood Park Cemetery, overlooking the city.

Cynthia waited for what she considered to be a respectable amount of time; then she said to Reverend Davis, "It is a sad day. I guess we have to start thinking about who is going to take over as pastor. I don't want to appear insensitive, but I assume we have your support for the nomination of Percy as Pastor Cleaveland's successor. I think he already has the support of most of the members of the board of trustees."

"Cynthia, please," Percy said, looking her directly in the eyes and squeezing her hand tightly.

She flinched from his grip.

"Show some respect for the man. His body isn't even in the grave yet."

"That's okay, Percy. Cynthia is right. We do have to start talking about this. I've been thinking about it, since the pastor raised the subject. I have decided to recommend you to the trustees." He lowered his head in shame as he spoke the painful words.

Cynthia clutched Percy's arm and said, "That is wonderful, Reverend Davis. You won't regret it. Percy will make a great pastor."

26

If only her life could have been as neat and tidy as her kitchen. She had arrived in Los Angeles as a young girl from the South. Her mother wanted a better life for her, so she sent her to live with relatives in California. She was smart and beautiful her entire life, but she never really knew it. Her shyness was often mistaken for conceit. Boys found the shy, attractive Southern girl captivating. Her naïveté and soft voice garnered proposals of marriage long before she turned eighteen.

At nineteen, she became secretary for Hezekiah Cleaveland. Scarlet was smart and efficient. Hezekiah was immediately attracted to the young beauty and pursued her from the start. Scarlet was flattered by the attention from the handsome minister, but she flatly refused his constant advances. She often cried after work, and wondered what she had done to elicit such carnal responses from the man she admired.

After a year Scarlet could resist no longer. She gave in to the pastor and began a two-month affair. Hezekiah was the first man she had ever been with. He was gentle and attentive, and never made her feel cheap. Scarlet soon learned she was pregnant. Hezekiah offered to put her up in an apartment until the baby was born. After that, he told her, she would have to put the baby up for adoption.

She was devastated. Not because she was pregnant, but because the man she had fallen in love with did not share her joy. Samantha had soon learned of Scarlet's condition and immediately fired her. Scarlet then married a man who had pursued her since she was fifteen. It wasn't easy, but she convinced her new husband that the baby she was carrying was his.

For five years the couple lived a turbulent life filled with physical abuse and mistrust. Her new husband never believed the cute little girl named Natalie was really his. In a violent argument he threw Scarlet and Natalie out on the street. Scarlet never loved her husband, so the divorce came as a relief, but the pain of her secret lingered. She still held it close to her chest like an unwanted family heirloom that she had been entrusted to protect.

The death of Pastor Cleaveland only served to reopen the wounds that had taken her years to heal. Her feelings for Hezekiah flooded back, as if she were nineteen again. Over the years she never stopped hating Samantha. The woman who had treated her so cruelly. The woman she had once admired.

Scarlet rejoined New Testament after her marriage ended and soon became a trusted and valuable member of the church. Hezekiah, who never lost his deep feelings for her, eventually appointed her to the board of trustees.

She had harbored loathing for Samantha Cleaveland for years, and now that intensified. She always suspected that Samantha would want to take over the church if Hezekiah ever died, and Scarlet vowed to do all within her power to prevent it if she ever tried.

As the teakettle on her stove simmered, the telephone rang.

It was Willie Mitchell. "How are you, Scarlet?"

"I'm fine." Like everyone else, Scarlet knew that when Willie called, he wanted something.

"I'm calling about the trustee meeting this week. We've got to decide who is going to replace Pastor Cleaveland, God rest his soul. I wanted to know who you were going to support."

"What do you mean, who? There is only one obvious choice—Reverend Pryce."

"Scarlet, you know I never like to disagree with you, but how about Samantha? She is much more qualified, and I think Pastor would have wanted her to replace him."

Scarlet leaned against the counter and laughed. "Samantha Cleaveland? Why would we do that? I never have, and never will, consider her for the position. Also, we need someone right now. The woman must still be in shock. Her husband's body isn't even cold yet, and she already wants to be pastor."

"You know Samantha better than that, Scarlet. She's a fighter."

"I know that. But she's not a pastor. I've never trusted her to have the best interest of New Testament." Scarlet grew impatient. "You've caught me at a bad time. We can talk about this at the trustee meeting."

"All right, Scarlet. Just think about it, would you?"

"I've already thought about it. Good-bye."

Scarlet sat down at her kitchen table and wondered why Reverend Mitchell was so intent on Samantha becoming pastor. Had she bribed him? Her concern grew. Typically, if Reverend Mitchell wanted something from the board, he usually got it. She would have to work twice as hard to convince them not to select Samantha Cleaveland.

27

Willie Mitchell slammed the conference table and jumped to his feet. "Everyone, please, please be quiet. If this room does not come to order, I'm going to end the meeting right now."

It was the Thursday after Hezekiah's funeral. The five members of the board of trustees exhibited their frustrations by throwing pens onto the table, slamming notebooks, and rolling eyes in disgust. They had gathered to decide who would replace Hezekiah. Reverend Davis, Scarlet Shackelford, and Hattie Williams each spoke adamantly in favor of appointing Reverend Pryce. Reverend Mitchell and Rev. Larry Sullivan supported the appointment of Samantha Cleaveland as pastor.

Percy Pryce and Samantha did not attend the meeting. Samantha had already given Willie instructions not to adjourn the meeting until they appointed her as pastor. "Do whatever it takes, Willie. I'm counting on you."

Willie wiped the sweat from his lip and went on. "Now, I'll be the first one to agree that Percy has served this church well over the years, but, no disrespect to Reverend Percy, he is no leader. He never did anything around here without asking permission first. We need someone who can inspire us through this difficult time. We need someone who can take charge and show the world that New Testament Cathedral is here to stay. We need Reverend Samantha Cleaveland to stand in the pulpit as pastor and tell the world that New Testament is going to be all right."

Scarlet Shackelford responded, "Samantha Cleaveland is in mourning. We need someone right now. There's already talk of some people leaving. We can't wait for Samantha to pull herself together. It takes time for a woman to get over the loss of a husband—"

"I spoke to Samantha before this meeting," Willie interrupted, "and she said, if appointed, she would be prepared to assume the position immediately. You know she's a strong woman."

Reverend Davis jumped in. "Yes, but how will members react when they hear we've appointed a woman as pastor? Sorry, Sisters, but you know it's the truth."

"Come on, Reverend Davis," said Larry Sullivan. "There are women pastors all over the country. And remember this isn't just any woman. Samantha Cleaveland helped Hezekiah build this ministry. I think we owe it to Pastor's memory to at least appoint her as interim pastor, and give her a chance."

"Reverend Sullivan makes a good point." The room fell silent as Hattie Williams spoke. "I admit I have concerns about Samantha Cleaveland, but this isn't about her. It's about the survival of New Testament. It's about keeping people coming in those doors every Sunday. The church needs to regain some stability. And if that means putting another Cleaveland in the pulpit, then, I guess, I'm in favor of it."

There was silence. Willie's stomach muscles relaxed. He knew no one could resist the wisdom of Hattie Williams. Now that she was on his side, his battle was almost won.

Scarlet felt betrayed. She never imagined that Hattie would side with Samantha Cleaveland. She had seen the way the old woman looked at Samantha every time she saw her.

Willie broke the silence. "Scarlet, are you at least willing to support Samantha as interim pastor? We'll all keep a close eye on her, and if it doesn't work out, we'll find someone else."

Scarlet did not speak.

Willie went on, "How about you, Reverend Davis? Are you willing to give her a chance? Remember, it's for the church."

Reverend Davis avoided looking into the red eyes of Reverend Mitchell. They had been there for almost four hours, and he was exhausted. He closed his folder and said, "I'll agree only as interim pastor, and only if we review her performance every month."

Willie slammed the table and said, "Good. I knew you'd do the right thing. Come on, Scarlet. You're the last vote. This has to be unanimous."

Scarlet searched the eyes of her fellow trustees. They all avoided her glance, except for Hattie.

Scarlet finally spoke. "All right. I'll agree on one condition—that you appoint me as head of the committee in charge of her monthly evaluation, and finding her replacement."

"Wait a minute, Scarlet. You're getting ahead of the process. Let's take this one step at a time—"

"No, she isn't, Willie," Hattie broke in. "Somebody has

to do it, and I trust Scarlet. Appoint her the chair of the Evaluation and Search Committee and you have my vote."

Signs of agreement were seen around the table. Relieved heads nodded yes and eye contact was made, again. Willie had no choice. "All right, then. It's unanimous. Reverend Samantha Cleaveland is now interim pastor, and Scarlet Shackelford will head the Evaluation and Search Committee to find a permanent pastor if we, as a board, determine that Samantha is not suited to serve as permanent pastor. Meeting adjourned."

He hit the table with his fist. Samantha would not be pleased, but he had done his best.

Samantha received the call just after nine o'clock that night. She'd been clutching her phone and chain-smoking cigarettes in her study.

"Samantha, you're in, baby. It was unanimous. You're the new interim pastor of New Testament Cathedral."

After the word "interim" registered, Samantha spoke. "What do you mean, interim?"

Willie's stomach churned. "It was the only way I could get Scarlet Shackelford and Hattie Williams to agree. They almost ruined it."

"I knew you would screw it up." Blood began rushing to her head. "Why did you let them get away with that?"

Willie's voice began to shake. "It's not as bad as it sounds. We can drag this out for years. Pretty soon they'll forget it's a temporary position."

It was now time for Samantha to perform her final chore. Willie had been a bundle of nerves since the murder. She hoped now to give him the final push over the edge. She steadied herself and said, "Willie, I've been thinking. You're the only person who can connect me to Hezekiah's death, and that makes me nervous."

"What are you talking about? I'm in this shit as deep as you are. Who the hell am I going to tell?"

"No, Willie, you don't understand. I'm not involved in this 'shit' at all. As a matter of fact, I might make a call tomorrow to my friend Jack, the chief of police. I'm thinking of telling him I remembered an argument between you and Hezekiah in which you threatened to have him killed. After they start snooping around, it won't take the police long to figure out that you murdered Virgil Jackson too."

"Why are you saying this? You know I love you. I'll never say anything to anyone." Pain in his gut caused beads of sweat to form on his brow. The walls in his living room began to move closer around him. He gasped for breath, and managed to choke out, "You fucking bitch, I'll kill you if . . ."

Samantha laughed. "Thank you, Willie. Now I can honestly tell Jack you threatened me too."

"I'll tell them everything," Willie sputtered. "I'll tell them you paid Virgil to kill him . . . that the whole thing was your idea."

"You are as dumb as I thought. You forget, I never paid anyone anything. Besides, who would believe a fat, sweaty, good old country boy like you over me?"

Willie dropped the telephone and jolted to his feet. He kicked over the coffee table in a rage and began ransacking his living room. He then retrieved the phone from the floor and cursed aloud. "You fucking whore, how could you? I did all this for you and you threaten to fuck me over like this."

Samantha listened calmly for a moment and said, "Willie, you sound upset. It's late and I just lost my husband, so I'm going to bed. Good luck with your trial."

Willie heard the dial tone and threw the phone across the room. His stomach convulsed as he continued the rampage. Pictures were knocked off walls, the television was tipped over, and lamps pulled from sockets and thrown to the floor. He violently lifted the sofa from the floor and saw the gun he had hidden there. He grabbed it and randomly fired a bullet into a mirror. The sound of the gun caused the room to spin around him. The pain in his gut made him drop to his knees. He tried to focus, but the walls only twirled faster.

The pain felt as though he had been kicked by a wild horse. He placed the gun between his sweating lips. The last bullet in the chamber went through the roof of his mouth and out the top of his head. It lodged in a wall, and the room suddenly stopped spinning.

28

The white gloves swung open the double doors once again. The faithful stood to their feet. The choir marched down the center aisle and sang: "We are on our way. We're on our journey home. We are on our way. We're on our journey home."

Reverend Pryce stood firm in a black suit behind the podium as he spoke. "Brothers and Sisters, this is a sad time for New Testament Cathedral. We have lost two of our leaders, and our friends. The tragic death of Reverend Willie Mitchell is a sad reminder for us all never to let go of God's hand. No matter how heavy the load gets, we need to hold on to his hand. Hold on to Jesus, and He will never let us fall."

Through muffled tears the congregation responded, "Amen, Preacher. Amen."

"God also saw fit to call home our beloved pastor. Now, it's not our job to question why."

"Tell it, Reverend," echoed from the rear of the sanctuary.

"It's our job to look to God and say, 'Whatever my lot.'"

"Yes, Lord," came the reply.

"Thou hast taught me to say, 'It is well. It is well with my soul.'"

Cries of agreement erupted throughout the room.

Reverend Pryce went on. "As hard as it may seem, we've got to go on. We've got to let the gentle hands of God heal our hearts and get on with the work of the church. Our beloved first lady, Sister Samantha Cleaveland, has suffered a great loss. Sister, we know your heart is heavy right now. But know that God is going to see you through. Just hold on, Sister. Hold on."

Samantha sat in the seat of honor on the pulpit. The gold braiding on her white robe glistened in the light.

There was a hush in the room as Reverend Pryce continued. "She's a strong woman. She's a godly woman, and the Lord is going to bless her greatly. In spite of her grief, and in spite of her sorrow, Sister Cleaveland has agreed to do what is best for New Testament Cathedral. Ladies and gentlemen, Brothers and Sisters, it is with great pleasure I present to you our new interim pastor, the Dr. Reverend Samantha S. Cleaveland."

Samantha approached the podium, and the faithful jumped to their feet. Applause burst from the back of the sanctuary and rode like a wave to the front and up through the choir stand.

The crowd chanted, "Thank you, Jesus. Yes, Lord. Yes, Lord."

Scarlet Shackelford's hand reached past the mints and hand lotion in her purse for a tissue. *How could this have happened?* she thought. *How could this woman who has tormented so many now be standing in this sacred place of honor?*

The congregation continued to show their approval for the next moments as Pastor Samantha Cleaveland basked in the glow of the stained-glass windows and bright lights. She stretched out her arms and the long robe unfurled to its full and radiant splendor. Her eyes looked upward, then back to the adoring adulation of the faithful.

Samantha interrupted the praise and spoke her first words as pastor. "Good morning, New Testament Cathedral! Does anybody here know that God is still a good God?"

In response to her question the congregants jumped once again to their feet and released a thunderous round of applause.

The silk flowers in Cynthia Pryce's hat trembled as she struggled to contain her rage. She searched the room for a sympathetic face but found none. She loathed the grace with which her husband relinquished the podium to Samantha, and she wished she had married a man more like Hezekiah Cleaveland.

Samantha interrupted the clamoring mass a second time. "I am a living witness that God is in the business of healing. I wouldn't be here this morning if it were not for Him."

Jasmine held the bottle of sleeping pills in her hand. Her bedroom was dark. She had succumbed to the grief of losing the man who loved her so much. The man who held her hand when she was a little girl and protected her, as best he could, from the dangers of the world. *How can I go on without Daddy?* she silently questioned.

She had always believed that only her father would notice if she were no longer on earth, and now that he was gone, there was no reason to remain. She could either die in the dignity of her own room or in a crack house in South Central. Thoughts of her mother did not enter her mind as she swallowed the handful of blue tablets. Her fears were soon replaced by the warmth and comforting embrace of sleep.

Samantha adjusted the microphone and said, "Yes, my heart is heavy, but I'm going to praise God, anyhow. I'm going to continue the work of my late husband, Hezekiah T. Cleaveland. We are going to finish the construction of our beautiful new cathedral, and then continue to spread the gospel of Jesus Christ through this country and throughout the world."

Hattie Williams sat quietly while those around her danced and shouted praises in the sanctuary. Her eyes were closed, but her heart was open. Light from the windows touched her hands as she looked up and prayed silently, *God have mercy on New Testament Cathedral this Sunday morning.*